I0604109

ALSO BY TC PARKER

Saltblood
Hummingbird
Salvation Spring
Maiden (with Ward Nerdlo)
The Long Con: An El Gardener Omnibus

THE EL GARDENER TRILOGY
The Debt (Book 1)
The Push (Book 2)
The Remembrance (Book 3)

A PRESS OF FEATHERS

TC PARKER

PUBLISHED BY NEFARIOUS BAT PRESS

2022

A PRESS OF FEATHERS
Second Paperback Edition

Published by Nefarious Bat Press

Copyright © 2020 by TC Parker
Cover design by Kealan Patrick Burke
Interior art by Edward Lorn
Interior design by Todd Keisling | Dullington Design Co.

All rights reserved.

For Ana & Kate, my cheerleaders

And for my mum, the firmest but fairest of first readers

FROM THE GATES: A WELCOME HANDBOOK

We're not like other neighbourhoods.

At The Gates, we believe in 3 things: kindness, reciprocity and authentic human connection.

We don't want you to participate in the life of our community – we expect you to.

Taking your place at The Gates means becoming part of The Gates.

It means caring for your neighbours, not just getting to know them.

It means making a contribution - helping to foster a dynamic, nurturing ecosystem that brings out the best in all our residents, whether by attending our weekly Co-Life Dinners and Resident Sharing Assemblies, or by pitching in wherever you can to our Healing Moments sessions.

Most of all, it means opening your heart and mind to a more meaningful and more spiritually nourishing way of life.

Now, we know what you're thinking.

But meaningful doesn't mean austere – at least, not for us.

We've reimagined modern luxury for the next generation of home owners through our thoughtful, beautiful and sustainable design. At The Gates you'll experience every imaginable convenience - from our on-site heated swimming pool and sauna to the energy-efficient appliances integrated as standard into every property, from the largest to the most streamlined.

In return, we ask you to commit to our Fraternity & Fellowship Philosophy, details of which you'll find below.

We're very happy to have you.

PART I

CHAPTER 1

There was no reason for the spikes, that Bea could see.

She'd heard of similar initiatives before: tapestries of long metal studs, sharpened to vicious points like the inner door of an Iron Maiden, laid carefully down on the sills and pavements of high-street banks and supermarkets to deter the homeless from sleeping there or frightening the customers stopping to rest their bones. Hostile architecture, she thought it was called; social engineering through urban design.

But they were way out in the countryside, here - ten miles from the city centre and a fifteen-minute walk from the nearest shop. There were no homeless people around to deter, no customers to alarm - and, if she'd understood the letting agent's spiel correctly, no other homes on the development but hers and the half-dozen others that surrounded it. The rest of The Gates was flattened brownfield: fifty acres of construction site, thus far undeveloped, with not so much as a length of tarpaulin to offer shelter from the elements.

Which made the presence of the spikes... peculiar.

They ringed the house like a flower bed, the perfect circle they made interrupted only by the stretch of concrete slab that led from the pavement to her front door. The neighbouring houses had them too, she saw: little rivers of spurs enclosing both the wide redbrick three-storey to the left and the more modest pair of semis to the right with the belligerence of a Medieval moat.

Very, very peculiar.

There were none around the pool-house, at least, nor any girdling the squat, steepled building across the road that declared itself a Community Hall - though any relief she might have felt at *that* was tempered by the knowledge that the pool-house, if not the Hall, was off-limits. To her, and to the other renters at The Gates.

"It's a condition of the lease," the letting agent had told her, apologetically. She was a young girl, a school leaver or a recent graduate in an off-the-rail work suit that was too loose at the waist and too tight around the shoulders, and she hadn't known how to handle a client like Bea - one whose age and impatient, faintly arrogant demeanour suggested a woman with a maximum monthly income far in excess of the figure she'd submitted on her application form.

"A condition of the lease?" Bea had asked, astonished. "It's a condition of the lease to keep us out of sight of our betters? I've never heard of anything so Victorian."

"It's to do with the service charge," the girl had explained, squirming awkwardly in her seat. "The home-owners pay a surcharge each month that gives them access to the facilities, whereas the renters... don't."

"That's disgusting," Bea had said. But she'd signed the lease, regardless.

She couldn't afford *not* to, by then. Jeremy's solicitor had been pushing her to put the Oadby house on the market, even as Jeremy himself told her to *take her time*, that there was *no rush*; she'd needed somewhere to live, immediately. And the affordable rental market - as the letting agent had reminded her, when she'd taken her first, astonished look at Bea's budget - was on its arse, from a renter's perspective; there were precious few places in her price range out there.

The two-bed detached at The Gates, when the girl had phoned to offer it, had fallen on her ears like manna from heaven.

"It's just landed on my desk," the girl had said, haltingly. "Only…"

"Only what?" Bea had replied sharply. "It sounds ideal."

The girl had hesitated.

"It's not a normal application process," the girl had said eventually, sounding terrified out of her wits.

"What does *that* mean?"

"There's no credit check. They don't care about your financials."

For Bea, this last statement had come as something as a relief, given the precarity of her finances since Jeremy had moved his toothbrush and his Propecia prescription into the (no doubt grimily Bohemian) bathroom of that little whore in Enfield. But there was no reason to share as much with the girl.

"Isn't that a good thing?" she'd said. "If we want to expedite the process?"

The girl had swallowed, releasing a gulp so pronounced it echoed down the line.

"There's… an essay," she'd said, almost whispering. "And a test. A psychometric test. Like one of those Myers-Briggs things."

Bea had almost laughed aloud.

"A psychometric test?" she'd repeated.

She'd read about hoops like this, she'd realised: scanned tweets and forum posts and newspaper articles detailing the unreasonable, excessively exacting, sometimes disconcertingly sexual and occasionally outright unhinged demands made of tenants by their would-be landlords. Had even taken a certain voyeuristic pleasure in the reading; safe, then, in the knowledge - idiot that she'd been - that it could never happen to her.

"It shouldn't take long to fill in," the girl had offered, conciliatory - pleading, even. "And the price is incredible. Three-fifty a month for a furnished two-bed in that area… it just doesn't happen. I've seen *bungalows* go for a quarter of a million in that postcode."

Bea had ended the conversation there; had told the girl she needed time to think about it before she started any paperwork.

It was all for show, though; the pretence of other options deployed solely to protect what little was left of her pride. Three-fifty for a house - not just a room, but a *house* - in a part of town she'd have been delighted to move to with Jeremy, back when money represented something more than an ever-present source of anxiety and she could bring herself to actually *look* at her bank balance... it was better than a good deal. It was nigh-on miraculous.

Whatever hoops there were to jump, she'd known, she was going to jump through them. And jump through them with a smile on her face.

Now, hoops navigated and tenancy secured, she took the freshly-cut key from the manila envelope the letting agent had given her and slid it, with no effort at all, into the polished lock of her new front door. With a turn of the handle, she pulled the door open, releasing a gust of untrodden floorboards and just-dried paint into the open air of the driveway; paused to breathe in the alien scent of what was now, apparently, her home.

"Just moved in?" said a woman's voice behind her - lilting and girlish, a Birmingham accent with the edges rounded off by a private education.

Bea spun around. There was a couple behind her: a South Asian man and woman in their late twenties or early thirties, standing a polite distance from the house, at the edge of the concrete path that led to her door.

They'd been running together, by the look of them - their slim, toned bodies wrapped in black and purple Lycra that clung at the thighs and stomach and their faces shiny with fresh sweat. *Wholesome* sweat, she corrected herself; the liquid glow that comes of energetic activity in the summer sun, and not the more unhealthy - and, she considered, altogether uglier - kind that poured from her neck and the small of her back when she ran for the bus or sat for too long in an overheated office.

The woman was small, delicately built and catalogue-pretty, her nose retroussé and her long black hair pulled back from her face in a ponytail.

The man was taller, broader in the shoulders but equally pretty, his jaw finely sculpted and his cheeks darkened by a spray of carefully contoured stubble.

If the developers had any marketing nous at all, Bea thought, they'd have plastered them both across every bit of promotional material they intended to distribute.

"Moving in now," she answered, giving them a smile that felt painfully unpractised.

"Watch yourself on those spikes," the man said, smiling back at her with white, orthodontically-enhanced teeth. He was more local than the woman, by the sound of it; a Leicester boy, though equally well-spoken.

"What are they even *for*, anyway?" she asked him - realising after the fact how rude she'd sounded, how unwittingly interrogatory.

"It's horrible, actually," the woman jumped in, with a wrinkle of her lovely nose. "They're for the birds. The foxes too, really, but mostly the birds. They keep them away."

"The birds?" Bea said.

"Crows and magpies. Well, I *say* crows - they're big enough to be ravens, if you ask me, although Raj will never believe me when I tell him, will you?"

She prodded the man - Raj - gently in his gleaming upper arm.

"I'm just not sure you're enough of an expert to know a crow from a raven from a golden eagle," he told her. "She's not exactly a country girl," he added to Bea.

"And you're David Attenborough, are you?" the woman replied, with faux indignation.

"There are crows?" Bea said, interrupting them. "Or ravens, or whatever?"

"All over," said Raj. "I don't know what it is about this bit of land, but they seem to flock to it. Scared the crap out of Aarti when we first moved in, didn't they? Before Jordan put the spikes up."

The woman nodded her agreement.

"You won't have seen them yet," she told Bea. "They only seem to come out at night, which I suppose makes sense for the foxes? But they get everywhere: on your roof, in your bins, scratching at your windows. We've woken up to a load of crows on top of the Audi before, haven't we?"

"It was nasty, properly nasty," Raj said, the memory of it sending a ripple of disgust across the Cupid's bow of his lip. "I was up early for work one morning, trying to beat the traffic into town, and I couldn't believe what I was looking at when the security lights came on. There must have been ten of them on the roof-rack - big black things, the size of my head. I had to scare them off with the car alarm."

Bea's eyes shifted, involuntary, to the sparkling silver Audi parked on the pavement beside the neighbouring three-storey. She pictured it carpeted with enormous, sharp-beaked birds – black as pitch, their spread wings shedding oily, obsidian feathers onto the chassis. The image repulsed her; sent a short, sick shudder through her bones.

"But the spikes keep them away from the houses?" she asked - hoping for reassurance, for Raj or Aarti or both to tell her that the spikes were as good as a dog whistle for deterring the deluge of unwanted wildlife.

"They seem to," Aarti said. "We still get a few dead ones now and then, the ones that fly into them and skewer themselves. But they mostly steer clear."

"Must be the price you pay for moving to the sticks," Raj added, smiling again.

"Must be," said Bea noncommittally, remembering the Somerset village she'd lived in until she'd left for university, and where her parents and sister still lived: a rural, mud-splattered slice of nowhere that, while occasionally troubled by pheasants and marauding badgers, had never fallen prey to Hitchcockian hordes of corvids.

She passed a minute or two more with the Arolkers, as Raj and Aarti had introduced themselves, before excusing herself on the pretext of unpacking - promising, in response to Aarti's seemingly sincere invitation, to pop around to theirs for a glass of wine as soon as she'd settled in.

"And don't stress yourself out about the handbook," she shouted back to Bea, as she followed Raj across the threshold of her own house. "It's quite nice, really, the eating together - like being back at home with all your family 'round. And you can take the rest of it with a pinch of salt. I know *we* do."

The handbook? Bea thought, as the Arolkers' door closed. What handbook?

It was waiting for her in the living room: a coffee-table hardback in cream and crimson vinyl, balanced - considerately - on one of the cushions of the sofa. Its front cover was dominated by a computer-generated visualisation of the estate, as seen from above - not incomplete, as it was now, but fully-developed, row upon row of chestnut trees and new-build houses taking the place of the displaced soil and open trenches dug in anticipation of foundation-laying.

The Gates, its title screamed at her from its unnecessarily gaudy mint-green typeface: *A Welcome Handbook.*

She let herself fall onto the sofa beside it; picked it up, appreciating the heft of it, if not its design aesthetic, and skimmed through, stopping at a section marked *House Rules.*

Of *course* there are rules, she thought, flashing back to the application essay she'd written, the many protracted exchanges she'd had with the increasingly nervous letting agent before she'd claimed the keys. Capital-R Rules, even. I'd have expected nothing less.

By Rule #3 ("Unless indicated otherwise, Co-Life dinners are held every Tuesday at 7pm in the Community Hall, and we count on everyone to attend except where work, illness or incapacity prevents it"), she'd lost the will to read on any further, and - vowing to get the highlights from Aarti Arolker, where necessary - closed the book and placed it, face down, on the floor.

She got up from the sofa; stretched, cracked her knuckles and set to unpacking.

There wasn't much to unpack, though. Along with their friends, his signature on the mortgage and the promise of his unwavering lifelong affection, Jeremy had taken with him the bulk of their collective worldly goods when he'd left, up to and including the South American travel guides they'd bought but never opened, much less put to use, and the erotic tableware they'd received as a wedding present from Jeremy's great-aunt Elizabeth. Bea had encouraged him to, at the time - had pelted him with books and plates and ornaments as he'd loaded the Volvo with everything he'd thought he'd need for his extended stay down south with *her*, scraps of paper and shards of bone china accumulating at his feet as he'd dodged the projectiles she'd hurled his way.

"Please don't," he'd begged her, trying to sound calm, to sound *reasonable* - as if it were irrational of her to want to hurt him. As if she ought to be *happy* to stay surrounded by the things he'd owned, the things he'd touched.

Her anger had been boundless, infinite; a gaping, gluttonous hole in her that would never be filled, never be sated. So wildly dissimilar was it from any emotion she'd felt before that she struggled at first to name it - could conceive of it only as a *thing*, both part of her and not, a blood-red symbiotic thing that screamed and sickened and cried to be fed.

She was angry, still - the rage now more a steady hum than the roar of the sea in her ears, but there all the same. Rage at Jeremy and his wandering cock and the little bitch who, knowing what a good thing she was onto, had stopped taking the pill and pricked holes in every condom in her bottom drawer to lure him permanently away; at herself, both the nagging tone she'd let creep into her voice whenever she spoke to Jeremy and the fat she'd allowed to accrete, complacent in the security of their marriage, around her almost-middle-aged belly. Rage, ultimately, at the life she'd been left with in his absence: the unending evenings and weekends spent alone in bed, the unexpected stabs of pain and the constant low-level humiliation of her new, entirely unforeseen penury.

It was too much, sometimes; too much to bear.

In the kitchen, she unboxed bread and cereal, jam and butter; stacked cutlery in trays and bowls in cupboards, wincing all the while at how *little* she had now. How few artefacts - functional as well as personal - there were to rearrange.

When she'd finished, she sat down to eat, and thought, suddenly, of the Arolkers: their toned abs and long lashes, their SUVs and their matching athleisurewear. Her gut - her fat, stretch-marked gut - reacted to the residual image of their bodies - churning and shaking, releasing bubbles of bitter gas up into her mouth and throat.

They're just young, she told herself; young, and pretty, and still sufficiently in love to want to exercise together. None of these things are crimes.

She glanced around the kitchen, scanning for something - anything - that might distract her from the anger, from the taste of her own rancour. Her eyes landed on an earthenware pot on the window ledge: an inoffensive terracotta container housing what might have been the ugliest cactus she'd ever seen. It was bright blue, furred and distended - a lumpy, herniated testicle of a plant dotted all over with pus-yellow flowers, wholly out of place in the cultivated neutrality of the house.

It would have to go, that much was clear. Perhaps not immediately, while she was finding her feet in this collectivist high-end hippy utopia, but soon, once she knew for sure that removing it from its exalted position in the window wouldn't offend her neighbours' sensibilities or violate any of the ludicrous rules laid out in the community manifesto she'd pledged to uphold.

She squinted, trying to remove it from her field of vision by sheer force of will, and peered out through the glass into the street beyond.

The sky was darker and the sun lower in the sky than it had been when she'd met the Arolkers; amber rather than canary, sinking down into the farmland to the west of The Gates. Nearer, something squawked, an owl or a wood pigeon, and another something responded in kind: a crow - or even a raven, if Aarti Arolker could be believed - cawing and rasping at the sunset.

She was surprised by how close it sounded, how *near* it must have been for the noise to have carried so clearly through the double glazing.

Then she saw it, perched on its skinny grey legs on her garden path, hemmed in by the spikes: an enormous crow, oleaginously shiny, its open beak tilted upwards and towards her.

She took a step backwards, alarmed - and the crow hopped forwards one step closer in response.

It's watching me, she thought.

Her hands shot reflexively to the monstrous cactus, her fingers wrapping tight around the terracotta pot - preparing to tap it against the window to scare the bird away, or (hesitant though she was to admit to so irrational an impulse, even to herself) throw it *through* the window, right at the thing's dark head.

The crow moved a second time; spread its horrible ribbon of wings and took flight, darting off in the direction of the Community Hall.

She blinked; took a long, deep breath and relaxed her shoulders.

And then it was back - a charcoal bullet, diving down towards the window.

Jesus fucking Christ, she thought. It's coming straight at me.

She took half a dozen more steps backwards, until her shoulders pressed against the door of the fridge. But perhaps three inches from the window, the crow changed course - turning sharply to the left, and then downwards again, beak pointed to the ground like an aircraft coming in for landing.

And impaled its thick black body on the bed of spikes beside the path.

CHAPTER 2

The boy's name had been Simon. Simon Henshaw.

He'd been a student: an undergrad from Sheffield, in the second year of a Fashion Design degree at De Montfort. He looked gentle, Lou thought, as she studied the pale, pixelated face that had done the rounds of the news sites - local, and then national - on the announcement of his death; soft-eyed and smiling, the sort of boy who wouldn't hesitate to share the last slice of his pizza after a night out or give up his seat on the bus for a pregnant woman.

A gentle boy, who'd died horribly.

Strangulation: that was the cause of death the press had given. But there had been other things, too - other injuries the papers had alluded to but not detailed, ritualistic elements to the killing they were apparently forbidden from naming explicitly.

She'd found out easily enough what these might have been - trawling forums and following the digital footprints of self-proclaimed police insiders until she found information that at least *sounded* halfway legitimate.

His teeth had been removed. Not smashed or chipped, as they might have been had he been hit in the face with a fist or a hammer, but extracted: each tooth pulled, manually, from the gum with forceps or pliers, almost certainly (given the volume of blood in and around his mouth) while he was still alive.

Four of his ribs were broken, and both shoulders dislocated - not, or so the inside source claimed, as the result of a blow to the chest or the over-zealous application of a restraint technique, but because they'd been compressed, his arms secured so tightly around his torso with a material thus far unidentified that they'd squeezed the bone around and underneath them until they splintered.

A straitjacket, Lou had thought as she'd read the insider's description. Whoever killed him put him in a straitjacket and tied it so tightly that he'd asphyxiated trying to escape.

His was the third body to have turned up in the city centre over the course of the summer. Like him, the other victims were young and male: the first, John Seward, was the head chef of a gastropub that doubled as a rock venue; the second, Paul Knight, was another student, an aspiring archaeologist studying for his master's.

Their wounds were different, but equally unpleasant.

John Seward had been exsanguinated, losing more than 60% of the blood in his system by means of a hundred or more small but deep incisions carved into his chest, neck, thighs and stomach with a knife or scalpel, or another sharp object altogether - his naked, greying remains abandoned one week-night in June in the doorway of a herbalist store, and discovered the following morning by the store manager when she arrived to open up.

Paul Knight, by contrast, had no obvious physical wounds at all. His cause of death, withheld like Simon Henshaw's from the general public, was hyponatremia - a dilution of the blood, brought on by water intoxication. Post-mortem examination, the inside source indicated, had uncovered evidence of intracranial swelling and damage to Knight's kidneys, as well as internal bruising to his mouth and windpipe characteristic of force-feeding - indicating that whoever had attacked him had shoved a tube or funnel down his throat, and then poured water through that tube or funnel into his stomach until his brain and organs had literally burst.

His body had been left in the chapel of the Royal Infirmary. The choice of dumping ground in this case had, according to the source, caused police to consider a possible religious motive, for Knight's murder if not for Seward's - a line of enquiry that investigators were still pursuing.

The three men, it seemed to Lou on the basis of what she'd read, had next to nothing in common.

Not ethnicity: Henshaw was white British, Seward second-generation Black Caribbean, and Knight part-Irish and part-Malaysian.

Not sexuality: Henshaw was gay and single, Seward engaged to his long-term girlfriend and Knight so deeply immersed in his studies that he had, or so his former flatmate told the tabloids when he sold his story, no social or romantic life to speak of at all.

And certainly not intersecting interests. Henshaw was creative, a designer and amateur graphic artist who baked and attended the occasional dance class in his spare time; Seward was athletic, a martial artist and middle-distance runner, and a talented musician who'd taught guitar during his A Levels. Knight, whom Lou had mentally tagged as the most introverted of the trio, was a gamer - spending upwards of three hours a night, once he'd made sufficient headway with his course reading and essay-writing, plugged into MMORPGs and city simulator titles on his PC.

Their paths, she considered, were unlikely to ever have crossed, at least while they were alive.

She drained the remainder of her tea, which had cooled to a lukewarm slush topped by a thin skin of calcified brown while she'd been examining Henshaw's features; took a bite of her sandwich and closed the laptop.

It was a good sandwich: thickly buttered and structurally sound, neither the fried egg nor the ketchup subordinate to the bacon inside. But it wasn't *her* sandwich; she hadn't made it herself, made it *for* herself, the way an adult woman was supposed to when she was hungry. Instead, her Mum had made it: grilled the bacon, fried the egg, slathered on the sauce and then, when her work was done, carried the finished product up the two flights of stairs to Lou's attic bedroom to place it, with quiet maternal kindness, on the desk beside the laptop screen.

It was humiliating, being fed; endlessly humiliating. She was grateful to both her parents - would never *stop* being grateful - for taking her in when, entirely unexpectedly, her contract at the media agency she'd been temping at had been terminated and, too broke to afford even the next month's rent on her studio in Acton, she'd been forced to take the train back to Leicester and beg them for shelter. But, while there was nothing any of them could have done to make it otherwise, the experience was never less than infantilising - every folded pile of laundry and home-cooked plate of spaghetti Bolognese a tangible reminder of her failure to cope in the world on her own.

There was nothing unusual about it, her friends had assured her, when she'd eventually cracked and told them where she'd vanished to, why she hadn't been around for game nights or post-work cocktails or impromptu day trips down to Brighton. A lot of people moved back home at twenty-five; some when they were even older. And it made sense financially, didn't it? Moving somewhere cheaper to regroup, to build up a few cash reserves so she could bounce back stronger, fitter, more solvent?

You're right, she'd told them with a smile - resisting the urge to add that this bouncing back, the building up of these reserves would be possible only if she managed to find another job that paid well enough for her to save, not just survive.

Because there *were* no jobs out there, as she'd quickly discovered - or rather, no jobs for which she was appropriately qualified. There were professionalisms, specialisms: junior doctor positions, and quantity surveying placements, and mid-level accountant posts available in the Finance division of the county council. And there were minimum wage opportunities and zero-hour contracts, in warehouses and factories and supermarkets, most of them advertised through recruitment consultant intermediaries who laughed, in some cases literally, in the face of Lou's total lack of prior experience in shelf-stacking and order-picking - and who ended their interviews, invariably, by asking some career-specific variation on what a nice girl like her was doing in a place like theirs.

Neither advertising copywriters nor digital marketing assistants, it seemed, were a particularly hot commodity in the here and now. And, since these were the only roles she'd taken since graduating, her employment prospects were beginning to feel less bright than they had previously.

Her parents had been patient and supportive; had done everything right. They'd told her time and again how happy they were to have her back; reminded her more than once that her brother had moved back home for a while himself while he trained for his pilot's licence, before he moved to Stockholm; assured her in no uncertain terms that she could, as far as they were concerned, stay under their roof for as long as she needed to, no questions asked.

But it was suffocating, being home. Suffocating and stifling, a suspension of normality - of real life - that made her feel like she was drowning, slowly, while her body aged and her resume stagnated.

The initial murder, when she'd heard about it - when John Seward's dimples and pleasantly fox-like face had popped up on her newsfeed - had been a shot of excitement; a break from the monotony of day after day spent filling in application forms and sending speculative emails into the ether, in the hope that some HR underling somewhere would open them. The subsequent, profoundly strange killing of Paul Knight had made her sit up straighter in her chair and pay attention; might, had she had the money to go out, have made her just a little apprehensive about venturing into town after dark.

Simon Henshaw's death, though, had given her an idea.

She'd spent a lot of time reading, since she'd been back in Leicester; reading, and watching TV, and listening to podcasts, many of the latter focused on true crime and historical cold cases long put aside by traditional detectives.

What if, she'd thought when the Henshaw story had broken, she could make her own? Pull together a podcast or an online serial, not about a cold case but a *live* one - a real, ongoing investigation into killings that were *still being committed*, and committed in her own backyard?

True, she wasn't technically an investigator, or even an investigative journalist - but neither in many cases were the podcasters whose narratives she'd been devouring, and it never stopped *them* from going digging. They were citizen journalists: ordinary people with a civic interest in crimes already documented in the public domain, generally armed with nothing more elaborate than a set of notes, a decent camera and the audio recording function on their smartphones. If they could do it, why couldn't she?

And if the story she unearthed - the content she created *from* that story - was compelling enough to draw in an audience, to build a brand, and she could find a way to leverage that brand to bring in a little extra money or attract the attention of a radio producer or a senior editor who appreciated her talent and her chutzpah... well, so much the better.

First, though, she needed to find out what that story *was* - what sort of human-interest angle she could bring to the murders of Seward and Knight and Henshaw, beyond the grisly but ultimately unsatisfying fact of their deaths. She needed to find out more about them, about the men they'd been and the lives they'd led before the blood and breath had been drained out of them. She needed them to be personalities, not just bodies on a mortuary table, and she needed viewers and listeners to care about them - if only so they could care, in turn, about *her* and the work she was doing.

She couldn't go straight to their friends and families; she knew that. There'd be reporters - *traditional* reporters - sniffing around them already, trying to incentivise whomever they could to spill the beans on Paul Knight's childhood or the intimate specifics of Simon Henshaw's sexual proclivities. And the police would most likely be there too, still, asking questions and following whatever meagre leads they thought they had already. The best she could hope for if she went to any of the Sewards, the Knights or the Henshaws directly was a door slammed in her face; the worst, a night in the cells and a grilling on where *she'd* been and what *she'd* been doing on the night each boy was murdered.

The digital footprints of the victims, though, were another matter. Social media accounts, dating profiles, blogs and playlists, professional websites and direct-to-camera videos made and uploaded and then forgotten... *they* were there for the taking.

And the crime scenes, the place each body had been found - they were public access, weren't they? She had every right to be there. Nobody could stop her going; stop her looking around and drawing her own deductions from the things she saw. Or even sharing those deductions with other people, if she wanted to.

She had every right.

CHAPTER 3

The Community Hall was modelled on a Viking longhouse – or, perhaps, a very expensive Japanese restaurant. Its ceiling was high and crisscrossed with exposed beams; the rugged wood panelling below was unvarnished and hung with multicoloured tapestries, while a single rectangular bench peppered with low stools for seating bisected the room down its centre. There was even an open fire, Bea saw: a raw hole and rough-hewn chimney carved out of a section of wall, fed with logs and framed by three asymmetrical chunks of granite that could have been standing stones in miniature. Smoke curled and rose from the logs, forming thin, greyish puffs of smoke that hung above their heads like rainclouds.

That's *got* to be a health hazard, she thought, with no small amount of disapproval.

At the head of the bench, as craggy and weathered as his backdrop, sat Lawrence Jordan, a goblet of Pinot Noir in his hand.

Bea had come across his name from time to time, before The Gates appeared on her horizon, in local paper headlines and regional news reports. He was, or so she'd thought then - where she'd given him any thought at all - the archetypal entrepreneur: a working-class boy made good through hard slog and canny investment, primarily in quarrying and construction. He was in his mid-fifties, she vaguely remembered, short and wiry and brimming with the kinetic energy of a Method actor – the hunch of his shoulders, the messy black hair brushed back from his forehead and the Mephistophelean goatee encircling his lips and chin giving him the look of a Shakespearean antihero, an Iago or a Richard III leaning in to confide, in conspiratorial soliloquy, his plan to overthrow the ruling monarch.

The Gates was his latest baby, the letting agent had told her: an experiment in co-living and community economy inspired by a trip he'd taken to Copenhagen's Free Town commune two years earlier, one so close to his heart that he'd build himself a property on the site so he could watch it grow and thrive first-hand.

"It's all about sharing," the girl had said, as if reading from a script. "The problem with modern living, Mr Jordan says, is that it's too atomised - everyone cut off from everyone else in their own little bubbles. He wants to go back to more of a village model - everybody pitching in, looking after each other, that kind of thing."

"Then why aren't renters allowed to use the pool or the sauna?" Bea had asked, sceptical of the whole proposition, and of Jordan himself. "Doesn't seem very egalitarian to me."

"Look," the girl had said, lowering her voice to stop the agent in the adjoining cubicle from hearing, "I didn't tell you this, alright? But I don't reckon it's fair to keep it from you, since you're moving in."

Bea had stayed silent, letting her talk and wondering, privately, whether the girl might be better suited to a career outside of property sales and management.

"We're not sure that he ever actually *wanted* rentals on the site," she'd continued. "We *think* he wanted all homeowners - you know, so everyone'd be properly invested in the whole community living thing. But a lot of councils have been clamping down on luxury developments lately, making the developers ring-fence sections for tenants - local authority sometimes, as well as private. So we *think* he might have had to agree to take on however many renters, so they'd give him permission to build in the first place."

"He doesn't actually *want* people like me living there?" Bea had replied, a new conflagration of outrage stirring. "Even after all the bloody paperwork he wants to put us through, the *essay* he's making us write?"

She'd felt a sudden, unexpected empathy for the other tenants of The Gates, her fellow second-class citizens; a sense of solidarity that had transformed her, in the moment, from an *I* to a *we*.

"I didn't tell you that," the girl had said, eyes dropping guiltily to the contracts on the desk between them.

Tonight, with all the current inhabitants of The Gates assembled on the bench around her, it seemed to Bea that it would have been painfully obvious which of them were renters and which were property owners, even if she hadn't seen the majority of them emerge from their differently-sized houses on the short walk across to the Community Hall – or received a truncated biography of each in advance of the meal, courtesy of Aarti Arolker.

The Arolkers themselves, she guessed, were owners, and probably mortgage-free to boot. Though young, they were obviously wealthy, both of them *from* money as well as well-equipped to earn it. Raj was a pharmacist, Aarti had said; *owned* a pharmacy, in fact, somewhere along the Narborough Road, and would be investing in a second unit when the time was right. Aarti herself was an accountant, a client manager with one of the larger firms in town - although, as she'd told Bea over the promised glass of wine, all that would change when she and Raj finally succeeded in conceiving the baby they'd been trying for over the last few months.

Bea, who even before Jeremy's impregnation of his Enfield whore had loathed the phrase *trying for a baby* - and the attendant mental image of the *trying* couple plugging joylessly away day and night until their goal was reached - had winced, but nodded enthusiastically, and wished her and Raj the best of luck with their undertaking.

Opposite the Arolkers sat a second couple, the Harris-Hindochas, both male and both older - one in his late thirties and the other in his forties, if Bea had to guess - but equally affluent in appearance. Their suits were designer, Paul Smith and Alexander McQueen, and the diamonds on their matching solitaire wedding rings sufficiently large that the cut of each was visible to her from ten feet away.

Amit, the older-looking of the two, worked for a sexual health charity, or so Aarti had said - not as a fundraiser, nothing so boots-on-the-ground, but as the CFO, managing budgets and coordinating bids. He was an attractive man, Bea thought, and made more so by his willingness to embrace rather than try to stave off the ageing process - the crow's feet under his eyes and the streaks of silver in his black hair a testament, she decided, to robust self-esteem rather than a lack of self-care.

Luke, his husband, was baby-faced by comparison - a thick-set, curly-haired bear-cub of a man, his full reddish-brown beard growing up his cheeks and down his neck like copper ivy. He was an IT consultant: a network specialist who worked primarily from home and, as per Aarti's slightly breathless description, could be regularly spotted lifting weights in his living room around lunchtime each day, shirtless and glistening with sweat.

Beside him sat the first of the renters, Bea herself notwithstanding - an elderly woman named Joan McTierney. She was small, white and fragile: her grey hair sparse and her face as liver spotted as her hands and wattled throat. She looked threadbare, Bea thought - as if a long, tiring working life spent on her feet had worn her that bit too thin. She'd been a cleaner before she'd retired, Aarti had said, and before that a stay-at-home mother to a son and two daughters, the latter of whom had secured her a place at The Gates when she'd fallen, unknowingly, behind on her rent and been promptly evicted thereafter from the council house she'd lived in almost all of her life.

Next to her, dour and dowdy in a hooded top and pale-blue tracksuit bottoms, was the other renter, Kajal Sawiak, whom Aarti had said was *still* a cleaner: her two jobs taking her away from The Gates and her nine year old child six days a week, from 6am until dinner time. She was thin, too thin in Bea's opinion, her wrists like twigs and the skin pulled tight across her jaw and cheekbones; South Asian, but decidedly pale and sickly-looking. Her hair was short and greasy, dark roots cropping up through blonde bleach, and her fingernails were marked with the small white spots of mineral deficiency. She seemed, to Bea, as if she'd prefer to be anywhere else but at the table.

"She hardly talks," Aarti had said, when Bea had pressed her for details, "so we know almost nothing about her, not compared to everyone else here. She's divorced, I think, but the ex-husband isn't around, from what we've seen. The daughter's a bit chattier, though. And just between us," she'd added, "I wouldn't be surprised if he used to hit her – the husband. She's not said anything to me about it, obviously. But she's got that *look* about her, if you know what I mean. Sort of... beaten-down."

The daughter, Karolina, sat to the left of her mother. She was solid, where her mother was skinny, and to Bea's eye altogether healthier in appearance: her brown hair thicker and glossier, her teeth straighter and whiter. She wasn't smiling, though; was making little effort to make conversation or hold eye contact with the others in the Hall, her blank gaze fixed instead on the bowl of foraged mushroom soup and chunk of home-made sourdough bread on the wicker placemat in front of her.

Both bread and soup had originated with the last two people around the bench: Ivan and Elaine Davenport, joint owners of one of The Gates' more substantial properties and nominated by Jordan himself to feed their neighbours at this particular Co-Life Dinner. They were pink, plump and in their early sixties, early retirees and the dictionary definition of empty nesters. From a distance, Bea might have taken them for characters from an Agatha Christie adaptation: the bluff former colonel and his well-kept wife, she the enthusiastic treasurer at her local Women's Institute and he an avowed outdoorsman, often to be found shooting grouse or clay pigeons on the grounds of his country estate.

In fact, Aarti said, they'd been importers and wholesalers - providing exotic fruits, vegetables, meats and pulses to some of the most expensive restaurants in the country at a comfortably high profit via a distribution network now overseen by their eldest son. Ivan wore tweed, a thin white moustache and an Argyle sweater draped around his shoulders; his wife, in true Christie style, was in pearls, her tawny perm a near-perfect colour match for the silk of her blouse.

"I really think," she was saying, her face turned to Jordan's, "that we ought to do something about the magpies."

Bea's stomach convulsed, briefly, at the word magpie: at the memory it conjured of the bloody, impaled crow at her own front door, the gore and innards that had spilled from it like melted cheese from a pizza when she'd scooped it up with a bin bag.

"*Just* the magpies?" asked Luke Harris. "What about the other birds, the crows and that?"

He was another local, then, Bea realised as she listened to him speak - very local, by the sound of it.

"I've spoken to a pest control company," Jordan said, waving his goblet at them both magnanimously - a Medieval king resolving a dispute among the peasants. "They've recommended we install ultrasonic devices on the perimeter of each house - sound wave generators, to scare the birds away. They're typically used for cats, but apparently crows have very sensitive hearing, as sensitive as ours, so they may work on them too."

"Wouldn't that mean *we'll* have to hear them as well, if we're all on the same frequency?" said Joan McTierney.

Jordan ignored her, and the others followed suit.

"I'm more concerned," he continued, "about our security issue."

"What security issue?" said Luke.

"What *security*?" Raj muttered. "Our place didn't even come with burglar alarms."

"*By design*," Jordan answered, sounding irritated. "What sort of village would we be, if we didn't trust each other enough to leave our doors unlocked, figuratively speaking?"

"It's not *us* I'm worried about, mate," Raj countered. "Or have you not been reading the news?"

Jordan held up a hand to quiet him.

"And there, you've hit the nail on the head," he said. "The security issue we have isn't with any individual house, it's with The Gates itself. Until the construction guys can fit a fence around the site, more or less anyone could walk in whenever they want. And what with all the trouble in town…"

"Those boys who got murdered, you mean," Joan McTierney corrected him.

"*Yes*, Joan," he said, impatiently. "Those boys who got murdered. I'm not expecting anything like that out here, before anyone asks," he added. "The only crimes I've ever known happen 'round this way are fly-tipping and the odd toolbox getting nicked out the back of a work van someone's been daft enough to leave wide open. But that doesn't mean we shouldn't be sensible."

"What is it you were thinking?" said Luke.

Jordan grimaced, as if about to outline a complication of intractable difficulty.

"We can't erect a fence or build a wall, not while the work's still going on," he said. "And it'll be months before the rest of the plots are finished. So it strikes me that we've got two choices: we can either hire someone to come in, a security guard or a nightwatchman or something like that, and take the money out of the service charge… or we all club together and shell out for some CCTV cameras, get the lads to hang them up around the site, and one of us can take charge of looking over the footage every couple of days, just to make sure no-one's been sneaking around or trying to rob us."

If it's *your* development, Bea thought, should *you* be the one to sort this out, and pay for it? Why are you putting it on *us*?

"And it would be covered by the service charge as is, would it?" asked Aarti carefully.

"No," Jordan said. "No, we'd have to adjust the charge, if we wanted to accommodate additional costs. Adjust it upwards. Right now it only covers maintenance of the common areas - this place, the pathways, the recycling area... and the pool-house."

Bea's own hackles rose at the mention of the pool-house. She glanced down the table to Joan McTierney; saw the old woman's lips, too, were pursed in displeasure.

Raj, though, seemed irked for a different reason.

"You're saying you won't pay for security yourself, then?" he asked Jordan, faintly aggressively. "Even though it's *your* land, *your* development, and it's *your* pocket our mortgages are going in," he looked over at Bea and then, seeming to realise what he'd said, looked quickly away again, "you're not willing to sort it?"

"We share our resources," Jordan told him, "and we share our responsibilities. That's what *makes* us a community. I'm not some nineteenth-century landlord trying to squeeze you for your last penny. I live here too; I'm one of you. How are we supposed to learn to work together, to find solutions together, if I swoop in with a big wad of cash every time we run up against a stumbling block?"

Except you *are* my landlord, Bea thought. I quite literally pay you rent. All this *I'm just one of you lot* rubbish would be a lot more convincing if that wad of cash you're talking about didn't come directly out of my bank account.

She was genuinely angry now; incensed even, both at Jordan's refusal to meet what were so clearly his obligations and at the possibility of having to pay herself - pay money she could ill afford - to mitigate against being burgled or slaughtered in her sleep.

The sensation rose up in her like hot liquid, lava or molten steel; flowing upwards from her toes and the muscles in her calves to her stomach, her chest, the top of her head, until she was boiling in it, caramelising in her own rage. For a moment or two, she could happily have murdered Jordan - put her hands around his neck and squeezed, taken the large serrated blade from the breadboard in front of her and hurled it between his eyes with the strength and surety of a circus knife-thrower.

And then it passed, and she came back to herself, aware of a pain in her jaw where she'd ground her back teeth together, of blood in her mouth where she'd bitten the side of her tongue.

"So that's it, then, is it?" Raj asked, no less confrontational than before. "Cameras or a nightwatchman, and either way it's us paying for it?"

Jordan took a slow, contemplative sip of his wine.

"Cameras, and you'd pay less," he said. "For a purchase, an *item*, it's only fair that all of us contribute, owners *and* tenants - which would lower the overall outlay for everyone. A security guard, though - that's a service. An ongoing expense. And since only property *owners* are liable for the service charge..."

"We'd pay more," Luke Harris finished. "We'd pay more, and this lot..." he gestured to Joan McTierney, to Kajal Sawiak - though not, Bea noticed, to her, "they'd get the same benefits, the same protection, but they'd pay nothing."

And the alternative is - what? Bea thought. Throw the serfs to the wolves? Hire a guard and tell them to ignore our houses when they do their rounds?

"I can't afford no cameras," Joan McTierney said. "Not on my pension."

"And we can't, either," Karolina Sawiak added indignantly, apparently speaking on behalf of her mother.

"I'm sorry," said Elaine Davenport, addressing Joan rather than the girl, and obviously not in the least bit sorry, "but community spirit or not, your personal finances are hardly *our* responsibility. And who's to say that Ivan and *I* can stretch to these extra charges, either? We're on a fixed income too, you know."

You can stretch to that Hermès scarf around your neck, though, can't you? Bea thought. And that year-old Range Rover I saw parked in your driveway.

"Look," said Jordan, raising his hand again, "we don't have to decide straight away. Just have a think about it, everyone, alright? And we can take a vote at the Sharing Assembly on Friday. I don't know about the rest of you, but I'm starving, and I don't know how much longer I can sit here looking at this feast Elaine's cooked up without drooling down my own chin."

He's playing the peacemaker, Bea told herself - the beneficent leader. Or trying to seem like he is.

But she'd seen something else in him, too, or so she believed: a flash of... not pleasure, exactly, but a sort of calculated watchfulness. A concentrated interest in the chaos he'd unleashed, the cat he'd set among the pigeons - the focused consideration of a Logic professor as he manoeuvred an unsuspecting group of students into a round of the Prisoner's Dilemma.

She'd studied game theory, briefly, at university; had a dim recollection of the principles, the case studies her own lecturers had wheeled out.

Maybe that's what this is, she thought. Game theory in action. Him pitting one group's interests against another's and seeing what happens next - which way each one of them votes, how each one of them reacts.

Each one of *us*.

The thought was both discomfiting and puzzling. Why, after all, would anyone do that? What would be the benefit, especially to someone trying to cultivate the sort of community ethos The Gates was purportedly built on?

Or was *why* the wrong question for her to be asking? Was Jordan just the kind of guy who liked to sow discord for discord's sake?

The remainder of the meal passed comparatively uneventfully: Jordan guiding the table's conversation into the less controversial waters of the late summer heat and the presumptive assault-by-fox on the Arolkers' garden waste bin that had unleashed a tsunami of twigs, leaves and cut grass onto the lower body of Raj's just-cleaned Audi.

Elaine Davenport's desserts, a double-bill of Eton mess and vanilla cheesecake, were unveiled and lavishly praised by the Harris-Hindochas for their depth and complexity of flavour; Amit, who seemed to Bea the friendlier of the couple, made a concerted - and, she thought, faintly apologetic - effort to engage with her, expressing interest in her work at the museum and backtracking immediately, and with a discretion she couldn't fail to appreciate, at the earliest mention of Jeremy and the divorce.

"Folklore?" he asked, after grilling her - gently - about the exhibition she'd most recently overseen. "How absolutely *fascinating*. Were there, you know... big cats and things? I go straight to the Beast of Bodmin Moor, when I think about folklore."

"Mostly elves and pixies," she told him, smiling. "The occasional black dog, but mostly elves and pixies. Sorry to disappoint."

He'd placed a hand on hers and squeezed it companionably. It was, it occurred to her later, the first time she'd been touched with anything like intimacy since That Sunday: the day Jeremy had sat her down at the kitchen table and told her, gently but firmly, that he was leaving her, and why. For whom.

"My office is nothing but condoms and STI testing," he said, smiling back. "Honestly, my love - I'd give my right arm for a pixie or two some days."

Luke, picking up the tail-end of their conversation, shot Amit a warning glance, and glared at Bea over his cream and strawberries.

Neither Kajal Sawiak nor Joan McTierney said another word for the rest of the evening.

Bea had left her phone on charge at home for the Co-Life Dinner, conscious of wanting to avoid embarrassment by having it beep or rattle in her handbag while they were eating. The sort of people that would choose to live in a place like The Gates, she'd reasoned (and the sort of people, in the case of Jordan, that would choose to build a place like The Gates in the first place) probably wouldn't take kindly to the presence of technology in the Community Hall; would consider it a distraction from the enjoyment of one another's company, or the development of authentic and spiritually-enriching human connections, or whatever other bollocks it was they believed.

There were, consequently, three new messages waiting for her when she finally arrived back at the house: one from her father, still on extended vacation in Marseilles, and two from Jeremy.

She let her father's message play - realising, after the several seconds of muffled voices and background noise that followed, that he hadn't intended to call her at all, and that his voicemail had been left entirely by accident.

Jeremy's messages she simply deleted. Anything he had to say that might be worth hearing, she reasoned, he could say to her face. *He* had her new address; if he had to speak to her, in pursuit of whatever end-goal, he could get in his bloody Volvo and drive back up to Leicester. The little whore could fend for herself for a few hours, even deprived of his company. Besides which: his solicitor had made Jeremy's legal position abundantly clear in *his* correspondence. On that score, at least, there was nothing left to say.

It was tiring, following the train of thought along its track and past the same stations it inevitably travelled: Jeremy; the divorce; his parasitic lawyer; her own, entirely useless brief, the one who'd seemed so content to submit to *an equitable division of assets* even though it was *her* who'd been left, *her* who'd had her life so unexpectedly scooped out from its moulding and its component parts incinerated. Tiring, and stressful, particularly as the epilogue to the strange, nerve-shredding dinner she'd just suffered through – to the profound peculiarity of both her new neighbours and her new neighbourhood, and to her own dawning awareness of what exactly she'd signed up for at The Gates in return for cheap rent and a desirable postcode.

Of the incessant petty squabbles and deranged power-plays that being part of a community, or certainly *this* community, apparently entailed.

A bath, she thought. I'll take a bath.

Her new bathroom, at least, was a comfort, an oasis of calm amid the wider madness: a clean, minimalist exercise in Modernist design, its marbled coral-pink tiling and deep oval washbasins built around a freestanding claw-foot bathtub that was clearly intended as the centrepiece of the room. She hadn't used the tub yet; had spent the last week showering, saving the bath for a time when she most needed it. For the moment when a long soak in liquorice-scented bubbles with a tumbler of whiskey in her hand might be the only thing she could rely on to relax the muscles in her shoulders and bring her resting pulse down to an acceptable level.

Tonight felt like that time.

She turned on the taps to let the water run and made her way downstairs to pour the whiskey. Satisfied with its potency, she began to undress in the living room, revelling in the sensation of having a house entirely to herself, a house in which she was free to go as naked or as fully-clothed as she wished at any hour of the day or night, and in any room she wanted - providing she, unlike Luke Harris, remembered to close the blinds.

Clothes and underwear shed, she padded back up the stairs to the bathroom, sipping from the tumbler and humming lightly to herself in anticipation of pleasure, her bare feet luxuriating in the feel of the unworn carpet under her toes.

And stopped, dead, in the bathroom doorway, the sudden motion spilling half the whiskey in the glass onto the tiled floor.

There was a woman in the bathtub: a young woman, as naked as Bea, no older than twenty but bald and toothless as a fairy tale witch, her mouth sunken and stubbly clumps of regrowth gathering in random constellations on the surface of her swollen scalp. Her skin was grey, tending to mottled-green and bruised-blue around the armpits, breasts and thighs, her eyes corpse-grey down to the iris. She was, it seemed to Bea, very obviously dead.

Nevertheless, she was moving: shivering, the water around her vibrating with every violent shake of her rotting body. She looked, Bea thought - inasmuch as she was able to form thoughts, to reshape what she was seeing into an image she could reconcile with a semi-sane universe - very much as if she were frightened; terrified, in fact, and in no small amount of physical pain, despite the soothing warmth of the water.

Bea blinked; squeezed her own eyes shut and held them there for a beat, then another.

When she opened them, the young woman was gone, and there was nothing but feathers in the place she'd been: dark, oily feathers, a blanket of them, floating like rose petals on the surface of the water.

CHAPTER 4

Like the others, Simon Henshaw had been left in the open after his death: his crushed, toothless body dumped in a trolley outside a pet shop on the outskirts of the city centre, and stumbled upon in the early hours of a Sunday morning by a group of teenagers on their way back from a night of clubbing, their systems still so saturated with MDMA and the damage to Henshaw so pronounced that they were unsure, in the first instance, that what they were seeing really *was* a body, and not a scarecrow or a mannequin or an abandoned sex doll.

The pet shop owners, Lou had learned from her hours spent trawling the forums, had been interviewed, and presumably exonerated by police; the teenagers, too, had been released, after an initial round of questioning.

There was nothing symbolically significant about the dump site itself, as far as she could tell. The pet shop was unremarkable: a small, scruffy store topped by a striped canopy coated in dust and old exhaust fumes, squeezed in between a halal butcher and a vape shop that had once been a Polish supermarket, and before that an Australian-themed bar that Lou remembered visiting, in the days before she'd left for university. There was a small skatepark on the opposite side of the street, and beside it a Catholic church with an adjacent, overgrown graveyard; either one of them, she thought, would have made more sense as a dumping ground than the pet shop.

In the doorway of the church, her own vape pen clasped between her teeth, she took out her phone, pressed Record and began to replay - in the kind of slow, slightly hesitant narrator's voice that podcasts seemed to necessitate - the few things she'd seen at the site that had struck her as even remotely interesting: the use of the trolley ("a killer's critique of late capitalism?" she asked herself and her future listeners); the proximity to the butcher ("animal rights activism?"); the straw and sawdust in the pet shop window ("comment on the fragility of human life?")

John Seward's body had been left by a herbalist dispensary and Paul Knight's in a hospital, both medical surroundings - albeit in her opinion tenuously, in the herbalist's case. This, she reasoned, might suggest the beginnings of a pattern: a murderer with a propensity to deposit their kills in healthcare contexts after the fact, possibly even one with a grudge against the medical establishment. And if that *was* the murderer's pattern, then it would be logical to conclude that Simon Henshaw, as their third victim, would have turned up in a similar location: near a dentist's office, or a physiotherapist's, or a podiatrist's store front.

Instead, he'd been found outside a pet shop. A *pet shop*.

It made no sense.

She took a long, deep drag on the vape pen - the sound of which, she hoped, would add a noir-ish note of jaded frustration to her commentary on the audio recording, the world-weariness of a Philip Marlowe or an Easy Rawlins - and slid her phone into the pocket of her jeans.

She'd driven the six miles into Leicester in the dented little Citroën she'd inherited from Dan, her brother, and was halfway back to her parents' house in Countesthorpe when she remembered the *other* reason she'd made the trip to town: she had a date.

The girl's name was Josie, or she'd said it was - Lou was never sure how much stock to invest in the word of a stranger on a dating app. She was roughly Lou's age, twenty-six; an assistant librarian with novel-writing aspirations who volunteered with a children's theatre company in her spare time and who seemed, on the basis of the dozen or so messages and pictures they'd exchanged, very pretty, very nice and very thoughtful, if a little over-earnest and unlikely to set Lou's world on fire conversationally.

Though she hadn't said so explicitly, Lou suspected that she, too, lived with her parents - and it was this, more than anything else, that had convinced her to agree to a drink when Josie had suggested it. A date with a proper, adult woman - one with a salary, a home of her own, maybe even her name on the deed - would lead almost certainly to Lou's humiliation, in her current, much reduced circumstances; a date with another overgrown child felt safer and more manageable by comparison, even in the absence (at least from Lou's perspective) of any overwhelming romantic attraction.

She had no plans, however, to share the latter point with Josie.

Once she'd turned the car around, driven back into town and found somewhere close enough to the place they'd agreed on to park, she was fifteen minutes late - and, she realised as she pushed through the doors, had entirely forgotten to alert her date to her lateness.

She was waiting for Lou in an alcove by the bar, her phone in her hands and her eyes glued to the screen. It wasn't until Lou had pulled up a chair and sat down that she looked up and registered Lou's presence.

"I thought I'd been stood up," she said, grinning. It *sounded* understanding, at least, or so Lou thought; more understanding than Lou herself might have been, in similar circumstances.

She was dressed much like Lou, in jeans and a long-sleeved shirt that was slightly too warm for the summer heat - and not, as Lou had been expecting, in an ankle-length skirt or a fluffy sweater or any of the other accessories she'd subconsciously associated with librarianism. She smiled more than Lou had imagined she would, too; gave the impression, on first glance, of taking neither herself nor Lou particularly seriously.

"Sorry," Lou replied. "I..."

She stopped herself, mid-sentence. What *was* it she'd been doing, exactly? Snooping around a murder scene with a camera-phone, hunting for clues? Gathering material for the true crime show she'd been thinking of launching, after she'd read about some men she didn't know who'd been tortured and killed not far from where she grew up?

Either explanation, she surmised, would send Josie running - probably very sensibly - for the hills.

"I got lost," she finished weakly.

Josie's smile broadened.

"Aren't you *from* here?" she asked. *She* was from Northampton, Lou recalled; the more legitimately able of the two of them to plead geographic uncertainty, should she need to.

"Yeah," Lou said, embarrassed. "But I was away nearly seven years - a lot's changed. Makes it hard to navigate, when everything's different than you remember it being - when the school uniform shop's a bubble tea cafe and the HMV's a macaron stall..."

She stopped again; let the words trail off into the ether. There was something there, in what she'd just said; something important. Something she knew but didn't *know* she knew - something her brain was trying to tell her, but that the conscious bit of her couldn't quite hear. Something to do with the murders; with the scene she'd just visited.

"Everything alright?" Josie asked, a flash of worry pressing her smile into a straight, flat line.

What *was* it? Lou thought. It was there, on the tip of her mind - the proximity of it itching and prickling like an insect bite, a hidden splinter under her skin.

"Sorry," she said, a second time. "Just..."

"Retracing your steps?" Josie supplied, the smile back in place.

"Something like that," Lou answered, smiling back. "Should probably get my eyesight checked," she added.

"God, don't - I went to the optician yesterday about my contacts, and they took about an hour getting my prescription ready..."

The prickling intensified, and Lou felt herself edging closer to... something. An answer. A memory, maybe?

Prescription, Josie had said.

My prescription.

And there it was, suddenly, no longer on the edges of her understanding but fully-formed and concrete: what the butcher's shop next to the pet shop was, what it hadn't been in fifteen years but what it *had been, once*, when she was a crying kid with an ear infection and her Dad had rushed her there in the back of his cab because it was after six o'clock on a Saturday and there was nowhere else open.

"A chemist," she said aloud. "It used to be a chemist."

The anxious look reappeared on Josie's face, and a flash of puzzlement with it.

"What did?" she asked.

It was called Solanki's, Lou remembered. Solanki's Pharmacy. It had been small and stacked, the shelves overflowing with creams and gels and sanitary towels; had smelled of mouthwash and disinfectant fluid. There'd been lollipop whistles on display beside the till.

And if it used to be a chemist... then there was a pattern to the body dumps, after all. Whoever killed Simon Henshaw and Paul Knight and John Seward was trying to say something with their choice of location - something about health, about medicine. They were out to make a point.

What that point might be, she couldn't fathom - not with the information she had.

But if she kept digging...

She reached for the phone in her pocket; shot up from her chair with the force of a bullet.

"I'm sorry," she said for a third time, ignoring the look of absolute bewilderment creeping over Josie's eyes and mouth as she spoke, "I think I need to go. I'm really sorry."

She almost tripped over her legs in her race for the exit; barged through the door, shoulder-first, and sprinted down the road towards the car.

CHAPTER 5

The feathers were gone: vanished from the bath without a trace, as quickly and cleanly as the rotting woman had vanished before them.

And, three large whiskies and a cigarette later - from the emergency packet she'd brought with her in the move, the packet she'd told herself she'd never smoke - she almost had herself convinced she hadn't really seen them, that they were never really there at all.

Almost.

She was, she told herself, as if talking herself down from a high ledge, a prime candidate for a stress-induced hallucination: thirty-nine and flooded with fluctuating hormones, the hormones in question almost certainly playing havoc with her emotional state as well as the condition of her body; in the middle of a scarring relationship breakdown that had cost her her home and her savings as well as her stability. She was psychiatrically medicated, if it came to that - albeit on the lowest dose of the antidepressant her doctor had prescribed when she'd rocked up at his surgery complaining of headaches, a racing heartbeat and insomnia.

On paper, she considered, she was every inch a Hysterical Woman - her hyper vigilance and neuroticism conjuring otherworldly threats and indescribable horrors around every corner.

Except... there was a flavour to the air, in the bathroom.

There were no visible traces of crow or corpse in the tub, it was true: no pitch-black down or grease-marks on the bottom, no drifting flakes of greying skin or tell-tale fingerprints on the porcelain. Just cooling water, slick with bubble-bath residue - water Bea had no intention of draining. The thought of touching it at all was horrifying; the possibility of breaking the surface with her fingers, of dipping a hand into the space where those feathers and that body had been - where she'd *imagined* they'd been - was unspeakable.

But there was a smell, or the lingering memory of one, as faint as the scent of rain the day after a thunderstorm. It was something like sweat, and something like burning, and it hadn't - and this she would swear to - been there in the bathroom before, not even when she'd first turned on the taps and stepped out to the kitchen to pour herself a drink.

It was possible, she knew - though she was no psychiatrist - for hallucinations to be olfactory as well as visual or auditory; for the brain to invent a thousand synaesthetic ways to torment itself under pressure.

But she wasn't sure at all hers *had* done, was the thing. And a part of her suspected that, had someone else been there with her in that bathroom - Jeremy, say - then they would have smelled it, too.

It was almost midnight by the time she'd finished the whiskey - long past an acceptable hour to contact family or friends except in the event of an emergency. A *confirmed* emergency, she corrected herself; one whose existence could be verified in the real, physical world. Besides which: who *would* she have called or texted in her panic, were calling after midnight an option? Her father was in France, her mother dead, and her sister Kelly - pleasant though she was, when she and Bea bumped into one another at funerals and unavoidable family get-togethers - was as much a stranger to her as the Davenports or the Harris-Hindochas. What friends she'd had were Jeremy's friends, too, and they'd made it abundantly clear, in their silence - in the messages they hadn't sent, the questions they hadn't asked, the invitations to dinner they'd found more and more inventive ways to decline - whose side they'd be choosing, were it necessary for sides to be taken.

She was, at least for now, entirely alone.

It wasn't new information, the fact of her aloneness - and there were moments, like earlier that evening, when she didn't experience it as loneliness at all, but rather a temporary suspension of social expectations, a break - albeit an enforced one - from the obligations placed on her by friendships and intimate partner relations.

At other moments, though, she was lonely, and painfully so: the absence of people to talk and listen to an open, suppurating wound she lacked the means to heal. The absence of Jeremy - so often Jeremy, by her side in bed and at dinner and in front of the television on a Saturday night, his arm around her waist or his lips pressed against the back of her neck.

She'd never been scared to be alone, though - not before tonight. Had never worried that a privation of company might equate to vulnerability; never conceived of the presence of a warm body next to hers as a defensive shield, a bulwark against the terrors waiting for her in the dark or springing, unbidden, from her own mind.

The thought that it might be - that having no-one to rely on but herself might leave her not just melancholy but exposed, unprotected - only frightened her further; seemed to amplify the original dread she'd felt at the sight of the dead woman. The dread she still felt, now, in recalling it.

She couldn't bring herself to go to bed, not with her bedroom so close to the bathroom; to the bathtub and the water, to the abiding traces of that strange and somehow terrible smell. So, with every light downstairs switched on to its highest beam and the weight of the whiskey in her stomach muffling at least a little of the fear, she edged her way to the living room, trembling at every soft tread of her feet on the carpet, and sank down onto the sofa, knees gathered tight to her chest and a picnic rug she'd yet to find a place for in the house tucked behind her hips and shoulders like a shroud.

She wouldn't sleep, she thought; how could anyone, in her place? But she could rest - lie still and quiet until morning, until the sun rose and the world woke and she could reasonably and legitimately, and without undue alarm, take herself out of this house and away from The Gates, and perhaps even into the fellowship of other, categorically living people until such time as she felt certain of her own sanity. Until such time as she was definitively equipped to banish the image of the woman - her green-blue skin, and the black of the feathers all around her.

She closed her eyes. Opened them again, experimentally - and saw the room around her receding, the robin's-egg wallpaper of the lounge giving way to bare white stone and a small barred window that reminded her, absurdly, of the walls of a monk's cell she'd seen once on a visit to an abbey in Siena. She blinked; felt, then saw the sofa cushions under her begin to writhe and undulate, the padding and upholstery reshaping and reconfiguring itself until there *were* no cushions, *was* no sofa, but was instead a hard, thin mattress on a rusting metal bed frame, its khaki top-sheet crawling with black bugs just large enough to be seen, but too small to be accurately identified. Her legs, the legs that had been stretched out in front of her only seconds before, were now, she saw, tied to the ends of the bed frame by two torn strips of a tough brown fabric; her wrists, likewise, were strapped to the metal slats above her head by a pair of battered leather manacles.

She looked up. On one Baroque, floral-patterned and incongruously ornate cornice in the ceiling above her perched a crow - fat, black-beaked and shiny as an oil-slick.

She twitched, unintentionally straining against the straps that held her, and it cawed - opened its beak to hiss, then unfurled its wings and flung itself towards her, shedding feathers as it flew.

She screamed.

It landed, horribly, between the bare flesh of her ankles, its greasy plumage brushing lightly against her skin, and seemed to settle there, wings retracting back against its gently pulsing sides.

She opened her lips to scream again, but nothing came, her throat closing as firmly as if it had been stuffed with cotton. There was something wrong with her mouth, she realised, running the dry tip of her tongue along her gum line; an unfamiliar absence, something missing that ought to have been there.

Her teeth. Her teeth were gone.

Often, in the anxiety dreams she'd had since Jeremy's leaving, she'd shed and lost, watched helplessly as the ancillary components of herself withered and fell away: tufts of hair, cascading into her hands as she tugged at her scalp; layers of muscle and fat and epidermis, as she dug nails into her cheeks and clawed at her face; fingers and toes, wrinkling and mummifying and contracting in on themselves until they came apart from the tendons that had held them and fell, painlessly, from the trusted moorings of her hands and feet.

But never teeth. Not before now.

Devoid of pulp and minerals, the sockets of her gums were hollow, tasting of old blood and the remnants of whatever stale food had caught in them. And they ached - not badly, the way a legitimate toothache might, but enough to give her the impression that the missing teeth hadn't fallen away, as the hair and teeth and nails had in her dreams, but had been actively removed. Had been pulled out.

At the base of the bed, the crow shifted position, its feathers ruffling. It cawed again, and to Bea's horror, another of the creatures, invisible to her from where she lay, cawed loudly back in response - not from outside, where cawing might have made at least a kind of sense, but from inside the room. From under the bed.

She watched, paralysed, as the new crow insinuated itself into the mostly-empty room; as first its beak, then its slick, dark head and finally its claws and feathers - filthy feathers, she saw, coated with dust and dirtier by far than the first crow's - poked out from where it had hidden itself below the bed frame.

It didn't fly; kept its wings sheathed. Instead, it seemed to hop from the bare floor to the mattress - joining its companion between her lower legs and then, apparently unsatisfied with the level of comfort this position afforded it, actually onto her ankle bone, resting there like a cockatoo on a perch.

She found she couldn't move; couldn't so much as jerk a muscle or kick out to dislodge it, to *get it off* of her. Could only lie there, still as a statue in this place she didn't know and hadn't asked to be taken to - her toothless, useless body nothing but an obstacle for the birds and insects to negotiate. Until, that was, one or other of them decided she was carrion.

She felt terror, of course; absolute, and almost all-encompassing, a terror so vast and so utterly shredding that she failed to see how any one self could contain it.

But not just terror. There was something else there, too, lying just below the stratified deposits of her fear.

Anger.

No; not anger. Anger was... not enough, somehow. What she felt wasn't hot and sharp, but deep; not the molten spew of a volcano when it finally ruptured but the steady movement of the magma in the chamber, the building force of ancient pressure as it grew and gathered under the rock below.

Rage.

Rage at her confinement; at the straps holding down her wrists, the strips of fabric cutting off the oxygen to her legs, the bars on the window. Rage at the insects and the crows that crawled and scratched at her with no regard at all for her discomfort or her pain. Rage, most of all, at the men who'd done this to her: held her down until she thought her arms would break and pulled her teeth from her mouth with their pliers, left her in this hole to rot with the birds and the foxes that came sniffing around the bars at night, and with nothing to eat but the stale crusts of bread she couldn't chew.

Wait, though.

Wait.

What men? Held her down *where*?

She let her eyes close again; tried to block out, inasmuch as she was able, the gnaw of the *nothing* that was left in her gums, the scratching of the insects behind her back and knees, the terrible caress of the crow feathers against her ankles.

Tried to *think*.

Whatever this bed was, whatever this cell was... she wasn't in it. Not really.

She was on her sofa, in her house; in The Gates, in her own body. Her body, ageing and pharmaceutically enhanced as it was – a body she knew and one she trusted, at least some of the time. One that had never undergone so much as a root canal, let alone suffered the wholesale removal of all twenty-eight of its teeth.

Not in *this* body - this mutilated, animal-worried sack of meat and discomfort, this set of limbs shackled to an alien bed in a whitewashed dungeon, seething with hatred for the unnamed men who'd done her wrong.

She was Beatrice Alexander, neé Gulliver. She was thirty-nine years old, curator of exhibits and mother of no-one, married - albeit now in only the most technical of senses - to a man called Jeremy, whom she'd once loved more than she knew how to articulate and who had left her one day, with no warning at all, for a girl ten years younger and a hundred miles away, a girl now carrying his baby in her belly.

And perhaps she *was* angry; perhaps there *was* an ocean of rage broiling red and molten under the surface of her. But it was anger at *him*, at Jeremy and what he'd done to her. At him, and no-one else.

She was herself. Herself, in her own home, and not here, in this cell that couldn't be real, with bugs she shouldn't be able to feel on her skin and crows she shouldn't be able to see at her feet.

Because those things... those things weren't possible.

She forced her eyelids upwards, and found she was right: she *wasn't* there, and therefore - logically - *hadn't* been. She was, instead, in her own living room, on her own sofa, just as she should have been. Her body whole, teeth and all; her arms and legs untied. And not a trace of beaks or feathers anywhere.

It hadn't been real.

She'd dreamed it, then. Dreamed it, or imagined it, or hallucinated it, just as she had the girl and the crow-down in the bathtub.

Which was bad, yes - very bad, possibly, if these things were indeed hallucinations, a product of her own mind turning against her, finally. A problem, certainly.

But a *real-world* problem; a problem that could be addressed through expert intervention, through drug regimens and cognitive-behavioural therapies. Not an illusory monster made of fog and shadow.

If they were hallucinations; if she really *had* imagined them.

Another thought struck her - one that hadn't previously, in the panic of the bathroom and the insanity of the cell, but one which seemed, as it sunk in, a more plausible explanation for what she'd experienced even than a descent into madness.

Mushrooms.

They'd had mushroom soup for dinner, hadn't they? Foraged mushroom soup; the mushrooms picked, as she'd heard first-hand at the table, by the Davenports themselves – both ardent hunters and gatherers of naturally occurring crops since their retirement from the food industry.

She'd believed Elaine, when she'd announced - with no small amount of pride - that she and Ivan could tell a chanterelle from a poisonous Jack O'Lantern at ten paces. Because why on earth would anyone make that kind of boast, if it wasn't true?

What if they'd made a mistake, though, when they were out foraging? What if, instead of the penny buns and oysters they thought they'd been collecting, they'd happened on a psilocybin crop instead?

Bea had never taken hallucinogens; had never been drawn to the prospect of losing herself in alternative realities, especially not when there was a chance of those realities turning on you when you least expected it. The real world was malign enough; there was no point, in her opinion, in ingesting any substance that could, even potentially, make things worse.

But if the mushrooms in the soup *had* been hallucinogenic - that would explain everything, wouldn't it? The girl in the tub, and the bathful of feathers that was somehow just as frightening, just as sickening as the girl's mouldering skin; the room not spinning but actually *changing shape* before Bea's eyes. Even the sensation of immobility, of beetles - as she'd mentally classified them - crawling over her where she lay. The things she'd seen and felt, over the last few hours: they ticked every box on the Bad Trip checklist.

And as for the crows... well, wouldn't it stand to reason that her mushroom-addled, overheated brain would choose *those* to torment her, after the bird she'd seen torn apart by the spikes on her front lawn? After she'd wrenched its leaking body from those spikes with her own two hands?

It would; of course it would.

The clarity of the thought - the sudden but certain knowledge of her temporary, fungus-precipitated insanity - was unexpectedly soothing. If she *had* been poisoned by the Davenports' soup - and really, was there any *if* about it? - then the effects would be short-lived; would wear off, just as soon as the toxins left her system. Whereupon she would wash - though perhaps not in the bathtub, not yet - and dress herself, and brush her teeth, and walk herself across to Aarti Arolker's house to see just how badly affected she and Raj had been by the offending meal.

And the others; she'd check in on them, too, in due course. Joan McTierney especially; the woman had to be eighty if she was a day, and looked to be in pretty poor shape. Who knew how easily someone like her would bounce back, if *she'd* been poisoned?

Comforted, Bea closed her eyes a third time, and willed herself to sleep.

Near, but overhead, she heard the caw of a crow. She blotted it out; pulled the picnic blanket higher over her head until it covered her ears.

Reminded herself, when she felt something like feathers brush roughly against the soles of her feet, that there was nothing there to feel. It was all in her head.

When she did eventually sleep, legs cramping and tensing under the rug, she stayed sleeping - waking only when the rattling of the dustbins outside grew so loud that her unconscious self could no longer ignore it, or repurpose it as a stitch in the wider tapestry of her dreaming.

Foxes, she thought, rubbing dried sleep from her the corners of her eyes. Didn't Aarti Arolker say there were foxes sniffing around the site?

She felt no abiding love for wild animals, though she'd grown up in the countryside - and none, certainly, for the scavenging kind with a tendency to leave trails of litter and decapitated rabbits in its wake. Nor, though, was she particularly frightened of them; armies of circling crows were one thing, but foxes, in her experience, were little more than large, flea-ridden dogs who'd grown overconfident around humans. She'd have, she suspected, no hesitation at all in shooing one away from her doorstep with a sufficiently long-handled broom.

The hallucinations seemed, to her relief, to have abated - the worst of them sweated out of her pores in the night, perhaps, as the mushrooms worked their way out of her bloodstream. There was nothing in the room beyond what ought to have been there: chairs, carpet, television, bookshelf. No crows; no institutional beds; no leather straps around her wrists.

Everything was, more or less, as it should be.

She didn't feel entirely right, though. Felt, in fact, curiously disjointed, as if she'd been pulled apart in a hundred directions and then reassembled in not quite the right order, not quite her earlier configuration.

But perhaps that was normal, with hallucinogens? She had no basis for comparison, no earlier experiences to draw on to make the judgement, though it seemed as if it might be normal. As if it could be.

She weighed up a shower, or even dipping her face and head under the cold tap in the kitchen to reset her faculties; was up from the sofa and halfway there before stopping dead, overcome with nerves at the possibility, at the thought of the water trickling into her mouth and down her neck.

It was the bathtub, she reasoned; the sense-memory of the bathtub, of the girl she'd thought she'd seen lying - floating - in the bathwater. What she'd seen hadn't been real, she knew that now, but the sensation of seeing it, of smelling it... it hadn't left her quite yet. Would need to fully run its course before the underlying fear it had left her with dissipated, just like the mushroom residue in her system.

She could live without washing, until it did.

Cold air, though - that was another story. A very quick immersion in the early morning breeze might be exactly what she needed to clear her head - and get her, moreover, briefly out of and away from the house and the memories it held.

She wouldn't go far; no further, certainly, than the edge of the development.

With any luck, she'd miss the worst of the crows. The *real* crows, she added mentally: the ones that settled on cars and pecked at windows, and not the dream-crows, the repulsive feathered things that had sprung from her mind and made a home for themselves on her body.

She didn't bother to dress herself, beyond shoes and jogging bottoms and a lightweight jacket buttoned up to the collar to protect her braless modesty. She *did* take a weapon with her, though, one she'd thought to cram into the pocket of the jacket on her way out: not a broom but a rolling pin, a satisfyingly hefty wooden model she and Jeremy had been given for Christmas one year by a relative too distant to know that neither of them really cooked.

She wouldn't need it, obviously. But what was the harm in being prepared?

The crows *were* out, still - she saw that immediately. There were six of them on her roof alone, roosting on the tiles; a cluster by the front door of Joan McTierney's little semi, pecking idly at the yellow roses the old woman had planted there, and still more congregating, just as Aarti had described, on the Arolkers' Audi, imperious-looking and entirely unfazed by Bea's presence.

They weren't threatening, it seemed to her; not exactly. They didn't stare at her, or hop towards her on their hooked, dragon-scaled talons when they saw her approach. But she squeezed her fist around the rolling-pin in her pocket that bit tighter as she passed them, just in case.

It was light out already, though not bright - the July sun leaving pinkish streaks across the sky as it rose over what few clouds there were. There were no streetlights on the development, not yet, only lampposts dotted between the few houses already built, but she found she could see perfectly, even as she crossed the long, uneven stretch of tarmac that would eventually connect one end of The Gates to the other.

The rest of the place really did look like a building site, she thought. Whole patches of the clay earth across the large, flat plot of land had already been dislodged to make way for the as-yet-unlaid foundations of future homes, leaving holes in the ground of worrying - and surely slightly dangerous? - breadth and depth. There were blue chemical toilets scattered between scaffold skeletons and piles of unfinished brickwork leading upwards but nowhere; a large red digger, left unattended beside a heap of planks, and an even larger abandoned cement mixer, topped by a second pair of crows that were themselves so tall and sturdy that they really could have been ravens.

She walked slowly, partly for fear of tripping and falling and partly because she no longer trusted her feet to guide her on autopilot. She felt better than she had, it was true - and had gone a good three hours without seeing things that weren't there - but there was an unsteadiness to her gait that hadn't been there previously; a queasiness in her head and gut that could easily progress to full-blown nausea, if she wasn't very careful.

Had she taken the walk at her usual speed, she thought later, then there was every chance she wouldn't have spotted it - or, perhaps, wouldn't have registered it as something of interest, as an object worthy of scrutiny.

But, at her current pace, and with her senses already attuned after the experiences of the night before to detecting alien aspects in the familiar, she *did* spot it; *did* stop to stare.

It was a clump of hair: a tangled, curly cluster of Rita Hayworth red that seemed, from the tiny bulbs of white she thought she could make out here and there, to have been plucked from its owner's head at the root.

She bent to examine it, though stopped short of actually touching it. It looked human to her, human and organic - the hair of a living woman or man, and not the woven strands of a wig or a weave.

It was flecked with blood.

She recoiled, her stomach turning.

It isn't real, she whispered to herself. It's another hallucination - you know it is.

Ignore it and move on.

It feels real, though, another and more sensible part of her replied.

So did the cell, and the body in the bath. But it's your brain, tricking you.

But the blood, and the roots ...

There were more strands around the larger cluster of hair, she saw - scattered like dandelion seeds across the clay and up, a fine trail of them, leading all the way to the cement mixer.

They're breadcrumbs, she thought - the idea triggering another soft lurch of her stomach. Like the ones Hansel and Gretel left on their way through the forest.

Follow the breadcrumbs.

Don't, the sensible part of her countered. *Whatever you think might be there, it won't be something you want to see.*

If it isn't real, she answered it, the strange anger that wasn't quite hers beginning to rise again, then it can't actually hurt me, can it? So what do you care, if I look?

The voice fell silent.

She took the rolling pin from her pocket; walked, very slowly, towards the cement mixer.

The crows - or perhaps they really *were* ravens - watched her, not moving an inch from their resting spot; their raisin eyes trained on the movements of her body, the jerking swing of her arms as she approached.

When she was close enough, she swung the pin - intending, if not to hit them, then to scare them sufficiently that they'd leave and not come back until she'd finished her explorations.

They scattered.

The pin struck the mixer hard in the space where they'd been, releasing a bass-note thud into the surrounding air and tilting the lip of the drum downwards.

Dislodging something; something that had been inside.

It fell to the ground almost soundlessly, collapsing in on itself as it landed with a muffled thump.

Another body.

And not an *it* but a *he*: a boy almost young enough to be her son, half the hair torn from the scabbing remains of his scalp and the length of bloodied string tied around the lower half of his face slicing his mouth into an open, involuntary Glasgow smile.

Eyes gone, and tongue missing.

CHAPTER 6

Hadrian Dawson. Six feet tall, twenty-two, white Scottish - transplanted from Dundee to the Midlands as a teenager, when his dad took up a teaching post at the medical school in Nottingham.

He'd studied biochemistry at Warwick, with ambitions to eventually move on to a PhD, but had been working at the time of his death on a construction site near Market Bosworth, intending to use the money he earned as a labourer to fund a three-month backpacking trip through Australia and Southeast Asia.

It was on this same site that he'd been dumped after his death - his body shoved into a cement mixer, only to be stumbled upon later by a local woman out for an early-morning stroll.

His eyes had been gouged out of his head with a blunt instrument: a chisel, or even a spoon, as one of the insiders had suggested on the police and local news forums Lou now haunted. A sharper object had been driven through one of the empty sockets into his brain, effectively lobotomising and eventually killing him; an amputated tongue and flesh wounds to his lips and cheeks, the result of a length of dental floss tied so tightly around his face that it dug into his skin, were among the more minor wounds inflicted upon him, pre-mortem.

He'd been at least partially scalped.

Because his body had been found at his place of work, and because the character descriptions delivered (mostly anonymously) by his co-workers had framed him as an aggressive, entitled and fundamentally unlikeable boy given to starting arguments and occasionally physical fights with the men around him at the slightest provocation, police had been reluctant to tie his killing to the earlier murders of Simon Henshaw, Paul Knight and John Seward - despite the severity and cruelty of his injuries. They thought it more likely, one of the insiders claimed, that Dawson had been stabbed through the eye in the heat of the moment by someone who knew him, perhaps even someone who worked with him - his eyes and tongue subsequently removed, and his mouth lacerated, in order to lend a more ritualistic, serial killer-like look to the crime, a trail false enough to - perhaps - throw the investigating officers off the scent.

Lou disagreed with this hypothesis.

Dawson's murder, she was sure, was connected to Henshaw's, to Knight's and to Seward's - not so much because of the severity of the tortures enacted on all of their bodies, severe as those tortures had been, but rather because of a particular common trait she'd discovered had been shared by all four of the men when they'd been alive.

All of them had been the children of medical professionals.

The killer had evidently wanted to prove a point in their choice of dumping grounds for Henshaw, Knight and Seward: the hospital and the herbalist and the long-closed pharmacy. Lou had determined that much from her own investigations, from her knowledge of the dump sites and their likely semiotic significance. A point about health, maybe, or healthcare; about doctors and patients, caregivers and the cared-for.

And if that were the case, she'd speculated, then wasn't it possible that the men themselves might have some connection to the medical world, too?

A day of assiduous online searching thereafter had confirmed her suspicion. Both Simon Henshaw's mothers were optometrists, the joint owners of an independent optician in Sutton Coldfield. John Seward's grandmother, his legal guardian, had worked as a mental health nurse in Coventry and Dudley before her retirement; Philip Knight's father, now deceased, had been registered as a dietician in Kuala Lumpur and Penang before a career change had brought him to the UK.

Hadrian Dawson's father, meanwhile, was an academic neuroscientist - a lecturer specialising in aphasia and associated language disorders.

They were disparate fields: optometry, psychology, dietetics, neuroscience. So maybe not obviously related, if you weren't already looking for a link between them. But she *had* been looking, and she *had* seen it - and didn't it make perfect sense that a link like that would exist, given where the boys' bodies had turned up?

The construction site was an outlier, sure - there were no chemists or doctor's surgeries there, just fields and wasteland that had always *been* fields and wasteland, at least as long as Lou had been alive. But killers sometimes panicked, didn't they? Panicked, or just made mistakes. They didn't always keep to the patterns they established in their early crimes. And sometimes they lost control of themselves and flew into a frenzy, mid-kill - they *devolved*, as some of the podcasts put it.

So maybe that was what had happened with Hadrian Dawson - a sort of devolution. And maybe the killer, in the aftermath, had ended up with no choice except to leave the body where it had been savaged, instead of moving it to somewhere more meaningful.

Maybe.

The site was an active crime scene, still - it had to be, less than a week on from the body being found. A crime scene full of police tape and forensics people and sniffer dogs; definitely no builders back at work, and far too far out in the middle of nowhere for her to pass herself off as a curious bystander who'd wandered into the place by accident, rather than by design. She'd stick out like a sore thumb, if she went looking around there with her camera out.

But the area *around* the site - that was another story.

It was a housing estate, or the beginnings of one: a place called The Gates, one of those co-living planned community things with a grandiose mission statement, designed for working adults rather than the students or graduates who usually flocked to places like it. Wealthy working adults, if the location and the home designs she'd seen on its website were any indication.

There weren't many houses there yet - less than ten, she'd discovered, with the rest to come as the construction work progressed, if it ever would now. But people lived there, was the point. People with friends and families and colleagues concerned for their wellbeing; people to whom the presence of visitors in the neighbourhood wouldn't seem at all unusual.

One of them might know something; might have seen something out of the ordinary, the night of Dawson's murder. Might even, if she presented herself neatly and politely and happened to remind one of them of their daughter or a much-loved grandchild, be willing to talk to her. To let themselves be interviewed.

She'd been up on the message boards most of the night, making notes and exchanging texts with Josie - who, against all odds, seemed to have written off Lou's sudden disappearance five minutes into their date as an act of idiosyncrasy rather than abject lunacy, accepting the apology Lou had offered with better grace than Lou herself would have been able to muster, in her position.

But Lou wasn't tired, not yet - not with six cups' worth of coffee still lighting up her bloodstream. And the prospect of actually going somewhere, of leaving her bedroom with a clear and active purpose in mind that wasn't just stocking up on the vape refills her mum refused to buy her from the supermarket... it was an appealing one, even this early in the morning.

And The Gates wasn't that far away, really. Not if she drove.

She tiptoed downstairs, hoping the sound of her footsteps on the landing wouldn't carry as far as her parents' bedroom. Her dad was out working, ferrying three generations of a family from Kilby out to Heathrow for a midday flight and probably stopping for a burger at the motorway services on his way back, but her mum was almost certainly still in bed, if not guaranteed to be asleep - and the last thing Lou wanted was her asking questions about why Lou was up so early and what she was doing taking the Citroën out in rush-hour traffic. She didn't think, somehow, that either parent would be all that supportive of their youngest child running off to the countryside to look for a serial killer who'd been cutting up boys not that much younger than she was. Especially not so she could make a podcast about it - if they even knew what a podcast was.

If her mum was asleep, then the roar of the Citroën's engine would almost certainly wake her up when Lou backed it out of the garage. But she'd be out of the house by then; out all day, if things went well, and with ample time to formulate a cover story.

The Gates, when she got there, was a slightly sadder sight than she'd anticipated: a semi-circle of buildings - that were, admittedly, larger and more beautifully designed than any on her own road - penned in on all sides by unmanned machinery, trade materials and excavated earth. The place reminded her, up close, of some of the unincorporated areas she'd driven through, the year she'd studied in inland California, but rendered in miniature: the long, dull stretches of sand and soil that belonged to nobody, punctuated only by the occasional clutch of stores and houses and cattle sheds. The ghost towns.

Stranger still were the spikes: strip after strip of them, sharp little nodules of metal planted in front of each house where lawn and gravel should have been.

Were they a security measure? she wondered. A deterrent? Or part of the anticipated aesthetic of the place?

Were the architects, whoever they were, going for a torture theme with the outdoor decor?

Figuring she'd be less conspicuous without an unfamiliar vehicle, she'd parked the Citroën in a lay-by next to a field opposite the entrance to the development and gone in on foot - her boots, much to her annoyance, sinking into the muddy, uneven clay with every step she took before she hit the pavement.

There was nobody around anywhere, that she could see - no pet-walkers or cyclists, no trios of elderly ladies stopping for a chat on their doorsteps. And no police presence at all, not so much as a panda car or an unmarked Ford with a blue light on the dashboard. Just traffic cones, red and bright orange, demarcating the construction site from the currently occupied sections of land.

It was a little creepy, if she was honest with herself - though she wasn't sure that observation would make it into the analysis of the crime scene she'd be planning for the podcast. It wasn't a found footage horror movie she'd be making; her listeners wouldn't want to hear her scared, or even nervous, as her investigation unfolded. A dependable anchor, that was what they'd be looking for: someone relatable but reliable, and comfortingly stoic. Someone to hold their hands and tell them everything would be okay as they followed her into the darkness.

Fear on her part wouldn't work; wouldn't work at all.

The place was making her skittish, though; there was no sense in denying it, not to herself, even if it wouldn't be prudent to admit as much in public.

Some of the skittishness came from knowing that she was standing on, or close to, a killing ground: a place where death and worse had been meted out to a boy who might have been only a couple of years below her at school.

But that wasn't all of it, or even the greater part.

The sky felt too low in the sky here, for one thing: bulging out and down and - or so it felt - virtually on top of her with a denser force than gravity, so that every step felt leaden, every rise and fall of her toe and heel like a trudge through marshland.

There was something about the trees, too. They weren't unusual, at least on the surface: were oak or chestnut, thick-trunked and sprouting green foliage, the kind of trees you might find on any suburban street in some of the nicer parts of town. But they were *moving*, or so it seemed to her; the higher branches shifting and rustling more loudly and more vigorously than was natural.

And the birds - they weren't quite right, either. There were crows and magpies *everywhere*, huge ones, nipping at the soil and hovering overhead. And okay, this was the countryside, but she couldn't remember ever seeing quite so many of either species congregating in one place before, in or out of the city. There were dozens of them, maybe hundreds, all over the estate, hopping and ruffling like pigeons on Trafalgar Square. They seemed harmless, or maybe just too lazy to want to pose a threat - but it struck her that, if they ever did decide to band together and attack, the person on the receiving end would be lucky to get out with both their eyes intact.

The thought took her back to Hadrian Dawson, the descriptions she'd read of what had happened to his body, and her throat tightened.

Imagine dying like that. Dying like that *here*.

For that matter: imagine *living* here with those birds, under that sky.

Jesus.

As if on cue, the front door of one of the houses nearest to her opened, revealing a woman in the doorway.

She was older - older than Lou, anyway. Early forties maybe, blonde and curvy, her hair pulled back into a ponytail and her lower eyelids puffy from too little sleep or too much crying. She looked like every manager Lou had ever had, if those managers had laid off the makeup and stopped getting dressed in the morning, but with none of the artificial jollity. She was in pyjamas, a red flannel top and tartan trousers that would have been at home on a toddler or an anthropomorphised bear; she'd put on slippers, in spite of the heat, and over the pyjamas wore a dressing gown double-knotted at the waist.

She saw Lou and flinched.

Which was odd too, wasn't it? Suspicion Lou could understand - they were expensive houses, it was an exclusive community even if it *was* half-built, and Lou was a stranger, potentially untrustworthy even in the ironed shirt and smart trousers combination she'd grudgingly exchanged for her own sleepwear before she'd left home. But fear? She was tiny: short as well as skinny and laughably easy to overpower physically. The woman was bigger, probably stronger - looked more than capable of fending off any attack Lou might throw at her.

So what the hell was she afraid of?

She looked back at the woman, determined to catch her eye and prove, through the openness of her expression and the creaking width of her smile, that she at least was nothing for the woman to worry about, no cause at all for alarm.

And realised, with a jolt, that it wasn't Lou the woman was looking at, but a spot just behind Lou, and up - something, and an apparently very frightening something, in the boughs of the tree above Lou's head.

Lou turned around - on instinct, rather than because any rational part of her considered it a sensible strategy. Cast her own eyes up into the thickest crop of leaves and branches, where the foliage shuddered and shifted, and felt her gaze land, unbidden, onto the thing that rested there.

It was as big as she was, maybe even bigger - that was her first impression. Bigger than a large dog; bigger, no question, than any bird she'd even seen that was capable of flight. And yet, somehow, it *was* a bird: sharp-beaked and black-irised, its face the colour and shape of a barn owl's, and feathers fanning up and out from the back of its skull like the tail of a peacock or the ears of a kangaroo. Its grey wings were folded, pressed into the white of its chest like a travelling cape; were they to spring open, she imagined, they would stretch out at least the length of a man in each direction. The claws that secured it to the tree branch below were bright yellow, a splash of toxic colour against the monochrome of its body. Each claw was the size of her hand.

It couldn't exist - that was her initial thought. It couldn't exist, because the fact of its existence was an impossibility. It was too large, too strange.

It couldn't exist, and she couldn't, therefore, be seeing it.

QED.

It was an argument she might well have found compelling, had the blonde woman in the doorway not so obviously been seeing it too.

Lou rotated her head, very gradually, back towards the woman - hesitant to tear her gaze away from the impossible thing, much less to attract its attention through any sudden motion, but sure, equally, that continuing to look at it would drive her somewhere close to madness.

The woman hadn't moved; seemed glued to the spot, her knuckles pressed against her lips in panic.

No help *there*, then, Lou thought.

She allowed herself to turn back, as slowly as she was able, towards the bird-thing in the tree.

Which was no longer there.

It hadn't left; couldn't have. She'd have heard it shift and rattle the branches, had it changed position; heard its wings cut through the air, had it taken flight.

But nevertheless, it was gone.

She spun around again, wanting - needing - to catch the woman's eye, to seek out confirmation not just of what she'd seen, but of what she could no longer see.

Except... now the woman was gone, too. And not just the woman: the whole estate was gone, from the houses to the dug-up land and scaffolding. There, instead, was something like a Gothic castle, flying buttresses and all: a tall, sprawling arrangement of stained brickwork and elaborate metal gates, luxuriant tendrils of ivy growing up the outer walls.

Between Lou and the place where the woman had been was a girl, or what remained of one.

She was upright, her eyes open and her blue lips moving, soundlessly mouthing words Lou couldn't quite hear, but she was in every other respect a walking corpse: grey-skinned and sunken, her black gums retracted to reveal brown teeth far longer than they should have been and the arms and legs that poked out from her stained grey tunic wasted to little more than puckered skin on bone.

A ghost, Lou thought. I'm seeing a ghost.

The girl's mouth opened wider, her lower jaw unhinging in a snake-like motion to unleash a high-pitched scream that was, paradoxically, both loud and far away - as if Lou was hearing a plane take off from the next town over, or listening to the remastered version of a recording that had been of questionable quality to begin with.

She felt a twinge of pain as the sound hit her eardrums, and then, inexplicably, a sudden shock of rage and hate, flooding her system like a line of coke or a shot of neat, clear alcohol - overriding every other instinct, every bolt of fear and urge to flee.

What the hell was this in front of her, this putrefying remnant of a person? And where the fuck did it get off, screaming in her face like that?

Did it think it could *frighten* her? That an optical illusion and a bit of wailing was enough to send her running back home crying for her mother?

Not that her mother would care, if Lou did come home crying. All she cared about was keeping tabs on her daughter and where she was going, trying to feed her up like a prize pig so she'd stay infantilised; never get herself back on her feet and never make it back to London. Never leave the nest, the way Dan had when he'd gone off to Sweden. Never grow up.

As if there was anything much to worry about on that score, anyway. Because what were the odds of Lou ever sorting herself out, really? Ever landing another job, let alone saving up the money to move out again? She'd tried to be an adult, tried to live in the world like a real person, and she'd failed.

Lesson learned.

The girl's mouth snapped shut, her brown top teeth clashing with the bottom pair as they met, and then the rage was gone - the hate and bitterness seeming to drain from Lou as suddenly as it had hit, so quickly that the transition back to herself, or to the self she *thought* she was, left her sick and faintly dizzy.

Behind the girl, the castle began to fade and blur - trace outlines of the Gates estate, the houses, even the blonde woman in the doorway reappearing within its frame.

Except... *within* wasn't quite the word for what Lou was seeing. The Gates, the woman, the doorway... they weren't edging out the castle or supplanting it, so much as co-existing with it in the same physical space: the modern development overlaid onto the older-looking building in a photographic double exposure. The effect, Lou thought, was not unlike looking at an autostereogram or a print strip of negatives folded down the middle. Both scenes were there, if you squinted, the houses and the castle. And, as impossible as the bird-thing of the moment before, were there simultaneously.

She found she couldn't look straight at the scene, not for long - the experience of parsing a single, cohesive image from the two coterminous sites too much for her addled brain. She closed her eyes, *held* them closed, and both the castle and the development vanished.

And something else materialised, something visible even through her squeezed-shut eyelids. Another scene from another place, teeming with movement, but the specifics of it hazy and unfocused, refusing to solidify - as if she'd fallen victim to a temporary flash-blindness that had left her able to discern no finer detail than the most basic of shapes.

Moving, breathing shapes. Organic and sentient.

She couldn't have said how she knew this about them; how she was able to infer anything like as much from the darting flickers that was all they were from where she was standing, the shifting agglomerations of light and shadow they appeared to be. But she knew. Was absolutely certain of it.

And they were *wrong*.

Like the bird-thing, they were big: too big, and strangely proportioned, the limbs (*too many limbs, too many*) flailing bonelessly away from the bodies (*if they* were *bodies, if they* had *bodies*) like the inflatable sleeves of a tube man. And they gave off heat - a heat she could feel not on her skin but in her mind. The *idea* of heat, the Form of it - not the mundane oven-and-mercury iterations she was used to.

They had voices, dry broken voices like the crackle of radio static, and they were sighing, whispering.

Whispering to her.

PART II

CHAPTER 7

Two Days Earlier

Bea hadn't called the police when she'd found the boy's body; not straight away.

The Davenports' mushrooms, she'd reasoned, were still in her - still working their way through her intestines, some residue of the active agent that had precipitated her earlier hallucinations still metabolising.

Which meant that her perceptions were still compromised, her judgement untrustworthy. And that, while she *thought* she was seeing a body - torn, eyeless, tongueless - it was entirely possible that what she was *actually* seeing was something different altogether, something gentler and more benign. A pile of dirty rags, perhaps, stuffed inside the cement mixer by one of the builders before they finished for the day; a pile of bricks wrapped in plastic sheeting, refashioned by her currently elastic mind into something more sinister.

And if she'd thought she could smell the body's blood, taste the early tang of its decay on her own, undamaged tongue - well, surely that spoke to nothing more than the potency of the psilocin. The strength of her imagination, under the influence.

What she'd done, instead of making the call, was turn and run: away from the mixer, and the circling crows, and the desecrated body that was - possibly, probably - nothing like a body at all.

She'd been halfway back to her house, damp clay spattering her pyjamas up to the knee, when a second thought nudged its way into her strained consciousness: that it might be wise, regardless of how certain she was that there *was* no dead boy on the site, to seek a second opinion. To enlist another person to cast an eye over the murder scene that was, in all likelihood, nothing of the sort.

An eye. Eyes. Eyes the boy with the raw, bloody sockets opening out into his skull didn't have and would never have again.

Had he existed.

Aarti Arolker, she'd thought. Aarti Arolker would come and would look, if Bea asked her to. Assuming, of course, that she wasn't currently in the grip of her own hallucinatory episode.

She might judge; might privately consider Bea a lunatic for knocking on her door so early in the morning to ask the question and to beg her to leave the comfort of her home to verify the non-existence of a corpse in the vicinity. Might spend the remainder of the day telling Raj and anyone else who'd listen about the lunatic next door and her false reports of dead boys and mutilated flesh.

But it would be worth it, to be certain.

In fact, Aarti had been kind - had taken one look at Bea, quaking on her doorstep and gesturing backwards to the building site, and slipped on a pair of espadrilles from the shoe-rack by the welcome mat before Bea had even finished making her request.

Aarti didn't *look* ill, Bea had thought; she'd seemed, in fact, well-rested and refreshed, nothing at all like a woman who'd been up all night vomiting bad fungus into a toilet bowl or spiralling into a panic about the cracks in the ceiling or the monsters under the bed.

Until she'd seen the body, anyway.

Then she'd vomited - her face shifting from healthy bronze to sickly wheat and her toned legs buckling at the knee as a spray of curdled orange juice and undigested cereal travelled from her perfectly-lipsticked mouth to the patch of hair-speckled earth beside the cement mixer.

It's real, Bea had thought, with terrible clarity. Then: that boy. That poor, poor boy.

It was Raj who'd phoned it in, once they'd weaved their way back to the Arolkers' house - Aarti leaning against Bea for support all the way - and his wife had told him, in shaking fragments stripped entirely of her usual confidence, some of what she'd seen outside. What Bea had *taken her* to see.

The two days that followed, from Bea's perspective, were almost as fantastical as the scenes that preceded them: a discontiguous muddle of police interviews and exonerating saliva swabs and confiscated clothing; of door-stepping journalists and salivating photographers and recitations of what she remembered of finding the boy's body. Of explanations of what had induced her to take a walk around an empty plot of land on her own to begin with, at the time of the morning.

She'd lied, of course: had said something about fresh air and a new exercise regime, and nothing at all about the mushrooms or the horrors they'd visited upon her. Partly to protect the Davenports from scrutiny, if it was indeed their soup that had poisoned her - but mostly to save herself the embarrassment or worse that would doubtless come of confessing that she had, in point of fact, been off her head when she'd unknowingly dislodged the boy from the machinery into which he'd been stuffed.

And she'd hoped against hope that nothing incriminating would show up on the samples she'd given.

No further horrors, at least, had presented themselves in her house thereafter, when she'd finally been allowed to return to it. This led her to conclude, with an overwhelming sense of relief, that the worst of the delusions had passed: that she was safe once again in both her home and her mind.

She'd avoided the living room except where absolutely necessary, though; keeping the lights on in every room, at every time of day. Had taken to showering in her en-suite instead of the bathroom, and only ever in daylight - escaping into work as early as she could, despite the ever-present crows that clustered around the wheels of her car and scattered only when she revved the engine, and putting in so much overtime at her desk that several of her colleagues at the museum felt moved to ask whether she was "you know, *coping*" with her recent change of circumstance and to assure her that they were always on hand, if she ever needed a friendly ear or a shoulder to cry on.

She, in turn, had assured them she was fine, if a little tired, and would absolutely reach out, if any reaching out were needed. At no point had she felt inclined to share with them the discovery of the body - and had been nothing but grateful, when the story of the killing broke, that she'd given none of them her new address.

Jeremy, who *did* have the address, had called her several times a night, every night, once the murder and its location made the papers - to *make sure you're alright*, as he reiterated in the texts that followed every other missed call. She declined to return the messages.

The boy's name was Hadrian, she'd read; Hadrian Dawson. A good-looking boy, if the photos accompanying the headlines could be believed: tall and strong and well cared-for. Nothing at all like the butchered husk he'd become.

She'd expected Lawrence Jordan to summon her and the other denizens of The Gates to a *community assembly* or a *grief-exploration session* or some other grandiloquently-named neighbourhood watch meeting, in the wake of the boy's death; to make one public pronouncement or another on the incident, in his capacity as Grand High Witch and Fearless Leader of their small non-hierarchical republic. She was surprised, when the invitation came, only that it had come as late as it had, and in the manner that it had: as three lines of vague, euphemistic text in a plain white envelope, slipped through her letterbox the Saturday after what was left of Hadrian Dawson had been driven away to the mortuary in a blue nylon bag.

Recent incidents, it had said, *have left all of us shaken, and in greater need than ever of the comfort and companionship of our peers. We invite you therefore to join your neighbourhood family at the Community Hall at 7pm tonight for an evening of compassion, consolation and catharsis. We ask that you BYOB as well as any food you wish to share with the group.*

Which was how, just after seven that night, Bea found herself back on a bench in the longhouse, wedged between Joan McTierney and Luke Harris - with Jordan once again at the head of the table, another goblet of wine in his hand.

The wine, Bea noticed - wherever it had come from - hadn't been offered to any of *them*; nor had any of them brought with them any of the food or snacks the invitation had suggested they might want to.

They probably weren't inclined to risk it after last time, she thought. None of them seemed as if they'd been ill in the last few days - not even Joan McTierney, whose age surely made her the most susceptible of all of them to a bout of food poisoning or a moment of mushroom-borne psychosis. But then, nor did any of them seem particularly well, or particularly happy to be there. Aarti looked to Bea as glazed and distressed as she had the morning that she'd seen Hadrian Dawson's body; her pinched cheeks and hollow eyes suggesting she'd lost weight she couldn't spare from her tiny frame even in those last few days. Raj was stiff and watchful beside her - one arm wrapped protectively around her wasp-waist middle and another resting on his own upper thigh, the fingers tapping a nervous rhythm against the soft cotton of his chinos. Luke Harris was positively green, under his beard.

"I know how you must feel," Jordan began, scanning the table with every appearance of empathy. "It's been a challenging week for all of us. Knowing what happened to that boy, and that it happened to him here, just a few feet from where we're sitting now..."

He shuddered, wincing at his own recollection, and Bea would have put money on it being an act, an affectation. Another performance.

"And for not one but two of our own to have seen him in that condition… Aarti, Beatrice: I'm so, so sorry you had to go through that. My heart goes out to you both, it really does."

He glanced first at her, and *then* at Aarti – his head tilted in consolation and lips twisted into something between a grimace and a tender smile.

Is anyone buying what he's selling? she wondered. Or am I the only one having trouble swallowing this ersatz sincerity, this *we're all in it together* bullshit?

Do the rest of them *believe* it?

"It must have been absolutely dreadful for you," Elaine Davenport chipped in, with a little shudder of her own. "I can't even imagine how you must feel, either one of you, with *that* in your heads. I hope you know that Ivan and I - that you're always free to lean on us, if there's ever anything you need to get off your chests."

Bea tried to tamp down her cynicism; to accept the offer at face value.

It wasn't Elaine's fault, she told herself, that Hadrian Dawson had been murdered, or that she and Aarti had seen what they'd seen. And if Elaine and Ivan *had* inadvertently poisoned her, *had* temporarily caused a gateway to a very particular kind of hell to open somewhere in the back of her mind through their scattergun approach to foraging and food preparation… well, they could hardly be blamed for it, could they? It had been entirely accidental. They'd acted in good faith.

She knew all this. But still, there was something about the woman that irritated her - something, perhaps, about the need Bea sensed in her to be *seen* to be kind and neighbourly.

"Thank you, Elaine," Aarti replied, and Bea noticed with no small amount of gratitude that she seemed to be speaking on behalf of both of them, and not only for herself. "And thank you, Lawrence. It's been a lot to process, I'm not going to lie. A lot. But we're getting there."

Are we? Bea thought.

"Dreadful business," Ivan Davenport added. "Dreadful. Rather takes us back to the discussion of the other night, doesn't it?"

She thought she saw Kajal Sawiak recoil very slightly at this; saw her daughter whisper something inaudible but soothing into the nape of her mother's neck.

"What discussion?" said Joan McTierney sharply. "What are you on about?"

"The cameras, dear lady," Ivan told her, with a fruity, antiquated trill that had to be a contrivance, *had* to be - and which, if Bea was any judge of countenance, might incite Joan McTierney to violence if it continued.

"The security cameras?" Amit Hindocha asked, to the visible consternation of his husband. "I thought we were talking about bringing in a guard?"

"*We* were," said Joan.

"I *believe*," Ivan Davenport said, "that we were still debating the appropriate intervention, security-wise. And didn't we agree that cameras might prove the more cost-effective option? And that it might be more prudent - not to say fairer - for *all* of us to make a small contribution towards their purchase? It seems, as I'm sure I recall mentioning at the time, somewhat unfair to insist that those of us already burdened with a service charge should pay out yet more to carry the rest, when all of us benefit. Not very community-minded."

I could punch you, Bea thought - flashing back to the state of her overdraft, the invoice she'd received only the day before from her incompetent solicitor for services still undelivered.

"Think you're carrying us, do you?" Joan responded. Her tone was aggrieved, openly hostile now, her wrinkled mouth puckered in disdain. "Think you're worth more than we are 'cause your cheque goes out to the bank instead of to a landlord?"

"We've paid off our mortgage, thank you," Elaine snapped, leaping in to defend her husband. "Through our own hard graft, I might add. Neither one of us has ever been *given* anything. Whatever we have, we've earned for ourselves."

The strained atmosphere Bea had sensed from the moment she'd sat down at the table, the tension she'd felt hovering like a wraith over the Community Hall - it was changing, or so she thought. Heating and thickening, no longer at a simmer but very nearly on the boil. They were frightened, all of them; frightened and anxious. And their fears and anxieties were threatening to turn, very rapidly, to anger.

She was angry, for that matter - though when wasn't she, these days? Angry at Jeremy and the chaos he'd rained down on her, yes. But angry, right now specifically, at the Davenports: at their tight fists and noses stuck up in the air, the obvious disdain they had for the riff raff holding out their begging bowls and sullying the ideological purity of the neighbourhood.

Joan McTierney felt the same about them, evidently - and Kajal Sawiak too, most likely, although the woman's mouse-like timidity made it almost impossible to tell.

Amit Hindocha's expression was unreadable - but his husband's was easier to interpret. Luke, it seemed, was angry, too: his lips pressed into a tense white line under his beard and his thick eyebrows knitted together in consternation.

But not angry at the Davenports, Bea thought. Angry at Joan and Kajal, the renters - the leeches, the ones who wouldn't pay their way. Angry, by extension, at her.

And then there was Jordan, presiding over them from the head of the table with the serene detachment of a circus ringmaster - primed and ready to whip his recalcitrant lions into shape if they wandered too close to the cheap seats.

"I'm conscious," he said, "that we're all a little on edge. This is obviously quite a contentious issue for everyone, and it could be that now isn't the best of times to be debating the ins and outs of it. But equally, I have to ask myself: given what's gone on, and knowing that at least one very disturbed character has had access to the grounds, not to mention the reporters we've had creeping around... can we afford to wait? My inclination is to say: no, I'm not sure we can. If it were just up to me, we'd have every bloke working the doors at the clubs in town doing patrols around the site from dusk 'til dawn, and cameras to boot. But it's not. We're a community, a democracy. We all get a say. And we all get a vote."

"You want us to take a *vote* on it?" Amit asked, alarmed.

Jordan shrugged; spread his palms out towards them in a peace-making gesture that, somehow, conveyed both a desire to placate and a sense of his own helplessness against the more powerful force of democratic will.

"It's the fairest way."

None of them, as far as Bea could ascertain from the expressions they wore, seemed happy with this development. But none of them complained, either - which seemed to be enough for Jordan to proceed as if the matter had been settled.

"Right, then," he said. "Show of hands: who'd like to bring in a security guard, and add the costs on to the service charge at the end of each month?"

Joan McTierney and Karolina Sawiak raised their hands; so too, after a moment, did *Kajal* Sawiak, and then - to Bea's surprise, and apparently also to his husband's - Amit Hindocha. Finally, Bea raised her own.

Aarti, she noticed, kept her hands clasped firmly in her lap, and her eyes lowered to the tabletop.

Jordan made a show of counting the votes.

"And now," he continued sombrely, "who'd like to opt for security cameras, and divide the costs among all of us?"

The Davenports' hands shot up, with exactly the alacrity Bea might have predicted. Luke Harris' followed suit, then Raj Arolker's - then, just as Bea was beginning to believe that she might have escaped the burden of the additional fees after all, his wife's.

Aarti's gaze, however, stayed firmly fixed to the table.

"Interesting," said Jordan, adding up the second round of hands. "Looks like we've got a tie."

He took a sip of his wine, surveying them over the rim of his goblet, and Bea was left again with the odd impression of being not just watched but studied, and her reactions logged and analysed. Of being the unwitting, nonconsenting subject of a social-psychological experiment.

"A tie?" Ivan Davenport blustered, his whiskery face reddening in a way that seemed to Bea entirely on-brand. "What are we supposed to do with *that*? You can't expect us to sit around and wait for some lunatic to come calling just because a handful of dissenters can't bring themselves to do the decent thing, surely?"

He didn't look at her either, Bea observed; nor at Joan McTierney, for that matter. His eyes flitted instead between Jordan and Kajal Sawiak - perhaps, she thought, because he'd determined the latter to be the weakest prey of the tenants, and unlikely therefore to put up a fight, should he decide to put the boot in.

"And does a child's vote really *matter*, anyway?" said his wife, with Karolina Sawiak in her narrow-eyed sights. "Really, Lawrence - democracy is one thing, and I know you believe that everyone at The Gates should have a place at the table, but the girl is barely old enough to ride a bike, let alone understand the consequences of her actions."

"I'm allowed a say," Karolina answered quietly. "I live here, so I'm allowed a say."

"Yes, she is," Jordan concurred. "You know the rules, Elaine. All of us agreed to them, and we all abide by them. You can't change them mid-way through the game because you don't like the hand you've been dealt."

Ivan Davenport scratched his moustache, apparently chewing the problem over.

"Look," he said, turning to Joan McTierney, his tone gentler than before, more conciliatory, "we're all sensible people. And I can appreciate that not everyone has been as fortunate as we have, financially. So how about this? You," his eyes flickered to Bea, then to Kajal Sawiak, "help us by chipping in for the cameras, and Elaine and I will... do what we can to help you in return."

Is he trying to bribe us? Bea thought, dumbfounded.

"What do you mean, *help us*?" Joan McTierney replied, suspiciously. "I don't need no *help*. I just don't want to be paying out money I haven't got for something I ain't even sure I need."

"It isn't just *your* needs we're considering," said Elaine Davenport. "The security here, or current lack thereof... it affects all of us. Honestly, Joan - I'm disappointed in you. We're a community, as Lawrence says - it shouldn't be all *me, me, me*."

Bea was almost impressed by the speed of her volte-face.

"What sort of help?" Karolina Sawiak asked.

"What?" said Elaine Davenport.

"He'd said you'll help us, if we vote the way you want. *How* will you help us?"

Perhaps because she was a child and neither of the Davenports was used to being addressed so directly by anyone under the age of twenty-one, or perhaps because Ivan Davenport had made his proposal before he'd fully formulated an appropriate incentive, the girl's question met with nothing but silence.

"Aren't you going to answer her?" Amit Hindocha interjected, when several painful seconds had elapsed - and Bea got the feeling, though with nothing but the evidence of his very faint smile to support the idea, that he was enjoying the chance to take a shot at the Davenports.

Ivan Davenport rubbed a nervous hand over his throat, seeming to realise he was cornered.

"I thought perhaps... one of our organic hampers?" he offered weakly. "They're really very good. The piccalilli is magnificent, and there's a chorizo Riojano in the cured meat selection that I'd recommend to anyone."

"A *hamper*?" said Amit Hindocha, flabbergasted.

"How much is it worth?" Joan McTierney asked.

"I beg your pardon?" said Ivan Davenport, his face growing redder by the second.

"This hamper. How much is it worth?"

Davenport spluttered, apparently unable to form a response - leaving his wife to sweep in on his behalf once again.

"Between a hundred and fifty and two hundred pounds," she answered, enunciating every phoneme with a crisp, cruel flick of her tongue. "With some variation, depending on the contents of each box."

Joan McTierney turned her attention to Jordan.

"And how much would we be paying for these cameras of yours?" she asked him.

"Two thousand," he answered - quickly, very quickly, as if he'd been anticipating the question. "Give or take."

She turned back to the Davenports.

"Two thousand quid, and you're telling me you'll give me a *hamper* for it? I think I'll pass, if it's all the same to you."

The thin, insincere smile Elaine Davenport had been wearing even as she'd argued with her neighbours cracked and splintered.

And Bea felt it again, the sensation that had overtaken her that night in her living room, when she'd imagined her hands bound to a bed that wasn't there, her flesh crawling with non-existent insects and her toes pecked by the beaks of illusory crows: *rage*. A hot, fathomless reservoir of it, coursing through her muscles and setting light to her skin from the inside out - a rage that wasn't entirely hers, that had no obvious internal point of origin but seemed instead to be flowing *into* her, entering her body through her mouth and nose and pores like mustard gas, like a miasmic fog of transmissible disease.

The others felt it too. She could see it in their faces; in their clenched teeth; in the fingernails they'd dug into their palms to stop them lashing out at one another with their fists.

Rage: thick, suffocating, barely controllable rage. Rage that wasn't entirely theirs - that wasn't commensurate at all with what was, the logical part of her knew, an entirely commonplace neighbourhood dispute.

Not rage they'd conjured themselves, from their own fears and anxieties and righteous indignation, but rage that had found them - and found *in* them, in their heightened state of tension, fertile soil for a host of other and more personal furies to grow and find expression.

Did they know? Could they feel it sinking into them, the way that she could? Feel it permeating their skin, taking their own emotions hostages?

She cast her eyes around the table, searching for clues, for something that would tell her that even one of them *did* - even if, like her, they didn't understand why.

And then, as before, it was over: the fury gone from her system, and by the look of it from theirs, evaporated like mist in summer breeze. And nothing left at the table but twelve resentful semi-strangers, feuding over who'd be left to foot the bill for a property upgrade.

Entirely ordinary people, squabbling over entirely ordinary things.

The meeting disbanded shortly thereafter, with no obvious resolution in sight. Not one of them protested, when Jordan suggested they go home and think things through overnight - not even the Davenports, whom Bea had thought would be the first to grouse and kvetch at having to *wait* to get their way.

There was a certain uneasiness to them all, it struck her, as they filed two-by-two through the heavy wood and metal door of the Community Hall. Not the tension she'd picked up on at the beginning of the meeting, but something closer to nervous agitation - a desperation to be out of there, to be as far away from their neighbours as the proximity of their houses would allow.

The Harris-Hindochas were arguing on their way out - guardedly, their voices dropped to low, vexed whispers.

"What were you thinking?" Luke Harris hissed. "Why the hell would you want to add an extra grand a month to the service charge? We get a big enough bill as it is."

"You'd rather put those people through the wringer for it, would you?" his husband hissed back. "We can afford it, you know we can. You're being cheap for the sake of it."

"It's the principle of the thing."

"Oh, screw your principles. These are people's lives you're messing with."

"They're your friends, now, are they?"

She strained to hear more, following them at a discreet distance as they crossed the road - so absorbed in their conversation that she jumped in fright when she felt fingers gripping her, lightly but firmly, at the elbow.

"Sorry, love," said the voice attached to the fingers - Joan McTierney's voice, cigarette-rough and papery with age. "Didn't mean to startle you."

Bea took a breath; tried as best she could to compose herself.

"My fault," she said. "I was... somewhere else, for a minute."

"Well, no wonder, is it? I'm feeling a bit that way myself, after all that malarkey in there. Penny-pinching bastards, they are - every one of them, but for that Kajal and her little girl. Lovely little thing, she is. Worth ten of the rest of them put together."

"You don't get along with the others?" Bea asked - conscious of the need to keep her own voice down, to keep out of earshot of the rest of her neighbours as they slunk back to their houses.

The old woman laughed - a parched, derisive clearing of the throat that could have been a witch's cackle.

"You can tell you've not been here long. No, duck - I can't say that I do.

That Amit's alright, when he's not with that other one with the muscles and the beady eyes, but as for the rest of them… I wouldn't spit on them if they were on fire, that Lawrence Jordan included. They talk up wanting to be a community or a co-operative or what have you, and it might be that they *do* like the idea of it, but they're out for themselves, every one of them. I was on the picket line at Endicott Road in the seventies, and believe you me - not one of them buggers would've been stood out there with a placard, if push came to shove."

Then what possessed you to move here in the first place? Bea almost replied - then remembered, almost immediately, that Joan *hadn't* moved of her own volition. That she, like Bea herself, had been forced there through circumstance. And that she'd been turfed, unceremoniously, out of the house she probably still thought of as her real home - saved from destitution only through the intervention of the children who'd managed to secure her one of the rental slots at The Gates.

"What did you do?" she asked instead. "When you were on strike?"

"For work, you mean?"

"Yes."

"I was a machinist, love. At Hassell's, up in town. I doubt you'd remember it, a girl your age, but we made hosiery - tights and stockings and that. That was before the place shut down, of course - before I started out here."

Out here? Bea thought, puzzled. What's *out here*?

"At the hospital," Joan added, seeing Bea's confusion. "Cleaning work, that was. When there *was* a hospital here, I should say - though I expect you don't remember that, either?"

"I've… not been here long," Bea told her, stuttering over the words. "In the city."

"Makes sense. I shouldn't think many who *do* remember'd be falling over themselves to live here."

She let out another dry, jaded bark of a laugh.

"It was a loony bin," she continued, by way of explanation. "A *psychiatric hospital*, I should say, though we weren't so fussed about how we talked about it back then."

"And it was *here*?"

Bea was shocked; faintly appalled, though aware of the utter irrationality of the reaction. What should it matter to her, after all, what The Gates had been, before it was The Gates?

"Right where you're standing. Huge place, it was. Victorian - a proper old asylum, like something out of one of them Vincent Price films."

Bea shuddered - an entirely involuntary motion that was, again, completely irrational.

"It must be strange, coming back," she said weakly.

"*Strange* don't come close, duck. If you'd have asked me before I got my house took away, I'd have said you were mad if you thought I'd ever set foot out here again."

"You didn't like working there? Or... working *here*, I suppose?"

And there it was again - that cackle.

"*Like* it? I couldn't *stand* it. None of us could. The pay was decent - that's why most of us stopped there so long - but it was a bloody horrible place. Always cold, always damp, always crawling with rats, and crows and what have you everywhere - flying in and making a nuisance of themselves no matter how many ways you tried to get rid of them, just like the ones you get here now. And as for the girls... I tell you now, it never felt right to me, how they got treated."

"The girls?"

"The patients. They were all girls - young girls, mostly. You never knew what was wrong with most of them, or what they'd done to get themselves locked up - *I* never did, anyway. But what got done to them, what those doctors put them through, and some of the nurses, too... it didn't sit well with me. Didn't then, doesn't now. I'm not one for gossip, but I'll say this, just like

I'd have said it at the time, if anyone had bothered to ask: it was no surprise to me, what them inspectors found, when they finally came in and shut the place down. No surprise to me at all."

CHAPTER 8

She wasn't going to stop - Lou had known that straight away.

Not because she was particularly resilient, or had any predisposition towards perseverance in the face of adversity: she'd walked away from enough crap jobs and dead-end relationships in the past to have gotten comfortable with the idea of quitting, and the Lovecraftian horror-show she'd stumbled into at The Gates had offered more than enough incentive to throw in the towel.

She wasn't going to stop, because there was a story there: a huge one. One people would listen to, regardless of whether or not they could bring themselves to believe it.

What she'd seen and what she'd felt had scared her, of course it had; had terrified her, even. She hadn't closed her eyes since then without running up against the after-images she'd been left with: the withered ghost-girl, the bird-thing in the tree, the burning heat of the creatures with more limbs than even their incomprehensibly large bodies ought to have been able to support.

The place wasn't just haunted. That much had been clear from the moment she'd run screaming from the row of new-build houses that was also, impossibly, a crumbling castle from an earlier era and, more impossibly still, a gateway to another *somewhere* altogether.

Just ghosts... they would have been frightening, sure. But *just* ghosts would have been a known quantity - familiar enough that she could recognise them for what they were, even if she'd never had cause before to think very much about them.

But there were more than ghosts, at The Gates; more than the memory of the dead coming back to trouble the living. She knew it, down to the bone - even if she couldn't put a name yet to what that *more* might be.

In the two days since she'd fled the development, she'd flung herself wholesale into researching its background - the murders of Hadrian Dawson and Simon Henshaw, John Seward and Philip Knight jostled to the back of her mind by the fresher hell she'd witnessed first-hand. Researching it on the laptop, to begin with; then, when she'd exhausted the seams of information she'd been able to find online, and with the aid of the student ID badge she'd kept long after she'd finished her master's, in the Special Collections section of the university library. Which - conveniently, for her purposes - housed in its archives a substantial accumulation of local history texts and newspaper cuttings.

What she'd found had only encouraged her to keep digging.

The Gates, as she'd suspected already, had been nothing but empty fields and waste ground for years - thirty years, no less, the land lying unused and unsellable since 1990, when the hospital that previously occupied it had burned to the ground in a fire suspected, though not proven, to have been set by a group of homeless men who'd been living unofficially in an abandoned wing of the building.

The hospital, Fox Lodge, had been founded, as its Neo-Gothic architecture suggested, in the latter 1870s, and had specialised until its closure in 1989 in the treatment of psychiatric disorders, administering primarily to female patients from across the East Midlands counties.

The closure, she'd learned, was enforced rather than voluntary: the consequence of a series of investigations into the mismanagement of the hospital that had uncovered both proof of patient neglect and unsubstantiated but widespread anecdotal accounts of outright patient abuse. Several patients, the investigation found, had endured treatment regimens that included regular ice-baths and unsanctioned electroconvulsive therapy, as well as more mainstream drug and talking-cure interventions; still others, it was rumoured, had spent days at a time tied to their beds on mattresses soaked with urine and filthy with faeces, unable to move, as punishment for transgressions as minor as disobeying staff orders or refusing to swallow the medications they'd been prescribed.

The investigations themselves had been launched in response to a violent incident on one of the lower-security wards of the hospital: the wounding of a consultant, stabbed in the eyes and throat with a pair of surgical scissors by one of his patients.

Details of the stabbing were sketchy - to protect the identity of the patient as much as the family of the doctor, Lou had assumed - but it was clear that what happened had been serious enough to trigger a wider audit of Fox Lodge's safeguarding practices. An audit which had, in turn, opened the can of worms which had led ultimately to the hospital's shutdown, and to the redistribution of its remaining patients across other institutions, similar but more competently run, up and down the country.

The 1989 report, though, hadn't been the first to lift the lid on a scandal at the hospital.

In 1921, three years on from the Great War, an investigative reporter for the London Evening Review, an American named Sally Rhodes, had been admitted to the Fox Lodge Asylum - as it was then - after suffering delusions so severe that she believed her editor at the newspaper to be George V himself. She remained a patient there for almost two months, receiving a discharge only when staff became convinced that she'd been lying to them by feigning her purported madness, perhaps for attention.

And in fact, as had become apparent not so very long after her release, she *had* been faking it - but not for the reasons the asylum board had surmised.

Sally Rhodes, it transpired, had been working undercover for the duration of her stay at Fox Lodge; conspiring with her editor to fabricate the symptoms of psychosis in order to gain entry to the hospital, and thereafter to produce for the Review, in serialised format, the ultimate insider's account of life in a madhouse.

The conditions she encountered at Fox Lodge, she revealed in the first of these serials - which would later resurface as the opening chapter of her 1929 book *Into Pandaemonium* - had shocked her to the core. The women there, she wrote, suffered tortures and mistreatments beyond any she'd witnessed outside of wartime: fractures and suffocations under the weight of straitjackets too tight and too heavy to bear; water cures and immersions in vats of liquid so hot they burned and so cold they brought on frostbite; forcible partial lobotomies that left the unfortunate recipients drooling and incontinent. Some of these measures, in her estimation, were more punitive than therapeutic: the forcible removal of fingernails from patients who lashed out at staff with their fists, for example, or the full dental extractions meted out to biters and hissers.

(*Like Simon Henshaw*, Lou told herself, as she read on - *their teeth pulled out and their chests crushed, just like his had been. And the water cure... wasn't that how Philip Knight had died in the end, his brain and belly flooded with so much fluid it had drowned him from the inside?*

It wasn't a coincidence. It couldn't be).

Worst of all the maltreatments Rhodes encountered, though, were the infestations: the flocks of birds, packs of rats and armies of insects left to roam the hall of the asylum and colonise the bodies of the inmates by nurses and porters who were, she believed, either completely disengaged from their surroundings or deliberately, pathologically sadistic.

It is often said, she wrote, *that those who work among the head-sick and unbalanced are apt themselves to succumb to their own form of head-sickness, given world enough and time. In the case of Fox Lodge Asylum, however, I would go so far as to declare the doctors and nurses and orderlies already as head-sick as their patients. Even more so, perhaps.*

There was almost no mention, in any of the books or articles Lou searched, of anything otherworldly or supernatural having happened at Fox Lodge or the empty site it had left behind when it closed - with a single exception. One contributor to the newly established Journal of Local History Studies, a Lisa Dunbar - Senior Lecturer in Regional Folklore at a university in Derby, according to her bio - had referenced in her essay a letter, printed in a June 1867 edition of the Leicester Chronicle. It described the asylum as not only "haunted" but "ungodly" - and concluded by urging the decent, God-fearing readers of the Chronicle to join the letter-writer in petitioning the relevant local dignitaries to shut the gates of the place, and permanently.

Of its ungodliness, to Lou's frustration, neither the letter-writer nor Dunbar herself provided further description. Nor was there corroborating evidence of any kind to be found in the pages of the journal.

But it was something, at least. A place to start.

CHAPTER 9

I t was unimaginable that Bea should have been able to sleep, after the things she'd seen: the eagle-like creature in the tree, bigger than any bird she'd seen outside of the Amazon basin, more intelligent and more knowing than any animal had a right to look; the way the air had swelled and rippled around the shaggy-haired, justifiably terrified-looking girl who'd been standing directly below the creature and the tree; the tall, thin shadows that seemed to emerge out of the air itself, elastic ctenophores and cephalopod silhouettes, their maybe-mouths pulsating as they surrounded the girl where she stood.

But she *did* sleep: slamming shut her front door the moment she'd seen the girl break free of the shadows - and begin to run, out of the estate and *away* - then shuffling on her knees to the living room, crawling towards the sofa and dragging herself up and onto it, her conscious mind rebelling against the scene it had been privy to on her doorstep by closing down the higher-functioning parts of itself. It was its only available act of self-defence; she thought later; of self-preservation.

And though it was barely eight in the morning, the sun was already scorching a hole in the sky; and, though she'd slept the night before, albeit lightly and fitfully, she dreamed.

She was in an alleyway: a narrow strip of pavement with high brick walls on either side and lined with overflowing industrial bins, cigarette butts and puddles of lager-smelling urine drying to stains on the uneven cobbles underfoot. It was dark, night-time, but not quite pitch-black, the orange sodium glow of the lamppost on the intersecting street giving her exactly as much light as she needed to see by, and no more.

The alley looked out onto a nightclub: a low, octagonal structure so nondescript it could have been a warehouse or a cash and carry, if not for the heavy bassline of the music pumping out from its wedged-open fire door and the vast rainbow flag draped across its entrance like an awning. The club had been busy that night; was busy still, although some of its patrons - some drunk, some high, some wide awake and ready for more - were now spilling out onto the pavement outside. Almost all of them were men, and almost all of them were young and beautiful: inked and pierced, their thick hair immaculate and their tight shirts cut to flatter their pecs and triceps.

There would have been dozens to choose from, had she needed to make a choice. But she knew who she wanted. Had been told already: his name, description and the place she could find him filtering unvoiced into her head only that morning.

The eye-doctor's son. The dark boy with the pale hair and the forever-serpent on his skin.

The serpent part had confused her, and she'd said as much. So she'd been *shown* - an image of the boy beamed right into her head. His smiling face and blond highlights; the silver barbell through his eyebrow; the hand-decorated t-shirt he'd ripped at the sleeves to better show the swirling black ouroboros tattooed onto his upper arm.

He was easy to spot, as he tumbled through the exit with a laughing friend on each side - though he was more clear-eyed than she'd hoped he'd be. Not a drinker, then; certainly not a druggie. Just a sober, apparently healthy young man in the prime of his life.

He separated from his friends outside the club; dropped Gallic kisses on their artfully-stubbled cheeks and waved them goodbye as they hauled themselves into a waiting taxi, then began a slow, meandering walk back to the flat on the other side of town that she happened to know he shared with another boy of a similar age.

She adjusted the pack on her back - a navy hiker's rucksack, loaded with the things she'd need - and followed him, keeping to the shadows wherever she could. Although she rather suspected it wasn't necessary: there were mercifully few other people around, so late at night.

The boy took a shortcut through a cemetery to the west of the city, stopping to empty his bladder against the stump of a tree, and she saw her opportunity.

She was on him before he'd even heard her approach, seizing him by his forearms and yanking them back and behind him - forcing him face-first to the ground, his wrists pushed firmly into the small of his back and her knees pressed down onto his thighs to stop him kicking out.

He was strong, for a boy so slight, but she was stronger, much stronger - her veins coursing with the strength she'd been given, the strength she'd need to get the job done. She could have wrestled heavyweights into submission without breaking a sweat; could have pulled an articulated lorry half a mile up the road before her legs gave out.

It was never less than exhilarating, this recognition of the power she'd never dreamed she'd have; the power she could wield, if she chose to.

He tried to fight back, but gave up early on - understanding, she suspected, that resisting her was useless, that it would do nothing but sap his energy, energy that might be better saved for later. For a strategic strike she wouldn't see coming.

Let him believe that, if it helped him in the moment. If believing it gave him hope.

The straitjacket was already untied, and she slipped it from the rucksack and over his head and arms with comparative ease. She heard the joints of both his shoulders pop as she tightened the straps; heard the crack of at least one rib as she tightened it further across his chest. He cried out, and she gagged him with the silk tie she'd brought with her, just in case.

She pulled him back around, onto his back, and straddled his stomach, pinning him to the ground. He looked up at her, taking her in for the first time, and his eyes widened, not quite believing what they were seeing.

It was always that way, the first time they saw her.

The pliers were buried deep in the bottom of the rucksack, their blades wrapped twice with duct tape to stop them tearing into the fabric of the bag. She drew them out - carefully, reverently – and pulled their jaws apart, ripping the tape as she went.

He screamed, through his gag.

She tipped back her own head and let it fill her: the rage, the burn of myriad wrongs still unredressed. It surged through her like quicksilver, cooling and hardening until she felt as if the bones of her were nothing but tungsten - tough, impregnable, unbreakable.

And she set to work.

The teeth came out easily, even with the gag in place - the keen bite of the pliers and the strength of her own two hands prising each crown and root from the surrounding gum as quickly and cleanly as petals from a daisy. The gag absorbed the worst of the blood; what was left trickled pathetically down his chin and jawline, his tears and streaming mucus leaving rivulets in the patches of red as they dried.

They were perfect teeth, beautifully kept. She took them with her when she left, every one.

It seemed to her, when the pliers had worked their magic and his mouth was nothing but a red-raw mass of tissue, that he *wanted* her to finish. He didn't protest at all, as she pulled the neck-straps of the jacket tighter around his throat; gave nothing but the slightest twitch and shudder and only the most involuntary spasm of the legs as his air supply dwindled and the life seeped out of him.

Perhaps, by then, it was a kindness.

She woke up crying, sweat pouring from her skin and the hot metal smell of the boy's blood in the back of her throat.

The residual horror of the dream was such that, for a moment, she had no recollection of what had driven her into unconsciousness to begin with, so that the memories, when they came, hit her with the force of a body-blow. She bent double where she lay, certain she was going to be sick, or worse; that some vital part of her would break under the strain of what she'd seen and what she now knew was out there, barely ten feet from her window.

She couldn't conceive of ever opening the door again; of ever setting foot outside.

But staying inside, where she was, with those things so close - wouldn't that be just as bad, in its way? *For now* they were outside, yes; *for now* she could close the curtains to keep them at bay. How likely was it, though, that they'd *stay* outside - the bird-thing on its perch in the tree, and the tentacled things in the unnatural light they seemed to carry with them? They might decide, at any moment, to try their luck at her door, or at Joan McTierney's, or the Arolkers' - and what could anybody do to stop them, if they did?

The bird-thing alone was the length of a house, with its wings spread apart. And how did you scare away a thing that looked like it was made of shadow?

She turned away from the window, burying her face in the cushions of the sofa, and the dream came back to her, as powerful and vivid as a memory: the boy; the teeth; the terrible strength she'd felt flood through her.

Simon, she thought, with no sense at all of where the words or the knowledge had come from. His name was Simon. Simon Henshaw.

The logical part of her - the same part that had kept her grounded, kept her sane through the hallucinations of the week before - insisted that she didn't know this was true. That she couldn't possibly know it.

But the rest of her - the parts that had seen with their own eyes a bird the size of a kangaroo, had heard the slip and glide of too many alien limbs slicing the air - maintained, with absolute certainty, that she *did*.

She retrieved her phone from the floor without thinking, her fingers unlocking the screen the way they'd done a hundred times a day, a thousand, since she'd had the handset. She opened her search engine with the same reflexive motion; had typed in "Simon Henshaw" and "murder" before she'd even realised she was doing it.

The search generated results; a lot of them. Newspaper articles and pictures, hashtags and social media tributes.

And more than one photograph of the boy's face - gentle and smiling, exactly as it had been before she'd taken the strap to his throat and the pliers to his jaws.

She read for an hour; perhaps longer. It was later, much later, before she realised that she should have been at work; that people would notice her absence and worry.

The boy *had* been killed; *had* been strangled and mutilated. But "mutilated" was as lurid and specific as the news reports got, even in the tabloids. There was no mention of the straitjacket. Or of what happened to his teeth.

But for those omissions, she could almost have convinced herself that she'd read about Simon Henshaw and his murder before she dreamt them -

that the dream had been inspired by a snippet of a headline she'd encountered, once and briefly, and then immediately forgotten she'd ever seen until the fragments of the story rearranged themselves in her unconscious while she slept and left her imagination to fill in the narrative blanks.

She hadn't, though. And she knew it, even before she saw the rest.

A further search around the terms "Simon Henshaw," "murder" and "teeth" led her, somewhat circuitously, to a thread posted to a true crime discussion forum on one of the lesser known and notoriously lesser-regulated social media sites. The forum was focused - or so its brief, misspelled description suggested - on Real Life Murder and the thread on Simon Henshaw himself; the main contributor a self-identified policeman who was, he claimed, tangentially connected to the Henshaw case and to the two other, related, murders that had preceded it.

He could have been anyone, of course; Bea had her doubts that any serving police officer, however young and stupid and narcissistic, would risk their career to deliver updates about an ongoing case to strangers on the internet.

But what he'd written about the teeth, and about Simon Henshaw's crushed ribs and dislocated shoulders... she believed it. She'd seen it happen.

She remembered it.

The boy had been dead for several weeks - his body found barely a minute's walk from the cemetery in her dream. He'd been killed somewhere in the hazy, interstitial time between Jeremy leaving and her moving to The Gates. She barely remembered any of it; had only the dimmest sense of how she'd passed the hours and days between waking and sleeping again. She must have gone to work, she knew; must have eaten, and showered, and combed her hair. But none of it had stuck. Rather, it was as if she'd experienced a temporary bout of anterograde amnesia: the trauma of Jeremy's confession and the chaos it had thrust upon her seeming to damage her so completely that it prevented her, for a while, from forming new memories.

What she *did* remember was the anger, absolute and unremitting as it had been. And the drinking: the bottles of wine and coffee cups of spirits she'd leaned on to get her through the first of the nights without him.

Was it possible that, sometime in that terrible interregnum, drunk and splenetic, she could have deliberately gone out and hurt someone - killed someone, even? She'd heard the stories about hysterical strength: stories of young mothers lifting cars to free the infants trapped underneath and women protecting their children from wolves and polar bears with nothing only their bare hands. Could she, in her fugue state, have carried out a darker variation on the same feat - leveraging the force of her anger to pull a boy half her age off the street and throttle him, perhaps as some sort of proxy for Jeremy?

And if she had - had that been the *only* time she'd done it?

There'd been three bodies, three murders in total - that fact she found impossible to ignore. Three victims, all young men of a similar age and all killed in similarly gruesome ways.

And that was discounting the boy *she'd* found, the boy tortured and murdered within earshot of her house. *His* death hadn't been officially connected - connected *yet*, anyway - to the deaths of the others. But surely it *would* be, eventually?

Nor could she ignore the other pressing fact about the night of *that* boy's murder, given what she knew now: that not only had it happened across the road from where she lived, but it had happened while she'd been caught in the grip of a hallucination, a break from reality. While the balance of her mind had been, by any legal definition, disturbed.

The thought that she might have been responsible for one death was itself a kind of torture. That *four* boys might have died because of her - not indirectly, not accidentally, but because she had deliberately harmed them - was unbearable.

Although, the logical part of her suggested, *if you* were *responsible - there might be one, very small consolation.*

What? she snapped back. What the hell kind of consolation could there *possibly* be?

Madness, it told her. *If you'd done it, if you'd killed them - without knowing that you'd done it, and with no memory of it after the event - then that would mean you were mad, wouldn't it? Thoroughly, thoroughly disturbed. Your mind, your judgement, your perceptions - not one of them would be trustworthy.*

So?

So: if you were sufficiently unbalanced to have butchered those boys and then convinced yourself you hadn't... well, it's hardly inconceivable, is it, that you might have simply imagined *that enormous bird in the tree, and whatever else you thought you saw in the shadows. That your mind just... made them up to trick you. To frighten you.*

No, she thought. No. *She* saw them, too - the girl. And she was a perfect stranger - it wasn't some folie à deux. She *saw* them.

The logical voice waited a moment before it answered.

And how sure are you, it said, *that she was really there at all?*

CHAPTER 10

r Lisa Dunbar looked very little like an archetypal academic, and very much like a '70s singer or a recently retired supermodel: tall, gaunt and angular, no longer in thrall to the bad boyfriends and the good heroin but not quite ready to leave behind the smokey eyes or the high-strength cigarettes, either.

She was vaping as Lou entered her office: leaning out of the wide sash window with a silver pipe in one hand and a heavy-looking hardback in the other, trailing dense clouds of strawberry-scented steam out onto the courtyard below.

"Can you shut that?" she said, when Lou had sidled through the door. She didn't *sound* like an academic either, Lou thought; or, at least, like many of the academics who'd taught her at King's. Her accent was local, as thick as Lou's Dad's; her voice was low and gin-soaked, a Marianne Faithfull rasp that Lou might have found attractive in more ordinary circumstances.

Lou closed the door behind her and took a half-dozen steps inside, waiting for Dunbar to finish with the ersatz cigarette before she led in with her cover story.

The office, at least, was what Lou would had expected of an academic historian: an Aladdin's Cave of books and DVDs, paper journals and computer equipment, framed prints of local landmarks and A1 posters advertising fairs and exhibitions that looked as if they'd taken place, if the antiquated typeface was any indication, at least a century earlier. There was a toy figurine on the desk, balanced unsteadily on a pile of notepads: a six-inch reproduction of an Edwardian gentleman in top hat and tails, wearing a monocle and riding a penny farthing.

"You're here about the master's, is that right?" Dunbar asked, not turning around.

It had been the most convincing lie Lou had been able to concoct, under pressure: that she was interested in studying in Dunbar's department, possibly applying for the MA in Researching Local History that Dunbar herself convened – and was drawn to the course especially by Dunbar's expertise in regional folklore, which just so happened to intersect with Lou's longstanding enthusiasm for the myths and legends of her hometown.

"Yes," she said - figuring that saying as little as she could get away with would help with the deception.

"Sit down, then, for God's sake. There's no need to stand there hovering."

Lou lowered herself into the chair opposite Dunbar's, on the visitor's side of the desk. Dunbar took one last drag on her pipe, blew a final stream of white vapour out of the window and dropped down into her own seat - a seat, Lou couldn't help but notice, that was far more comfortable and better-padded than her own.

"What was it you wanted to ask?" she said. "We haven't finalised the module materials, so I'm not sure there's much I can tell you yet about the course content."

And there it was: the question that would let Lou wheel out the second part of the lie, if she could see it through.

"I was wondering," she began, with a nervousness that wasn't entirely feigned for Dunbar's benefit, "how much scope there was on the course for independent research?"

"A hell of a lot, as it happens," Dunbar replied. "It's a research master's in all but name - the way we're envisaging it, the dissertation component of the course would make up half the overall grade, maybe more. Why do you ask? Have you got a particular project in mind?"

Lou slipped a surreptitious hand into her jacket pocket and set her phone to Record.

"It sounds daft," she said, "but there's this bit of land down in Leicester, where I live, and I reckon it might make for quite an interesting case study. It's just been turned into a housing development, but it was a psychiatric hospital for a long time before that, and I heard all these stories when I was growing up about it being haunted - about all the weird stuff people said they'd seen there. So I thought maybe I could use it as an example of how contemporary local myths develop? How a rumour can go from gossip to urban legend, that sort of thing."

She let herself hesitate, stumbling self-consciously over the words.

"Do you mean Fox Lodge?" Dunbar asked, scrutinising Lou over the piles of paperwork with a new curiosity. "Is that the place you're talking about?"

"Do you know it?" Lou answered, with every appearance of surprise.

"Not well. But I'm from 'round there myself, Braunstone Town. And I think I know some of the stories you're talking about."

"That's amazing!" Lou said, fizzing with all the puppy-dog enthusiasm she imagined her amateur mythologist alter-ego would have felt at the revelation of this shared knowledge and common micro-cultural heritage. "I didn't think anyone would have had heard of it, outside of Leicester."

"It's got a reputation - or it *had* one anyway, when I was a kid. The hospital, that is. Though nothing to do with ghosts."

"The hospital?" Lou asked, entirely disingenuously.

She said *ghosts*, she thought. Actually said the word out loud.

"There was a scandal - one of the patients attacked a doctor, something like that - and the police got involved, then *they* brought in whatever the regulatory body was that oversaw mental health services back then. Turned out there were some really serious systemic problems with the way the women there were being cared for - or *not* cared for, I should say. It's why the place got shut down."

Lou nodded, as if this were entirely new and fascinating information.

"I'm sure some of the stories floating around were tied up with that," Dunbar continued. "You see it a lot - communities turning all the human horrors that happen behind closed doors into monsters and apparitions. It's an easy way of understanding them, of assimilating the terrible things you can't avoid knowing about without having to stress yourself out about moral complexities or your own complicity in whatever's going on just up the road. And it can't have hurt that the building looked the way it did - looming over you from the top of that hill like something out of Bram Stoker."

"What stories did *you* hear?" Lou asked - her interest now entirely sincere.

Dunbar considered her, from the other side of the desk.

"How serious are you, about this research project?" she said.

"Pretty serious," Lou answered - then, hedging her bets, added: "I haven't done much reading around it yet. But I plan to, if I get on the course and I can find a way to pay for the fees."

Dunbar nodded.

"I can't help you much with that. All our school funding's been allocated already. But if you do manage to join us in September... it might be good for us to have a chat. I've read a bit on Fox Lodge myself, and there's a lot to dig into. Enough for a PhD, not just a master's dissertation."

She's interested, Lou thought. She's interested because she thinks *I'm* interested.

Because she might not look like an academic - but she is one. Whatever she likes, whatever's grabbed her attention lately - she'll want to talk about it. Talk about it at length, and in great detail.

If Fox Lodge has piqued her interest... odds are, she'll be dying to share a bit of what she knows. And students, even potential students - they're the most captive audiences of all, aren't they? They *can't* leave, even if they want to.

"What have you read about it?" Lou said. "I mean - it might be good to get a bit of a steer on where I should start, if you've got any suggestions?"

Dunbar leaned in towards her - very much as if, Lou thought, she was about to let Lou in on a secret.

"Do you know what it was, before it was a hospital?" she said.

Lou shook her head.

"It was a temple - a Roman temple. Not as big as something like the Mithraeum in London, and we don't know half as much about it as we do *that* one because the Augustinian order that founded the hospital, in their infinite wisdom, decided to build it right on top of the ruins. But it seems, at least from what I've read, like it might have been a bit of an unusual one, even by the standards of Roman cultists. Have you heard of Nox?"

"It doesn't ring a bell."

"Nyx, maybe? Greek goddess of the night, primordial child of chaos? Meant to have stood at the threshold of creation?"

Lou shook her head a second time, hoping her ignorance on matters of ancient Greek and Roman theology wouldn't count against her in Dunbar's estimation.

"Well, Nox... Nox was more or less Nyx by another name. Same powers, same biography. We don't know much about *her*, either - but we know the Romans tended not to worship her, which makes sense, when you think about what she was supposed to represent. But evidently at least a few of them *did* worship her, even if they did it covertly. One of the Augustinian monks I mentioned was a bit of a Classics scholar, so he was told to keep a record of some of the bits and pieces they found when they were digging the foundations for Fox Lodge... and he seemed pretty convinced that Nox was the temple's main deity. Though it goes without saying," she added with a wry smile, "that he thought the whole thing was a bit of an obscenity. A false god, a female one, *and* she's an agent of chaos? Definitely not getting a thumbs-up from the Vatican."

Lou smiled back at her, using her every effort of will to prevent the shock of this particular piece of local history from playing out on her face.

Goddess of the night. Agent of chaos.

Primordial.

Was that what she'd seen, at The Gates? Something primordial? Creatures dredged up from whatever chaos there'd been in the moments before creation?

"... the sort of thing that legends start from, isn't it? Some nineteenth-century monk lets on to his Brothers that the land they're standing on used to be a shrine to a dark, unchristian goddess, and before you know it, half the town's talking about the demons they've seen in the shadows or the prehistoric bird they just *know* is hiding on top of one of the oak trees."

"Prehistoric bird?" Lou said, her skin prickling.

"Sorry - I was being a bit facetious. It's from one of the reports of the hauntings on the Fox Lodge site, from the 1860s - I ended up reading it for an article I was writing on the geographic roots of Victorian and Edwardian myths in the East Midlands. A guy wrote to the Mayor via one of the local papers, begging him - the Mayor - to close the hospital. Burn it down and salt the earth, that sort of thing. Because, and this is more or less verbatim: it's an evil place, and no man should set foot there if he values his reason or his immortal soul."

"What did he mean by that?"

She was keeping the tremor out of her voice, just. But she wasn't sure how much longer she'd be able to.

"It's interesting, actually. If you read the whole letter - it's about a page long, I'm inclined to think the paper only printed it because it's so bizarre and they thought their readers might get a kick out of it - it seems like the first paragraph is him beseeching the mayor to listen to him, and the rest of it is him describing what happened to him one night when he took his dog out for a walk around the grounds of the hospital. Which, by the way, I'm sure he wasn't supposed to."

"What did happen to him?"

The tremor was obvious now, a stutter dicing each syllable into halves and quarters - but if Dunbar was aware of it, she didn't let on.

"What I could gather, from what he wrote and from reading a bit between the lines, was: he was walking his wife's spaniel up near Fox Lodge, and the dog saw something that made it bolt - sent it running off into the woods on the edges of the hospital grounds. He went in after it through a gap in the fence, trying to catch it, and ran headlong into some sort of giant bird - an owl or an eagle, or so he said, but the size of a wolf, and with scaled wings like a dragon. Again: *his* words. It didn't attack him, apparently - just stood there and watched him, like it was weighing him up, appraising him. Then it flapped its wings, and suddenly there were shadows everywhere - shadows with things in them. *Demons*, was how he described them, though I'm not sure how much stock you can put in his descriptions. He said there was evil in the air around them - that he could feel it. Then suddenly there are about a dozen crows dive-bombing him from the roof of the hospital, pecking and clawing at his head, and the dog's racing back towards him... only instead of whining and begging for comfort, it jumps at him and sinks its teeth into his neck. Nearly tears his throat out."

"He swipes at it with his walking stick until it lets go, and then he runs screaming into the woods, back home to his wife. And the next morning, for his own reasons, he sits down at his writing bureau, gets the whole story down on paper and sends it off to the Chronicle, who obviously find it entertaining enough to put out in its entirety, and... are you okay? You look like you're going to be sick."

Lou certainly *felt* sick; had felt a rush of blood to her cheeks and the rapid acceleration of her heartbeat the moment Dunbar had repeated the unfortunate man's description of the bird-thing. And though nothing had attacked *her*, when she'd found herself in his position - if anything, the anger she'd felt surge through her at The Gates might have induced her to attack *someone else*, had there been any living human there to set upon when the shadows fell - she believed everything he'd told the newspaper. Believed it absolutely.

"Fine," she said weakly. "It's just a bit... hot."

Dunbar stared, quizzically, first at her and then at the cool breeze blowing in from the open window, but said nothing.

"Do you know much about the development that's there now?" Lou continued, more anxious now than ever to mine Dunbar for as much information as she could, while she could.

"You know more than I do, I would've thought, if you're still living near there," Dunbar said, still studying Lou's face, her reactions, with a mix of bafflement and concern. "Lawrence Jordan bought it, didn't he? The businessman - sort of Richard Branson-ish, but not quite?"

"I think so," Lou said.

"I don't know why I said it like that – like I wasn't sure. I *know* he did. I remember talking to one of my PhD students about it when it was in the papers - she knows *him*. Knew him, anyway. She lived in one of his other developments down in Brighton while she was doing her undergrad, and apparently he was 'round there more than you'd think. A lot more."

"Oh?" Lou said - sensing, without understanding why, that Dunbar wanted her to ask about this, too.

"Yeah. He's got a lot of money tied up in student accommodation - at the higher-end, I should say. Luxury apartments with en-suite bathrooms and games rooms in the basement. Not your typical halls of residence. You wouldn't want to live in any of them, though - not from what I heard. It's none of my business, really, and I probably shouldn't be passing it on, but I'll say this: the way this student of mine tells it, he's a peculiar bloke, Lawrence Jordan. Very, very peculiar. And definitely not the sort of person you want hanging around your kids when you send them off to uni."

CHAPTER 11

Bea heard them before she saw them, shouting across each other on the pavement by her front door.

It had been two days since she'd left the house: two days without washing or dressing or brushing her teeth. Two days of barely eating or drinking; of getting up from the sofa only when she needed to use the bathroom, or take her medication, or check - as she'd taken to, several times an hour - that the door was locked (and chained, and bolted), the windows closed and the blinds drawn as tightly as they'd go.

She still wasn't sure what frightened her more: the prospect of the unreal *things* she thought she'd seen finding a way to get inside, or what might happen - what she might do - if she allowed herself to go *out*side.

She'd called in sick to work, pleading gastroenteritis - which wasn't, she thought, so terribly far off the mark, given what had happened to her the night of her first Co-Life Dinner. Her boss had been kind and understanding, insisting that Bea take as much time as she needed to recover, and that both the exhibition and her team *would* and *could* soldier on without her. He'd interpreted *gastroenteritis*, she suspected, as code for *divorce-related depression*, and had been driven to react as charitably as he had as much by the fear of an industrial tribunal as by his own innate compassion.

She'd tried, in the spirit of extricating herself even temporarily from the workings of her own mind, to watch television, and had actually made it through thirty minutes of an American sitcom too bland and inoffensive to trigger any memories or elicit any emotional responses. But then the show had segued into a documentary on the marine life of the Great Barrier Reef, and she'd been left shaking and sweating in terror until she'd somehow found the courage to switch off the set and unplug it from the wall socket.

Those tentacles. God, those tentacles.

In the absence of sound and other distraction, she couldn't help but hear the voices outside as they carried through the glass of the bay windows. Couldn't help but recognise them, though the words themselves were muffled: Ivan Davenport's pompous bellow steamrollering over Joan McTierney's sharper rebukes, with Luke Harris's baritone attempting to broker - or so Bea imagined - a détente between them.

She rolled off the sofa onto the carpet and crawled, slowly and quietly, towards the window, intent on being neither seen nor heard - by Luke Harris, by Joan McTierney, by the Davenports, and by whoever or *whatever* else was waiting for her on the other side of the glass.

The argument was clearer, the closer she got - still muffled, but intelligible.

"What's wrong with you, woman?" Ivan Davenport was saying. "Be glad for us all to be set on by a madman, would you, if it saved you a few pounds?"

Bea was overcome, suddenly and unexpectedly, by a vision of Davenport dead on the pavement: mouth caught in a petrified rictus and head smashed to a pulp, the skull sunk in on itself like the skin of a rotten strawberry.

More unpleasant than the image, though, was the realisation that calling it to mind brought her no real distress at all: that she was neither upset nor repulsed by the thought of Davenport's body laid waste like that. That it brought her instead only a peculiar sense of calm and satisfaction - a feeling of relief that the man had been silenced, and that she'd never again be subjected to his foghorn pronouncements and Little Englander entitlement over the dinner table.

This, in itself, was disquieting.

Was this who she was now? Someone who actively relished pain in other people, if she felt those people had wronged her, or simply got on her nerves?

Someone prepared to *bring on* that pain, if it was the only way to shut them up?

"I haven't got the money," Joan McTierney replied. She sounded composed, on the face of things, even as Davenport barked at her. In control of herself and her words.

But Bea could hear it in her voice, in the bite of her tongue and the click of her teeth - the fury. Joan was holding on to her temper, Bea thought, but only just. She couldn't - wouldn't - be pushed further.

"Are you honestly telling us that none of your children would be willing to contribute?" Elaine Davenport said. "I thought they were the ones responsible for your rent?"

The stress she placed on *rent* - the absolute contempt she evidently had for the very *concept* of renting - would have been enough to drive Bea to violence, in Joan's position. But the old woman said nothing.

"Why are you even pushing this?" Amit Hindocha said, and had he been there all along, listening to them argue? "Not everyone's in the same financial position as you two. Just pay for the security and have done with it."

"For God's sake!" Luke told him, sounding rattled. "Why are you getting us involved in this?"

"You're happy to let them bully her, are you?" Amit said, rounding on him.

"Nobody's bullying anyone!" Elaine Davenport roared back at him. "All we're trying to do is sort this mess out in the most equitable way possible. *Someone* needs to take the bull by the bloody horns, and men like you clearly don't have it in you."

"Men like *us*?" Amit said, dangerously.

Bea reared up onto her knees; pressed a finger to the lowest slat of the blinds and pulled down until the smallest glimpse of the altercation outside was visible through the crack.

They were arranged like fighters in a four-way boxing match: Elaine and Ivan Davenport on one side of the ring, their faces bright red with indignation; Joan McTierney and Amit Hindocha on the other, and Luke Harris at his husband's shoulder, watching the brawl unfold with mounting concern.

And across the road from them, in the open doorway of the Community Hall, stood Lawrence Jordan - watching them, his phone held out in front of him as if he were trying to snap a photograph of the scene but couldn't quite get the shot he wanted lined up in the frame.

What the hell was he doing? Was he *filming* them, while they were arguing?

None of them had seen him; that much was obvious. But *she* must have moved less stealthily than she'd hoped, twitching the blinds with less subtlety than she'd thought she had, because she saw, when she looked away from Jordan and back at them all, that Joan, Amit and both the Davenports were now looking her way - the former with surprise, and the latter pair with something like displeasure at realising they'd become a semi-public spectacle.

They think I'm spying on them, she thought. Then, with the faintest trace of an amusement she hadn't felt in days, weeks: how's *that* for irony?

She should have closed the blinds and walked away; she knew that. But she found she didn't *want* to - couldn't stomach the idea of slinking off with her tail between her legs under the weight of the Davenports' stares, of letting them glare her into submission.

So, instead, she stared back at them. Reached a hand up for the blinds' pull-cord and yanked it, hard, exposing both her face and her living room to the audience outside.

Yes, I'm watching you, the gesture said, as clearly as if she'd spoken it aloud. And maybe you should move your arses off my driveway, if you want me to stop.

Amit Hindocha met her eyes and smiled, while his husband frowned beside him. The Davenports grimaced: Ivan mouthing something at her through the window, and Elaine wrinkling her nose, her expression that of a woman confronted with a half-eaten cockroach in her panna cotta.

Joan McTierney seemed not to notice her at all.

She grinned cheerfully at the Davenports, and they turned away - Elaine stalking off stage-right with the speed of a dedicated power-walker, and Ivan following less briskly in her wake.

Amit Hindocha leaned in towards Joan and whispered something in her ear; she gave him a brief, strained smile, whispered something back at him in return, after which he - apparently satisfied with what he'd heard - touched her once, very gently, on the arm and took his own leave.

Luke went after him, his face like thunder and the veins in his thick, corded neck very visibly throbbing.

There's an argument waiting to happen, Bea thought.

And then it was only her and Joan McTierney left - the old woman now not only acknowledging Bea's presence on the other side of the glass, but giving her a strange little wave before she, too, set off back to her own house.

Lawrence Jordan was gone, Bea noticed - had slipped unseen into the Community Hall, or slunk off to his mansion to review whatever footage he'd managed to capture on his phone, for whatever purpose he'd had in mind when he captured it.

It occurred to her that, only a week earlier, she'd have been profoundly troubled by the sight of her landlord - the owner of the estate she lived on, no less - covertly filming his tenants and fellow residents for reasons she couldn't fathom.

Today, though, it felt like small potatoes: barely registering as a worry, when stacked up against the waking nightmares she'd at the very least *thought* she'd witnessed, and the very likely prospect that she was herself not only insane but somnambulantly homicidal.

Whatever voyeuristic inclinations Jordan might have, she thought, were probably quite benign – *quaint*, even - by comparison.

She stood up from her kneeling position on the carpet, ran a hand through her hair - hair desperately in need of a wash and a comb - and had begun the slow shuffle back to the sofa when the first sound hit her: a thud like a shockwave, reverberating through the left-hand wall of the living room, the wall closest to the Arolker house.

That was the trouble with new-builds, she thought vaguely: the walls were thin, paper-thin, and the houses arranged so close together that even the largest of the detached variants virtually abutted their neighbouring properties, with the result that you could hear... well, if not quite *everything* that happened next door, then certainly the louder highlights.

The noise could have been anything: a piece of furniture falling down a flight of stairs, a shopping bag dropped heavily onto the kitchen floor, even a door slammed shut with more force than the action required.

The *other* noise, though, was less ambiguous when it came: a bass shriek of pain, sharp and sudden and ending as abruptly as it began. The cry of an elephant shot with a tranquilliser dart; a farmyard animal tangled in barbed wire.

Or a human man, in agony.

She'd have to help, she realised. Would have to leave the living room, leave the *house*, and go next door to the Arolkers' to investigate the sound. To find out whether someone - Raj – really *had* been hurt, and what, if he had, it would be necessary for her to do about it.

It wasn't a pleasant thought - far less pleasant, in its way, than the thought of Ivan Davenport's blood and brains and cerebral fluid spilling out from his head onto the paving stones.

But there was no choice, was there? She could barely live with herself as things stood, and the guilt she'd be guaranteed to feel later at having left an acquaintance - if not exactly a friend - to drown because she was too frightened, too much of a coward to walk the ten feet from her own front door to his... it would swallow her. She wouldn't survive it.

Nevertheless, it took her longer than it should have to actually *do* what she knew she needed to: put on clothes; gargle with mouthwash in lieu of brushing her teeth; unfix the chains and bolts and locks that had been her only - painfully meagre - security blanket for the preceding forty-eight hours.

She looked at neither the spikes nor the tree opposite as she navigated the drive and the narrow stretch of tarmac separating the Arolkers' home from her own. Instead, she kept her eyes fixed firmly on the ground ahead of her - obsessively cataloguing every bump and crack and indentation that passed underfoot.

She reached the Arolkers' door; pushed the bell and waited.

There was no answer.

She pushed the bell a second time, more forcefully: jabbing at the buzzer three times in quick succession with the pad of her index finger.

Again: no answer.

She leaned into the door with her shoulder and elbow and pressed an ear against the varnished wood, listening through it for footsteps or voices or the wounded animal roar that had prised her from the safety of her own four walls.

The handle turned under the weight of her arm, and the door - apparently left unlocked - swung inwards, inviting her in.

She'd appreciated the aesthetic of the Arolker house, the first time she'd visited. It was a little *much* for her own, more straightforward taste: had too many bold colours and too much character, its confectionery-inspired furniture and copper pendant lights that bit too self-consciously quirky. But every design choice in it was unequivocally a *decision*: an active choice made by someone - Raj or Aarti, or both - with a very specific eye and a very clear sense of their own style.

It had also been clean, neat and impeccably organised, so much so that it had left Bea slightly ashamed of the few bits and pieces she'd neglected to put away when she'd unpacked - the Arolkers' every cup, magazine and umbrella stacked and stowed, and their every end-table placed *just so* with surgical, Feng Shui precision.

The hallway she found herself in now might have belonged to an entirely different household.

There were clothes everywhere, idiosyncratic items strewn in all directions across the polished wood flooring: shirts and trousers, underwear and socks, baseball caps and winter scarves. There was glass and smashed pottery, both on the floor and trailing up the stairs to the first-floor landing - broken wine glasses, cracked dinner plates and something Bea thought might once have been a salad bowl.

And everywhere, scattered like snowflakes, there were crow feathers, long, black and sticky with their own oils: on the staircase, in the hall and in what Bea could see of the kitchen, the densest patch of them concentrated around the closed door that, from what she remembered, separated the hallway from the Arolkers' lounge.

Dreading what she'd find there - and knowing, down to the marrow, that it would be nothing good, nothing harmless - she eased the door open, as gently as her shaking hands would let her.

The carpet was almost gone - that was the first thing that struck her, though it was certainly the least of the horrors the room now held. What had been a turquoise, intricately patterned Axminster was now little more than a bed of feathers; so many feathers that Bea wondered later how the fleet of moulting birds that shed them could possibly have fit in so confined a space. Fit, and then fled, leaving no other trace at all to say they'd ever been there.

There was more broken glass; more scattered clothes. And there was blood: great gouts and spatters of it, staining the feathers on the floor a gluey arterial red and spritzed across the walls like spray-paint.

Neither the blood nor the feathers were the worst of it, though.

In the room's centre, bleeding out into the feather bed around it, was a body: tall and broad, its arms brawny under a white t-shirt now stained the colour of rust and its firm calves bulging in cycling shorts. It was Raj, she was almost certain, though she couldn't be *absolutely* sure on first glance, because its head was missing - its neck ending at the throat in a ragged stump of muscle and sinew.

And in the furthest corner of the lounge, daubing bloody prints onto the lemon wall with her back and shoulders, sat Aarti: eyes closed, legs crossed and smeared from head to toe with gore, cradling her husband's head in her arms like a sleeping infant.

CHAPTER 12

She'd set up notifications on her phone and laptop for any news stories that might be related to the killings of Simon Henshaw and the other boys, and Lou had half-expected to wake up, the morning after her meeting with Lisa Dunbar, to reports of yet another murder.

And in fact, there had been one: a murder-suicide, up near Coalville. The details of the crime, though, suggested it was less an act of ritual sadism than of misery and despair.

The victim, Joseph Wren, was a teenager; not that much younger than Seward and Knight and Dawson and Henshaw, but still school aged. He'd been smothered with a pillow while he slept. The murderer, though, was not an unknown stranger but his own mother - his own mother, who had cut her wrists in the bath immediately after she'd suffocated him, unable, or so the papers had already concluded, to live with the knowledge of what she'd done to her only child.

Wren, moreover, had not only died but *lived* very differently from the other boys. He'd been severely disabled, a wheelchair user with limited mobility and a number of complex learning difficulties who'd required round-the-clock care. His mother, Kathy, had been his carer for the majority of his life, but appeared to have received only the barest minimum of support from the local authorities - even as she struggled herself with the anxiety and clinical depression that, the papers suggested, eventually drove her to take her son's life, and then her own.

It was a tragedy, all told, and probably preventable. But it wasn't *Lou's* tragedy. And its temporary dominance of the local headlines meant that updates on the other murders - *her* murders - were comparatively scant.

So, with not much more second-hand information available on Fox Lodge and its peculiar history than the stuff she'd seen already, and finding herself with not quite enough courage yet to go back to The Gates to find out more *first-hand*, she followed the other lead Dunbar had unwittingly given her: Lawrence Jordan, the man who'd created The Gates as his own personal kibbutz and who was, at least in Dunbar's opinion, someone you couldn't trust as far as you could throw.

Usefully for Lou's purposes, Jordan's digital footprint was enormous - her search engine returning over a million results for his name alone. And he wasn't shy of publicity.

The Gates, she quickly ascertained, wasn't his first shot at recreating an egalitarian paradise on Earth. Before he'd snapped up the decaying parcel of unwanted land that had previously been Fox Lodge and begun the construction of his new pet project there, he'd sponsored - exactly as Dunbar had told her - a group of student co-living communities across London, Sussex and the south east, taking a personal interest in the day-to-day running of the group's flagship operation: an apartment block named Haven House in the Coldean area of Brighton.

It had opened in a blaze of positive press - but closed barely a year after opening, with no explanation given by the management company and no public statement made by Jordan or any of the block's student residents.

Dunbar, though, whether she'd known it or not, had already given Lou what she'd need to find out more.

One of my PhD students knew him, Dunbar had said. *She lived in one of his other developments down in Brighton while she was doing her undergrad.*

It took only a little more searching before Lou had called up Dunbar's departmental profile on the university's website - and with it, a list of the PhD candidates Dunbar was currently supervising, and a brief biography of each.

There were six currently registered. Three were international students who'd done their first degrees in Prague, São Paulo and Jerusalem; these Lou disregarded immediately, since none had any obvious connection to Brighton. The remaining three were British: one with both an undergrad and master's from Durham, another a mature student who'd lived and studied in Derbyshire for the entirety of his academic career. The sixth candidate, a baby-faced girl named Sadie Adebayo, hailed from Birmingham - but had, Lou saw, a first degree in History and Philosophy from the University of Sussex.

Which meant she'd lived, in all likelihood, in Brighton. And not that long ago.

There were contact details for each student under their respective biographies: email addresses and social media handles. Before she'd stopped to consider whether doing so might be sensible, or whether the gossip Dunbar had imparted had been given to her on the understanding of confidence, Lou had clicked on Sadie Adebayo's address, called up her own email account and fired off a message.

Hi Sadie, she wrote,

You don't know me, but I was speaking to Lisa Dunbar yesterday and she mentioned that you used to live in a place in Brighton called Haven House.

I know it sounds weird, since we haven't met or anything, but I was wondering if you might be willing to tell me about it, if I bought you a coffee? What it was like living there, that sort of thing?

It's not for anything sinister, I promise. I'm just trying to find out a bit more about Lawrence Jordan and how he does what he does - a good friend of mine might be moving into one of his new developments, but it sounded a bit dodgy so I thought I'd best look into it for her.

Thanks a lot,

Louise Rinder (Lou)

It was a lame pretext, she knew; a story that would disintegrate the second Sadie Adebayo spoke to Lisa Dunbar about the strange girl who'd emailed her out of the blue to ask about a block of flats she used to live in, several years ago and in another city.

But what did Lou have to lose? She'd already spoken to Dunbar; had got all the information from her that she needed, at least for now. And if Sadie Adebayo ignored the message or messaged back to tell Lou to get bent and never reach out to her again… well, there'd be other threads for Lou to follow. Other avenues to explore.

She closed down her email and opened another search window. This time, rather than hunting for whatever she could find on Fox Lodge or The Gates or the recent murders, she searched for "Roman temple," "goddess Nox" and "Leicester" - a combination of words so specific that she had little hope they'd bring her much in the way of revelations. Especially if Nox really was as unpopular a choice for Roman supplicants to worship as Dunbar had suggested.

Almost all the results were unhelpful, or too vague to be of much use to her: encyclopaedia articles on Nyx, Nox's better-known Greek counterpart; innumerable essays on the Romans in Leicester and the ruins they'd left behind; video game websites outlining the strengths and weaknesses of Nox as a playable character and Wiki entries on Paganism and the significance of Nox for the contemporary Wiccan practitioner.

One link caught her attention, though.

Its search engine description was vague, promising visitors to the advertised site "a fond look back at the rich mythological heritage of Leicestershire and Rutland," and the layout of the site itself was so cluttered and so amateur when she clicked through to the relevant page that it could almost have been - but, she considered, probably *wasn't* - deliberately retro.

Its content, by contrast, was eye-opening.

Nox, it confirmed, had indeed been worshipped - albeit somewhat covertly, or so the site-owner speculated - by a small, cult-like collection of Romans in western Leicestershire: their temple occupying a small portion of a larger area of land that would eventually become the Fox Lodge Asylum, and thereafter The Gates.

Few will know much, she read, in a section somewhat wryly titled Nox & The City, *of the influence of the goddess Nox, daughter of Chaos, on Leicester and its surrounding regions over the centuries.*

Nor will many be familiar with the underground temple built more than 2000 years ago by her worshippers, when they settled close to what would become the village of Cuswell, now virtually unpopulated but equidistant to the settlements already established at that time at Appleby Magna and, it's believed, Market Bosworth.

Following the end of Roman rule in Britain and the arrival of the Saxons in the Midlands, the Temple of Nox and the villas that surrounded it were left to ruin until the 1670s, when the textile and leather merchants concentrated in the Midlands began to travel more regularly between Leicester, Derby and Birmingham via Bosworth, Appleby and the many villages that dotted the farmland between them.

By the late 17th and early 18th century, oral reports of peculiar activity in the Cuswell area were already circulating. Several merchants passing through the village reported flocks of unusually large and aggressive black birds descending on the covered roofs of their wagons and carriages, seemingly from out of nowhere. Others spoke of dissonant, inhuman voices whispering in their ears as they passed the temple ruins, and of more nebulous feelings of unease that resolved just as soon as they returned to more populated stretches of road.

No story of the temple of Nox at Cuswell, however, is more unsettling than the account relayed in 1829 by the poet Francis Gambon of his own encounter with the village - and, perhaps, with the goddess Nox herself.

Navigating the Cuswell Road on horseback late one night after an evening of drinking, Gambon became disoriented and, for reasons he was unable later to fully articulate, guided Dante, his trusty Friesian, into the patch of woodland that had sprung up since the departure of the Romans around what had once been the temple.

No sooner had he entered the woods, Gambon claimed later, than:

"... there came a rustling of leaves, and into my path stepped a young woman, naked as Eve; her eyes two solid spheres of gold, and her hair as black as if it had been cut from night itself and woven with the light of dying stars.

She smiled at me through the dark, and her smile was of such brightness that it illuminated all that lay around her, and I perceived that at the curved alabaster of her shoulder there rested a Beast such as I had never seen nor would ever see again: a Bird, much as a Barn Owl or a White-Tailed Eagle, but of a size so great that it seemed not of this Earth at all but of another Realm entirely, and in its strigine visage I saw a Knowing of a depth to challenge any Man's.

Beside the Lady, its needle fangs bright yellow in the moonlight and muzzle fleck'd with spittle, there stood a great Cat, broad as a bear and long as the Lady herself, its thick feline head reaching almost to her sky-clad breast. Like a lapdog, the Monster let itself be stroked, its flat nose nuzzling at the Lady's rib as her hand ruffled and caressed the luxuriant pelt that gathered at its neck and ears. Each one of its claws spanned the length of my leg from knee to ankle. And each one, I knew, might have slit me open, throat to privates, as easily as you or I might bat away a butterfly.

And starboard of the Lady, its great stomach scraping the ground, there nestled an Animal such as I am certain exists in neither forest nor desert, nor in the least mapp'd corner of the deepest parts of Africa. Its fundamental shape was that of an aquatic reptile, perhaps a crocodile - not one as might be happened upon today in the Nile Delta or the swamplands of America, but altogether more ancient, almost Antediluvian in demeanour. The Animal's armoured-plated body spanned no less than forty feet from tip to tail, some twenty of which comprised its snout and jaws, which held themselves the many sharpened teeth of a mako Shark. Its front legs were small by comparison, its webbed feet jutting from its chest at an angle almost delicate in look. But where, at its hindquarters, there might have protruded a second pair of legs, I saw instead the curling, suckered tendrils of a squid or cuttlefish, rising up to rest, it seemed to me companionably, on the pale curve of the Lady's hip.

Nor was this the only strangeness to the Animal. For from its tail there rose a swaying Medusa's head of cobras, a dozen or more, their forked tongues tasting the air and their crimson eyes trained dead upon me.

I might have cried out; I might have bolted. But a certain numbness had crept over me, rooting me to my saddle and extinguishing my screams.

I thank the Lord Above, however, that good Dante was not so afflicted. Without waiting for the tug on his bridle that might, had I been capable of such an action, have steered both of us free of the Hellish scene before us, he reared up onto his back legs, turned and fled the clearing..."

The laptop pinged, and Lou saw - with some surprise - that Sadie Adebayo had returned her email.

Hello Lou, the response read,

Bit weird, yes, and weirder still of Lisa to have brought it up when you two met. She's my supervisor, but I really don't know her that well, and I'm not sure why she'd tell you what she told you about me.

BUT... I can understand your concerns about your friend, sort of. If you want my opinion - and it seems like you do? - then she's best off giving anything Lawrence Jordan's involved with a seriously wide berth. The guy's a freak, properly shady, and to be honest I'm surprised he's managed to get away with what he has so far.

There's no need to buy me a coffee or anything like that, and I've got a conference paper due so am a bit pressed for time at the moment, but if you still want to talk I can probably spare half an hour if you don't mind coming back to campus? Chances are I'll be at the library, I usually am.

Best,

Sadie

Lou waited barely a second before returning the email.

Hi again Sadie, she wrote. *Thanks, that would be great. Happy to come to you. Can you do this afternoon?*

CHAPTER 13

The head - *Raj's* head, Bea reminded herself - had been cut from the body, *Raj's* body, with a cleaver: a sturdy, wooden-handled model she'd previously seen hanging from a hook over the Arolkers' sink alongside their other, equally professional-looking cooking equipment, and which lay now at Aarti's feet, blood and fragments of off-white bone sticking to the edges of its blade.

How much effort would it take, she wondered numbly, to separate a head from its body with only a meat cleaver? How strong would you need to be to cut through the spine with it, to hack through the gristle of the neck?

Stronger than Aarti, surely.

The other woman's eyes were still closed and her lips still moving as she rocked her husband's head back and forth in her cupped arms - as if, Bea thought with a lurch of her stomach, she was whispering it to sleep with a lullaby. The blood on her face had dried to war paint streaks across her cheekbones; her hands, Bea saw, were wet with it, Raj's severed neck continuing to leak its coagulating juices at a steady drip into her palms and the crooks of her elbows.

"Aarti?" Bea said quietly, gently - afraid to step forward any further into the room but afraid, equally, to leave the scene undisturbed, to abandon Aarti and poor, dead Raj to the bloody mess around them.

Aarti's eyes opened; flicked upwards to meet Bea's.

"He wanted to leave," she replied, in an unpleasant sing-song tone that set Bea's teeth on edge.

"I'm sorry?" Bea asked, keeping her own tone as calm and painfully neutral as she could manage.

"He wanted to leave me. He was *going* to leave me - he said so. But I didn't want him to."

Bea was aware of the phrase *dead-eyed*; had heard it used before, often to describe killers or particularly ruthless, unemotional politicians. But she'd never until now seen the phenomenon up-close and first-hand.

There was nothing *there*, in Aarti's expression; nothing recognisably human, no vestige of emotion. The blank gaze that came to rest on Bea's could have belonged to a manta ray or a deep-sea anglerfish.

Bea took several tentative steps towards her, then - spurred on by a twinge of self-preservation she was surprised to feel, after everything - reached down to the patch of sodden floor on which Aarti was sitting, grabbed the cleaver by the handle and, gripping it so tightly it hurt her wrist, backed away again.

That her fingerprints had now transferred onto what was almost certainly a murder weapon was, she considered, probably not something she ought to waste time thinking about, in her current situation.

"Aarti," she said carefully, holding the cleaver behind her back and out of sight, not wanting to present herself as a threat but inclined to keep her distance, "did you do this? Did you hurt Raj?"

Aarti smiled - a caustic upturning of the mouth that was more terrible even than her ocean-bed expression - and, keeping her eyes on Bea, ran a hand through Raj's hair, tugging lightly at the short black strands of it as they caught between her fingers.

"He was going to leave me," she repeated, with that same, horrible inflection. "He told me. He'd met someone at work, a sales rep. He wanted to move in with her. *Before it's too late*, he said. Before I got pregnant and it was too late for him to get out."

Bea remembered the lines that had spilled out of Jeremy, that morning at the kitchen table: the realisation he'd apparently had that *you only live once*, that it *wasn't fair to either of them* to carry on like this when they could *both be happier*. That he *owed it* to his little whore to *be honest* and *do things properly*.

Her heart broke for Aarti; and then, again, for herself.

"I'm so sorry," she said, and meant it.

"I didn't believe him, because why would he do that, when he loved me? But then he said he was going upstairs to pack his things to take to hers, and I was so angry all of a sudden, I've never felt anything like it, and I told him to wait there while I got something from the kitchen, and I went and got the cleaver from the side where I'd been doing the dinner, and..."

She looked down at the head in her lap - then, appearing to see it properly for the first time, let out a wail of mingled panic and absolute misery and threw it, horrified, away.

It landed on the carpet with a muted thud, scattering feathers as it rolled - nothing like far enough from where Bea was standing for her liking. She angled her body away from it, desperate not to see its face, to have her eyes drawn inexorably - as she knew they would be - to the torn flesh that ended where its larynx should have been.

"What did I do?" Aarti said, struggling to breathe. "What did I do to him?"

It's not what *you did*, Bea answered silently. *It's how* - how *did you do that to him? You're tiny, and not even a knife like that could slice through vertebrae.*

And, with a jolt, she remembered her dream, if it *had been* a dream and not a memory: the way she'd overpowered the boy in the cemetery, in spite of his age and the power differential between them; how fluidly she'd snapped his joints, and how easily she'd loosened his strong, white teeth from his soft, bloody mouth.

Except... it wasn't *my* strength, she thought. Not exactly. I'd been given it; loaned it. *Something* took the anger, *my* anger, and forged it into something else. Something hard and sharp and hungry.

Did the same thing happen to Aarti?

"I think," she said, not because she wanted to but because she knew she *had* to, because it needed to be done, "we ought to call someone."

"Call someone?" Aarti replied, seeming dazed now - not empty, the way she had before, but distant. Coming back to herself, but not all the way there, not yet.

"The police. And someone else, someone who can help you. A friend? Someone from your family?"

Aarti didn't answer - seemed hypnotised, now, by the sight of the blood on her hands.

"I can call them for you," Bea persisted. "If you tell me where your phone is, I can call them. *Now*, so they get here in time for the police."

"Upstairs," Aarti said, so quietly Bea had to strain to hear her. "On the drawer by the bed."

Bea nodded - and, much as she would have preferred not to let Aarti or the body out of her sight, slipped out of the lounge and up the stairs, wincing at every crunch of the glass and feathers under her feet.

She found the Arolkers' bedroom right away. The biggest of the upstairs rooms, decorated in navy blue and mustard, its expensively-reclaimed furniture and fifty-inch television was overshadowed by the four-poster bed in its centre - and the framed canvas print, as big as the television, showing Raj and Aarti on what had to be their wedding day. She wore a floral wreath and red-gold sari, he a white Jodhpuri suit and sandals; both of them smiled broadly at the camera in apparently delirious happiness.

Bea found it as hard to look at, in light of what she knew now, as the disembodied head.

There were at least no feathers up here, beyond the ones she'd trodden into the carpet on her way up. And the phone was exactly where Aarti had said it would be, on the bedside table.

She picked up the phone and pocketed it, intending to return immediately downstairs.

Something stopped her, though: a flicker of green, barely noticeable on the edges of her peripheral vision. So barely noticeable, she suspected she wouldn't have been aware of it at all, had she not been so hyper-aware of every inch of her surroundings, so absolutely flooded with adrenaline and cortisol.

She paused where she stood, and it flashed again: a nanosecond of emerald light emanating from the upper left-hand corner of the room, above the television. Gone almost before she'd seen it.

She stepped in towards the place she thought the light had been, and craned her neck upwards, balancing on tiptoes until her nose was only inches from what she saw, as she got closer, was a tiny plastic box - a slim cream rectangle built directly into the wall.

It's an emissions detector, she thought. It must be. Smoke or carbon monoxide, something like that. It must have come with the house.

Except... there was nothing like it in *her* house, as far as she was aware. And if the houses at The Gates were constructed along even broadly similar lines, to even roughly similar plans, then surely the same sorts of fittings would feature in all of them, not just in one?

And there was something *else* about the plastic box, too; something familiar.

She couldn't place it, at first; couldn't put her finger on where she'd seen anything like it before. It was nothing, certainly, like the smoke detectors she and Jeremy had bought for *their* house: those chunky grey discs she'd had to help him fix, holding the stepladder steady while he secured the alarms to the ceiling with glue and Velcro.

Then it flashed again, the tiny green flare momentarily illuminating the transparent window into which it was set, and it dawned on her that it hadn't been *at home* that she'd seen a similar alarm, a similar mounting and setup. Not in Oadby with Jeremy, and not at The Gates.

It had been at work.

Her museum wasn't much of a target for burglary, as even its own security team would admit. It held none of the treasures of a V&A, a Rijksmuseum or a New York Met, and what few rare pieces it had - an Egyptian sarcophagus, an Iron Age pottery collection, a selection of tapestries from the Middle Ages - would be somewhat difficult for even the most dedicated and knowledgeable of thieves to sell on to a fence.

Last year, though, there'd been an attempted break-in: a group of teenagers, drunk on discounted spirits and their own bravado, had smashed through the automatic glass doors at the museum's entrance, intent on stealing a dinosaur bone.

They'd been caught, detained and arrested almost immediately, all four boys lacking the necessary stealth for a successful robbery and a clean getaway - but the board had insisted, thereafter, on heightening security in the rooms that contained the museum's more popular exhibits.

A fleet of cameras had been installed therein: traditional CCTV, of course, but also more covert surveillance technology. Hidden cameras, for example: pinhole spy-cams, some as small as her fingertip, concealed inside rectangular containers that came disguised as fire alarms, smoke detectors, fuse boxes, even air fresheners.

This, she realised, was what she was seeing now, high up in the corner of the Arolkers' bedroom: not an alarm, a CO2 monitor or a fuse box, but a hidden camera. A spy cam, watching her - and presumably before her, the Arolkers' - every move.

CHAPTER 14

Sadie Adebayo was wary, and Lou couldn't blame her.

She was a tall woman, older-looking in the flesh than she'd seemed in her photo, closer to thirty than twenty, and more self-assured than Lou had been anticipating: her soft grey dress, matching head wrap and the discreet flashes of gold and silver at her wrists and earlobes suggesting a junior banker or a corporate lawyer, not an academic-in-waiting.

"And this is for your mate, is it?" she asked Lou across the table.

"Yeah," Lou answered, conscious of the sound of her own saliva passing through her gullet as she swallowed. She was a terrible liar, always had been. And so much of the loose plan she'd devised to launch herself as an amateur investigator relied on evasion rather than outright deception - on her never being asked a direct question outright, where that question might require her to play fast and loose with the truth.

Sadie's immaculately plucked eyebrows furrowed.

"Only," she said, raising her voice to drown out the gurgling of coffee machines and the snippets of other people's conversation that echoed through the library cafe, "I wouldn't want to be talking about this to someone who'd lied about what they were after, you know what I mean? Someone who'd introduced themselves as... something they weren't."

Lou crumbled.

"How did you *know*?" she said.

Sadie laughed. Not a cruel laugh, Lou thought; she wasn't angry, or didn't seem to be. Just amused; mildly puzzled. And a little curious, possibly?

"Don't take this the wrong way," she told Lou, "but that email was about the worst cover story I've ever seen - and I've used a few myself, when I've tried to book interviews with some of the local yokels who wouldn't want someone like me writing what's basically a book about their village's history. Like, seriously - who cares *that* much about where their *friend's* thinking of moving to? I wouldn't make that much effort for my *Mum*. A bit of googling, that's the best she'd get."

Lou felt herself blush and dropped her eyes down at the table, studying its false wood-grain pattern with furious intensity.

"I'm not mad," Sadie continued. "I mean, like I said in the email - it's weird, *very* weird, but it worked. I'm here now, talking to you. But if you're going to be asking me about Haven House or Lawrence Jordan, then I'd rather know who it is I'm talking to. He's not afraid of an injunction, Jordan, and I can't afford to get taken to court when I've got so many deadlines hanging over me."

She smiled, and Lou relaxed, very slightly.

"I'm not going to get you sued," she said. Then, realising honesty was one of the very few conversational gambits left open to her, added, "I was making a podcast. Thinking of making one."

"About Lawrence Jordan?"

"No. About... look, this isn't going to sound any less weird, okay?"

"Okay."

"You know there've been those murders lately, in Leicester?"

"I've heard about them," Sadie said, hesitantly - looking, Lou thought, slightly worried now. Wondering, maybe, if she'd misread the situation; if Lou was something more than she'd initially imagined.

"Well, I started looking into them. I thought maybe I could record a show about them, you know? A sort of Serial-type thing. So I went to a couple of the places where the police found the bodies. And one of them was The Gates, if you've heard of it?"

"Lawrence Jordan's new baby," Sadie answered, a glimmer of understanding beginning to dawn.

"Yeah. There was a guy killed there, not that long ago. Or left there, after."

"So you went to check the place out."

Lou nodded.

"I don't want to get into what I saw when I went," she said. "You wouldn't believe me if I told you, anyway. But there's some odd shit going on at that place. Really fucking odd. And I know how I sound when I'm telling you this, I can hear myself, and I realise I'm coming off like a lunatic or some sort of mad conspiracy theorist ... but I think that whatever it is, Lawrence Jordan's got something to do with it. Maybe."

She was sure, when she stopped for breath, that Sadie would get up and leave - perhaps urging Lou, as a parting shot, to seek help for her paranoia, her delusional thinking.

But she didn't.

"Sounds about right," she said instead. "I wouldn't put it past him, whatever it is. He doesn't have the sort of limits normal people do, I know that. Doesn't acknowledge any checks or balances. If he gets it in his head to do something, he just..."

She stopped herself, mid-sentence.

"Are you still making it, this podcast?" she asked Lou, suddenly mistrustful. "'Cause I don't want to be recorded for it, you understand me?" She leaned forward and raised her voice again, speaking slowly, as if for the benefit of a microphone hidden in Lou's lapel. "I do not consent to being recorded."

In fact, Lou hadn't even unlocked her phone since they'd been speaking, much less pressed Record.

There would still *be* a podcast, she thought, somewhere down the line. But she'd realised the night before that, however things had started, the show, the investigation, had ceased to be her primary motivation; was no longer what was driving her to find out about The Gates, about the murders, about Jordan. Not after what she'd seen; what she'd read; what Lisa Dunbar had told her.

"I don't know," she replied, injecting as much honesty as she could into her voice. "Eventually, maybe. But that's not why I messaged you - and I swear, I'm not recording you, and I won't *be* recording you, whatever you tell me. I just want to find out what's going on, and how Jordan fits into it. After some of the stuff I've seen... I need to know, you know what I mean? For my own peace of mind."

Sadie considered this.

"What do you want to know about Jordan?" she said eventually. "Specifically."

"Anything you want to tell me. About Haven House, maybe? What it was like living there?"

"And you'll keep my name out of it, if any of this goes public?"

"I'm not even sure anymore that it will. But yeah, of course."

"You'd better, that's all I'm saying. You'd better."

She took a deep, yogic breath, in through her nose and out through her mouth - steeling herself, Lou thought, for the story she was about to tell, the confidence she was about to share.

"The thing about Haven House," she began, "was that it was cheap, really cheap. Like, *suspiciously* cheap. But I was so desperate when I moved in, I didn't give as much thought to that as maybe I should've done..."

She was approaching the second year of her first degree then, and - despite the sessional bar work she pulled in at the student union and the job she'd held down that summer at a recruitment consultancy back home - was painfully skint. She'd resisted moving into a shared house with friends or signing a lease on one of the many bedsits in Moulsecoomb or Kemptown; Brighton was expensive, and neither of those options, she knew, came in a price range she'd be comfortable stretching to. She'd wait it out, she told herself, as September rolled into view and her return to Sussex grew imminent; wait for someone to drop out of their contract and leave their room going spare, then swoop in and save herself, at the very least, the cost of an upfront deposit.

That was the plan, anyway.

And then one morning, a fortnight or so before she was due to go back, an email she initially dismissed as spam landed in her inbox: a message forwarded on from a girl on her course, a girl who knew about her housing predicament and who'd listened, with every appearance of sympathy, whenever Sadie had offloaded her money worries on the trek to and from lectures.

Fwd: A New Way Of Living At Haven House, the message read.

Might be just what you're looking for? the girl had added in the body of the email - above a link to a website advertising a new, just-built co-living community for students in Coldean, a short bus journey and only slightly longer walk away from campus.

Sadie had followed the link, half-expecting to be taken to a phishing site requesting her bank details, or a set of flashing neon letters in Comic Sans congratulating her on winning a new-model Mercedes. But Haven House had seemed, on the face of it, entirely legit.

It was a group house - or rather, a group apartment block - comprising twelve one-room flats, a large communal kitchen and a dedicated lounge for drinking, gaming and socialising. Each flat had its own bathroom, but none came with cooking facilities - which were in any case unnecessary, the website said, because all residents were expected as a condition of their tenancy to contribute to the life of the community by cooking, eating and cleaning with one another.

Sadie had heard of similar places before; had known at least a couple of people in her sister's year at school who'd lived or temporarily stayed in them, in London and further afield, in equally wallet-draining cities on the east and west coasts of the US. The reviews had been mixed but had correlated, by and large, to the personality types of the people involved - the introverts suffering the regular parties and group-bonding sessions through gritted teeth, while the extroverts had a whale of a time *organising* the parties, *facilitating* the sessions and knocking on the door of any neighbour who might be tempted to opt-out of the scheduled fun with a party popper and a fishbowl full of margarita.

Sadie, who tended towards introversion and the enjoyment of her own company, had previously dismissed co-living living as not for her - as likely to cause her irritation, if not outright anxiety.

But at the prices Haven House was offering, it was a difficult proposition to refuse.

The monthly rental cost of each flat in the block, according to the website, was a fraction of the lease on a bedsit of the same size, and less than half of what she'd pay for a room in a shared house. Haven House, the site suggested by way of explanation for its price structure, was a test-case for its developers - a toe in the ever-swelling waters of the co-living market. If the experiment was a success, and the block managed to retain tenants beyond their initial six-month contract, then the company would branch out into further, similar properties, in the UK and beyond; if it tanked, Haven House would be closed, the tenants evicted, and the company's funds directed elsewhere.

For £200 a month inclusive, though, Sadie figured she could live with a little housing insecurity. And, at a push, with the fishbowl cocktails.

She submitted an initial expression of interest via the site's contact form and was called, that same day, by a woman from the letting agency operating on the developers' behalf.

"She was super eager," Sadie told Lou. "Really selling the place - the location, the amenities, all of it. If I'd had any sense, I'd have found that suspect in itself. I mean, why would you need to *sell* something, at that price? It sells itself. Or it should do."

The woman was warm, grandmotherly, her voice a gentle Wiltshire burr and eminently trustworthy. Once her sales pitch had been put to bed and she'd established that Sadie was already interested and really didn't need convincing, she asked: was Sadie familiar with Haven House's slightly unusual application process?

"I told her I wasn't," Sadie said. "But I was nineteen. How was I supposed to know what *unusual* looks like, when you're trying to rent a flat? I'd only ever lived at home, or in halls. And actually, I think that's why it was students Jordan wanted to recruit. He probably had a sense we wouldn't have any frame of reference for the situation we ended up in, the way older people would. Wouldn't know where the lines were - what was appropriate, and what was just bizarre."

Applying to Haven House, the woman explained, was a multi-step process. Sadie would need to submit to a credit check, provide a guarantor's letter from her parents and supply a list of previous addresses: all the standard stuff. But she'd also be asked to write an essay outlining a bit about who she was and why she'd be a good fit for the Haven House community, and, after that, to complete a brief online personality test.

"It's like a Myers-Briggs," the woman had reassured her. "Nothing to worry about, I promise."

Sadie, who at that point had no idea what a Myers-Briggs was, had hummed her assent, and the conversation had moved on to more practical considerations - including, and most importantly for Sadie's purposes, how long the process was likely to take, and when she might find out whether or not her application had been accepted.

"Shouldn't take long at all, my lover," the woman said. "Mr Jordan's very keen to get the slots filled up, so if all goes well and you get your paperwork done quickly... you'll know within the week, I'd say."

And she had. She'd completed the necessary forms, written the essay, ticked the right boxes (or what she'd *thought* were the right boxes) on the test, and had been offered a place at Haven House that same week.

She'd moved in almost immediately, eager to familiarise herself with her new living environment, and to grapple with the peculiarities of communal living, before the start of the semester.

The flat itself had exceeded all her expectations. It was beautiful: clean, freshly-decorated, far bigger and more airy than she'd thought a bedsit *could* be, and with a view of the surrounding woodland that reminded her less of a seaside town than of the lush Pacific Northwest forests her mum and dad had taken her to visit as a child.

Her new neighbours - though she'd supposed, given how they'd be living together, they were more like flatmates - had been less delightful. Split broadly along the introvert/extrovert fault line she'd predicted, they'd struck her a particularly unlikeable bunch of people: some loud, abrasive and arrogant, competing with one another to talk the loudest and longest on any given topic, and others so sullen, rude and withdrawn she'd been left with the impression that they'd hated her on sight.

If they'd been cherry-picked for their complementary personalities, she'd thought, then there was something *very* wrong with the Haven House selection criteria.

But still, she'd told herself: *I can do this. For £200 a month and no bills, I can do this.*

She'd been there a month before she'd met Lawrence Jordan: a month of shared vegetarian meals at the long refectory table in the dining hall, making polite conversation whenever she was spoken to, but never more; of twice-weekly getting-to-know-you sessions in the communal lounge, wherein she was compelled to share, over and over again, the details of her family life and how she felt about it; of enforced Thursday evening ping-pong in the games room with Cammie, the motormouthed Business student from Fulham who'd declared herself *fascinated* by Sadie's braids and who never stopped trying to touch them, and Richard, a stern-faced trainee dentist with hard-right (and, Sadie suspected, faintly racist) political inclinations who'd chosen Dentistry, or so he'd claimed, because "they make real money, dentists. *Real* money."

She hadn't known who he was, when he'd first appeared at dinner; had thought he might be someone's dad, or even - with his grizzled face and obviously dyed black hair and beard - someone's granddad, come to visit.

Instead, he'd introduced himself, over a bowl of faintly watery cashew nut curry, as "Lawrence - the bloke in charge of all this."

He wanted, he'd told them, to get a bit more hands-on in the day-to-day running of Haven House. He had plans, he'd said - and as Sadie had known already - to take the specific co-living concept he'd developed further: to London and Manchester, San Francisco and New York, Paris and Madrid and Barcelona. But only if it worked; only if the youngsters - that was the word he'd used, *youngsters* - were interested in living like that. In having the sort of shared experience a space like Haven House was offering.

And to know if it worked, he'd said, he'd have to keep an eye on it for himself, up close and personal.

She'd understood where he was coming from, or thought she had - and had been less surprised than she might otherwise had been when his appearances at the dinner table became more frequent, his questions about *how they were finding the place* and *how they were feeling about the setup* that bit more pointed and intrusive.

He's just looking for feedback, she'd told herself. *That's all he's after: feedback.*

Her position on Jordan had changed somewhat a few months later, however, when the first batch of new house rules had been introduced - not in person by the man himself, but by an email sent to each of the tenants, and reinforced thereafter by the yellow laminated posters that appeared one morning in the communal areas of the block.

There'd been reports, both the email and the posters had said - in a passive-aggressive, nominalising voice that had raised even the nineteen year-old Sadie's hackles - of certain residents not pulling their weight: of them ducking out of the washing-up when it was their turn, of conveniently forgetting to contribute to the shared weekly shop, of leaving bathroom stalls and shower cubicles dirty after they'd used them.

Communal living, both communications had reiterated, functioned smoothly *only* when all parties were prepared to make an equal contribution to the life of the community. Failing to do so was not only antithetical to the Haven House ethos, but also deeply unfair on those who *did* pull their weight - and who were left to pick up the slack, when others didn't.

"An *equal contribution to the life of the community*," Sadie told Lou, her upper lip curling in contempt. "Can you believe that? It's the sort of bollocks I'd run a mile from, if I heard it now. But like I said - I was young."

To nip this potential inequality in the bud, the email and the poster had continued, the management company would be nominating four of the residents as House Marshals: prefect-like figures tasked with monitoring how well their neighbours adhered to the house rules they'd agreed to, and with alerting Jordan and the management team to any problems if and when they arose.

Like prefects, they would have the power to hand out penalties for any infractions they witnessed. These penalties would be minor, the comms had stressed, and should be understood as symbolic rather than genuinely punitive. But it was hoped that the residents would take them seriously, nonetheless.

"Penalties?" Lou asked, appalled. "What sort of penalties?"

"Taking stuff away, mainly," Sadie said. "Not letting you put certain items on the group shopping list - crisps and chocolate and booze, mainly. *Inessential items*, that was how they put it. And doling out a bit of public shaming, if they thought they needed to. Gathering everyone together in the drawing room to name the culprit in the mystery of the uncleaned toilet bowl - that sort of thing."

The names of the newly elected Marshals had been listed in the email, though not on the posters - and Sadie had been dismayed to see among them at least a couple of the people she privately considered least well-suited to wielding even this most low-level form of power.

Bullies, and loudmouths, and self-important dickheads with an axe to grind. Not the quiet, sullen ones - who were, she'd conceded, annoying in their own, less obtrusive way - but the playground sneaks and persecutors: the petty tyrants who'd pull your hair and then tell the teacher you'd upset them when you cried.

"Cammie was on there, obviously," Sadie said. "And Richard, and this rugby-player guy, Ben, and another girl, Antonia. But they were all the same *sort* of person, you know what I mean? And you just knew they'd get off on being put in charge."

She'd been proven right about that, among other things. All four Marshals had taken to the role like ducks to water, scrutinising the behaviour of the others in the block with zeal and deducting from the communal kitty any number of luxury items requested by those they considered miscreants.

And that was only the beginning.

"It was like... you know the Stanford Prison Experiment, where they took those American kids and made them prisoners and guards to see how they'd react, and the guards went mad with power and the prisoners ended up rioting?"

"Sure," Lou said.

"Imagine that, but without the uniforms, and with a nice block of flats instead of some basement dungeon. The Marshals... I'm telling you, they were *this* close to going full-on Prison Warden..."

As in the Stanford Experiment, things in Haven House had escalated more quickly than Sadie would have thought possible, had she not lived through them. By their fourth day on the job, the Marshals had moved from refusing to add food to the shopping list to actively confiscating food already delivered - sweeping bars of chocolate and six-packs of lager out of the cupboards and into rubbish bags destined for the recycling bin or their own rooms.

"Some of us emailed the management company to complain," Sadie said. "And one girl rang them, but she went straight to voicemail. And nobody ever replied to our messages."

On the fifth day, Alan - another rugby player, but a prop, so broad and burly that he had almost no neck at all - had challenged Ben and Richard: squared up to them, so that he and Ben were chest-to-barrel chest, and demanded to know what the hell they thought they were doing, getting rid of his food.

Cammie had intervened; had managed, somehow, to calm him down. To defuse the situation, or so Sadie had thought.

Until late that night, when all four of the Marshals had banded together to barricade the boy in his bedsit.

"The doors to the flats opened outwards," Sadie said, "and they'd pushed the snooker table up against his and stuck a load of heavy boxes on top, so that even when he charged at it with his shoulder, it wouldn't budge. They'd taken his phone and his laptop, too - I guess while he was having his dinner - so he couldn't text anyone or ring for help. All he *could* do was what he did: shout and scream and bang on the door until they let him out. Which they did - but not until the morning. I think they must have thought one night locked up was just about enough for him to have learned his lesson."

"He didn't go to the police about it, Alan. I don't know what I'd have done in his place, but he'd convinced himself nobody would take something like that seriously, coming from a guy his size - that they'd call it a student prank and laugh him out of the station. He tried to speak to the management team, but no-one got back to him either. He said he'd made an appointment with someone at the welfare office on campus, to see if there was anything *they'd* do, but the waiting time for that was a fortnight, and by then..."

Two further locks-in had followed, both organised by Cammie with the support of the other three Marshals: one stretching to only an hour, the other - enacted on a studious, deeply withdrawn third year named Jin, who'd been accused of stealing orange juice from Cammie's carton after her own was confiscated - lasting an entire day. The Marshals, like the student-guards at Stanford, grew more confident and more sadistic by the hour. The rest of them, unlike the Stanford prisoners, grew more and more frightened of just how far things would go, how far Cammie and the others would *take* things - too broke to move out, and, or so they'd come to believe after Alan's experience, powerless to bring in outside help.

And then they'd discovered the cameras.

"Thank God it was Richard who found them," said Sadie, still - or so it seemed to Lou - relieved at this, despite the years that had passed. "If it had been one of *us*, not one of the Marshals... I doubt they'd have believed it. They'd probably have thought we'd planted them ourselves to stir up trouble."

They were tiny things, black pinhole spy-cams no bigger than fifty pence pieces and no thicker than an adult thumb. The one in Richard's room had been hidden in the smoke detector on his ceiling - and would have *stayed* hidden there, had he not decided to prise open the detector with a screwdriver so he could enjoy a spliff on his bed without having to crack a window to avoid setting off the alarm.

He hadn't known what it was, when it fell from the dangling wires of the alarm onto his floor; was worried that he might have broken the smoke detector with the screwdriver, dislodged some vital component that would prevent the thing from working and incur a charge he really didn't want on his rent bill.

He'd taken a picture of it; texted the picture to several of his more technically minded friends and asked them, very casually, what they thought it might be. And just as importantly, how he might go about putting it back where it had come from with no damage done.

One friend, a third-year software engineer on an industrial placement at a video games company, had texted back immediately.

Thats a hidden camera bro, he'd written.

Secret agent shit

U spyin on someone?

And Richard had panicked.

He'd alerted Ben, his fellow Marshal, to what he'd found; then Antonia and Cammie. A sweep of Ben's room had uncovered a similar recording device built into the smoke detector on *his* ceiling - though not in the bedsit of either girl.

They'd been paranoid, though - paranoid enough to start tearing apart their rooms to look for any cameras that might have been watching them.

And eventually, they'd found them.

Antonia's had been placed in a false plug socket secured to the *real* plug socket beside her writing desk - its tiny lens tilted upwards, to better capture in full the movements of anyone who might have been in the room.

Cammie's had been hiding in plain sight, fixed to the back of the bookcase by her easy chair like a 3D sticker, and so obvious that Sadie had wondered when she'd finally seen it how Cammie could *possibly* have failed to notice its presence - unless, of course, she just wasn't much of the reader.

Sadie never knew how long the Marshals had waited, before they'd shared what they'd found with the rest of the block - whether it had been hours, or even days. But what they'd found had evidently rattled them enough to want to know whether their neighbours - and in some cases, their former prisoners - had likewise been spied on. And to want those neighbours on board with whatever action they'd decide to take against whoever was doing the spying.

"I think we all had a feeling it was something to do with Jordan," Sadie said. "I mean, he was the one who built the flats, right? It was his company. Maybe if he'd been around less, if he hadn't kept turning up for dinner or to check in on us, we might've suspected someone else - a pervy electrician, or something. But once we knew about the cameras, it started to feel a bit creepy, him popping in like that whenever he wanted. A bit... I don't know, voyeuristic?"

Trying *again* to get in touch with the management company, they'd concluded - the non-Marshals with no small degree of bitterness - would probably lead them nowhere. They'd have to go direct to Jordan.

"You went to see him?" Lou asked.

"Yep. Not everyone was completely convinced he'd actually planted the cameras himself. But even the ones who weren't knew they were his responsibility, if they'd been planted on *his* property - and that the bucked stopped with him. So we went to his house."

"His *house*?"

"Don't look so shocked. We all knew where he lived - he'd more or less told us, one of the times he'd come for dinner. Not the exact address, obviously - but it wasn't that hard to track it down online, with what we *did* know. And it was in Surrey, in Reigate, so easy enough for us to get to on the train."

They'd turned up on his doorstep, all twelve of them, around eight that night - late enough that the presence of so many young people marching together up the private road his house had sat on, a tree-lined cul-de-sac heavy with spiked fences and security gates, had caused more than a few curtains to twitch, and Sadie had found herself wondering, briefly but with no small amount of unease, if one of the neighbours behind the curtains was going to call the police.

Jordan had let them through his own gates with neither questions nor hesitation - inviting them inside when they'd knocked on his door.

They'd declined the offer.

"We'd like to know," Ben had said indignantly, his fair face reddening, "why you've been spying on us. Filming us, no less."

Jordan had made no effort at all to deny the accusation.

"I see you found the cameras, then," he'd replied.

"So you *did* do it!" Richard shouted from the back of the group, sounding to Sadie's ears unnecessarily triumphant at having heard what he'd clearly understood as a confession.

"Well... yes," Jordan had said, mildly. "Is that a problem?"

Neither Ben nor Richard had responded; Cammie and Antonia, too, appeared to have been struck dumb by the question. Eventually it was Sadie herself who'd spoken up.

"You've been filming us, in our rooms, without us knowing, and you're asking if we've got a *problem* with it?" she'd said, incredulous.

Jordan had stared at them all, the clamour of aggrieved not-quite-adults thronged in his doorway, and hesitated, seeming to Sadie faintly bemused. He'd scratched the back of his jet-black head with one hand, then run a thumb along his beard, as if pondering a particularly challenging problem.

"I have to ask," he'd said. "Have any of you actually *read* the contracts you signed you before you moved in?"

Sadie had thought back to the paperwork she'd been sent when she'd submitted her application to Haven House; the dozens of small-print, densely-spaced pages of tenancy clauses and sub-clauses she'd scrolled through before committing her electronic signature.

"I'd scanned them," she told Lou. "Or, I don't know... *bits* of them. The highlights. But you know what it's like, with forms like that. No-one really *reads* them. You just want to sign them and send them off so you can get on with your life. And housing agreements... they're all pretty standard, right? That was what I thought then, anyway."

Evidently, it had been what all of them had thought - even Shoshana, the pretty Legal Studies postgrad from Marseille who, Sadie had considered, really should have known better.

"What do you mean, have we *read* them?" Richard had pressed. "Do you think we're *stupid*? *Of course* we've read them!"

But it had all been bluster, nothing but hot air, and everyone had known it.

"So you saw the part about there being no expectation of privacy, then, did you?" Jordan had said, still eerily calm. "About filming being permitted in *all* parts of the building, not just the communal areas?"

For that, not one of them had had an answer.

"He'd stitched us," Sadie said, her manicured hands shaking around the silver water bottle she'd set to rest on the table - shaking with anger, Lou thought. "Banked on none of us bothering to read through half the stuff the management people had sent us. Alan had his tablet with him, and he brought his contract up on the screen there and then, with Jordan watching... and of course it *was* true, wasn't it? Everything he'd said. There was a whole paragraph in there about cameras and filming and waiving our rights to privacy for the duration of the tenancy. It was buried in a load of other stuff about accidental breakages and what to do about lost keys, but it was in there, no question. We might as well have signed up for a reality TV show, for all the rights we had as tenants."

"But... why?" Lou asked. "Was it, like, a sex thing, watching you all?"

Sadie clutched her hands tighter to the bottle.

"That was what they thought - some of them, anyway. Cammie definitely did, you could tell. But me... I'm not so sure."

"What do you mean?"

"This is conjecture, you understand? I don't know anything for certain. Jordan wasn't exactly forthcoming about his intentions, and the management company never told us, not even when all of us packed up our stuff and moved out the next day. Some of the boys would have taken it further, I think - gone to the police, or got a solicitor involved, or something. But they were shit scared. We all were. Someone records you for months, in your own home, without you knowing... they've got a lot on you, if you piss them off and they decide to retaliate. A lot of material they could let slip out."

"They couldn't have done that, surely?"

"Not officially, of course not. But they could leak it - say they'd been hacked, or whatever. It wouldn't be their fault then, would it? They wouldn't be liable. *Jordan* wouldn't be liable. But we'd still be, you know..."

Humiliated, Lou thought - her mind turning, selfish though she knew it probably was, to the thousand things *she'd* done in the privacy of her room at home, her flat in London, that would just about kill her if they ever found their way out into the public sphere.

Publicly and permanently humiliated.

"What was it, then?" she asked. "Why do you think he *did* want the footage?"

Sadie's eyes broke away from the bottle and fixed on Lou's.

"Zimbardo, the guy who organised the Stanford Experiment... Do you know why he did it?"

Lou didn't.

"To understand power dynamics, or something?" she said. "Sorry, I've never done Psychology - it's not really my specialist subject."

"Close. It was more like... deindividuation. He wanted to know how people's behaviour changed when you put them together, when you offered them a group identity and gave them power over another group of people. And if it was a change for the worse... whether it was because of the situation, or whether they were just terrible people to begin with."

"So you reckon Jordan wanted to recreate the experiment? No offence, but wouldn't that be a bit pointless? It's already been done. Hell, it's famous. Even I know about it."

Sadie sighed.

"I'm not saying he was trying to do the exact same thing," she said, impatiently. "And I don't know for sure *what* he'd have been trying to prove with it, before you ask. Chances are, I'll *never* know. But why else would you stir the pot the way he did, making some of us Marshals and the rest of us not? Why would you make a bunch of students take a freaking isometric test before you decided whether or not you wanted them to move into your building? It was a screening process. He wanted to make sure he got the right candidates, the right mix of personalities - and if you ask me, he arranged it so the personalities he ended up with were guaranteed to rub each other up the wrong way. Reality TV... it's not actually a bad analogy, if you think about it. He was trying to create drama - fireworks. Create them, and film them, so he go back and watch them afterwards."

"But you don't know why."

"Right."

And neither do I, Lou thought.

But he's built himself a new community now, right? Another Haven House, up at The Gates.

So whatever he was doing, down in Brighton... he's doing it again now.

CHAPTER 15

More swabs. More confiscated clothing. More interviews down at the police station - these longer, more detailed and, unless she was imagining it, more interrogatory than they'd been the first time, when she was nothing to them but an innocent, unlucky passer-by. When one crime scene was all she'd stumbled on; when one corpse was the sum total of the corpses she'd found.

Raj's death, at least, was a more open-and-shut case than Hadrian Dawson's had been. Physical evidence aside - and there was an abundance of it, all pointing to the murder as a domestic incident rather than a stranger killing - the police had little reason to doubt that Aarti was responsible. She'd confessed, after all: not once, under cross-examination, but over and over again, from the moment two shocked-looking young constables had arrived on the scene after Bea had called 999 to the moment she was led out of the house to the Battenburg car, weeping and rocking.

Bea was surprised to find, when the police finally invited her to leave - albeit with the warning that she could at any time be recalled for further questioning - that she was no longer frightened. That the terror that had come to colour her every waking moment since almost the moment she'd arrived at The Gates had, without her noticing, dissipated, leaving her calm and cool. Calmer and cooler, perhaps, than she'd been for quite some time.

Possibly, she thought as she stepped into the taxi she'd booked to carry her home, there was only so much fear a body could take; only so much running headlong and screaming into the darkness you could do before the shadows parted and you emerged, clear-headed, on the other side.

If this was true, then it was a development she welcomed. She had work to do, after all; work that could only be done at home.

She made a point, upon leaving the cab by her spike-lined front garden, of looking directly at the chestnut tree across the road - its branches currently devoid of monstrous birds. Turned her face *towards* the Arolker house, now gift-wrapped in black and yellow barrier tape, and not *away* from it as she walked the path to her door, not so much as a shiver passing through her as she remembered Raj's severed head in Aarti's lap: the dead eyes that had opened involuntarily as the skull that held them rolled across the carpet, dripping blood and worse as it went.

It dawned on her that she wasn't now, in any sense, *staving off* the thoughts that had previously terrorised her; that she was no longer trying to avoid them, or muffle them, or drown them out. The thoughts, in fact, were still there, as present as they'd ever been. But she no longer felt herself affected by them - was able, instead, to consider them dispassionately, even analytically. To look *inside* them and take them apart.

Moreover, she realised, she was no longer afraid of herself: of what she might be, and of the acts she might have committed.

If you did it, she told herself, bringing Simon Henshaw's toothless mouth and broken body to the front of her mind with that same cool clarity, *then it's already done, and no amount of worry will undo it.*

So stop tormenting yourself. Now.

She locked the door behind her as she entered the house, a decision born not of fear but pragmatism, and drew the blinds she'd left open when she'd watched Joan McTierney and the Davenports shouting at each other in the street.

Then began, methodically, to tear the place apart.

She found four cameras altogether, though she imagined there were others - concealed in places she hadn't thought to look, or too well-hidden to be easily discoverable. One had been placed in the living room, in the tiny vents of an air freshener; another in the kitchen, between the slim black hands of the wall-clock; a third on the first-floor landing, in the frame of a sailing boat print she'd hated since the day she moved in, and the last - the last she knew of - in the sturdy metal base of her bedside lamp.

There were none, she noticed, in the bathroom.

Because even Peeping Toms have their moral limits? she asked herself. *Or because whoever decided we needed to be watched didn't think there'd be much happening in there that was worth watching?*

She took the cameras out, one by one, with a screwdriver; wrapped them in a freezer bag, placed them gently on the hard floor of the kitchen and then, with the heel of her still bloody but now slipper-clad foot, stamped hard on the bag until there was nothing left inside but useless fragments.

It wouldn't help, she knew; there were no wires that she could see, and if the cameras were wireless, there'd be a video feed. And, somewhere, very likely, a repository of video *recordings*: an archive of everything she'd done and everything she'd *seen* in the house since her move.

Somewhere, unfortunately, was too nebulous to be helpful, if she wanted to actually find the recordings - find them and delete them.

She'd have to speak to Lawrence Jordan, she knew; she'd known as much, on some level, since she'd found the camera hidden in the Arolkers' bedroom. It was unlikely, she considered, that Jordan had planted the cameras himself - though perhaps not impossible, given how Machiavellian she'd found him, how much he'd seemed to enjoy watching and studying them all from a distance.

But their presence in her home - and in the Arolkers' home, and quite possibly the homes of their neighbours, too - was unequivocally his responsibility. His complication to resolve; his mess to clean up.

And if he didn't want to *take* that responsibility... well, in her current frame of mind, she wouldn't feel bad about forcing his hand.

She locked up, threw the bag of broken camera parts into the bin outside and strode across the estate with more of a sense of purpose than she'd felt in a long time - fully intending to corner Jordan at home and demand an explanation. Almost immediately, however, she was thwarted: first by the small flock of crows that seemed to block her path with every other step she took, hopping and flapping and reconfiguring themselves as if determined to keep her from her destination, and then by the Davenports, rounding the corner by the Community Hall and apparently - improbably - out for an evening stroll.

Elaine saw her first; made a beeline for her, crossing the road to reach her more nimbly than Bea would have thought possible for a woman of her age.

"Oh, you're *here*!" she cried, throwing her arms around Bea's body in a perfumed embrace that was, at least from Bea's perspective, far more intimate than was warranted by the thin neighbourly bonds they shared. "We've been so *worried* since we saw them take you away in that police car, haven't we, Ivan?"

Ivan Davenport certainly *looked* worried. He was a good deal paler than usual, almost bloodless: his weather-beaten skin like curdled milk and limescale, and the skin of his lips red and peeling and pitted with tiny scratches that might have been teeth marks.

The Davenports, she thought, must have been watching the Arolker house as the police descended; must have seen Aarti led outside in handcuffs, coated in her husband's blood, and what was left of Raj carried out in a body bag while technicians in disposable coveralls swarmed in and out of the house with UV torches and forensics kits. Ivan or Elaine, or both of them, might even have spoken to the police by now, if some of the officers had already started canvassing the estate.

"I'm fine," she said, stiffening in Elaine's arms until the older woman let her go. "Just needed to answer a couple of questions, that's all."

There was no reason to say more; to give away any more detail than was directly solicited. If the Davenports were aware of what had happened at the Arolkers' house and were set on pumping her for a lurid inside scoop, then they could ask her outright. And if they weren't, if they *didn't* know yet why one of their own had been arrested and *her* home transformed into a crime scene, then Bea certainly wasn't about to tell them.

"We didn't know *what* to think, did we?" Elaine said, and her husband nodded, though without enthusiasm.

Perhaps *he* saw something, Bea thought, even if *she* didn't: a sliver of bloodstained wallpaper through a gap in the curtains, or a flash of Raj's body as it was loaded into the bag. Something that set him rocking on his heels; took some of the colour from his face.

"I'm fine," she repeated.

"And how *is* poor Aarti?"

It was a harmless enough question, on the surface. But Bea had no patience for it.

"Why don't you ask the police?" she snapped. "Or did they shut you down already, when you tried?"

Elaine bridled. Ivan, Bea observed, barely reacted at all. She wondered if he'd even been listening.

"*Well!*" Elaine said, quite literally clutching at the pearls around her neck. "Excuse *me* for taking an interest in the welfare of my neighbours!"

"No," Bea said levelly, taking a very deliberate step away from both Davenports, "excuse *me*. There's somewhere I need to be."

She made a sharp, ninety-degree turn, removing herself from the acid burn of Elaine's glare, and crossed the road, heading for Jordan's house.

"It's not my place to tell Lawrence who he should and shouldn't take to," Bea heard her tell her husband as the two of them watched her go, "but that girl has got no *class*, if you ask me. No class at all."

There'd been a time, Bea reflected as she passed through the brick-and-timber lychgate separating Jordan's home from the pavement, when words like that might have hurt her. When she'd worried about how other people perceived her, what they said about her in her absence. When she'd cared how she seemed to others.

And perhaps part of that was Jeremy: his fixation with appearances, with making sure their family and friends and colleagues saw them in the best possible light, both individually and as a couple. That the two of them not just as *Bea* and *Jeremy* but as *the Alexanders* were understood - and admired - as exemplars of professional, personal and marital success.

But part of it had been her, too. Jeremy had wanted perfection - for himself and her and them, together - but she'd gone along with it, hadn't she? She'd pretended to want it as much as he did. For his sake, at first - and then, over time, because she'd convinced herself that it mattered. That the opinions of people like Elaine Davenport were actually *worth* something; were more than just white noise, as easy to filter out as the hum of traffic or the buzz of a refrigerator.

She wondered, now - feeling the words wash over her, and acknowledging their essential emptiness as she let them drift away - whether she might have availed herself of just a little more happiness, had she cared just a little less.

Jordan's door had neither a bell nor a knocker, that she could see. Nor did there seem to be a handle she could turn to let herself inside. It was, to all intents and purposes, nothing more than a solid block of wood with a lock and a peephole - thicker by far, she couldn't fail to notice, than her own front door.

She rapped on the wood with her knuckles; waited a minute, and then rapped again.

There was no answer: no turning of the handle from the inside, and no sound from behind the door.

She knocked a third time, with no real expectation of a response, and was rewarded with further silence.

He's out, she thought. Out, or too busy to come to the door.

Or, a more suspicious part of her whispered, *he's avoiding you. Hiding from you. Because he's been keeping tabs on you, on everyone, and he knows you found his cameras.*

There's no proof of that, she thought.

He built *those houses, didn't he? And you know he likes to watch - you've* seen *him watching. How much more proof do you need?*

A sound drifted her way from the bushes by the lychgate, interrupting the internal debate: a crackling, a breaking of twigs and a crinkling of leaves, the rustle of an animal trampling a forest floor.

A large animal. Too large by far to be a crow or a magpie. Too large even for a fox.

The bird, she thought, with none of the panic she'd felt before. The bird-thing in the tree, whatever it is - it's back.

Calmly, she turned, and walked down the path, not away from the sound but towards it, fully prepared to find the creature waiting for her on the gate, its vast wings folded and its claws gouging trenches into the brickwork as it perched.

But saw instead, as she drew closer to the gate, the shaggy-haired, studenty girl over whom the bird had hovered; the girl she'd half-convinced herself had been nothing but a figment of her overwrought imagination.

The girl who, seeing Bea approach, pulled her jacket tighter around her body and - in a way that struck Bea as entirely human, and the very opposite of illusory – smiled at her, nervously.

"Hi," she said, sounding very young and very unsure of herself. "We haven't met, not properly, but... do you think we might be able to go somewhere and talk? There's some weird stuff going on - weird like the stuff you saw when you saw me outside your house the other day - and I know this is going to come off as a bit mental, but I think you might be caught up in it, somehow. You and everyone else who lives round here."

CHAPTER 16

Staying away from The Gates hadn't been an option, after what Sadie Adebayo had told her.

Lou couldn't have said for sure what some of what she'd heard *meant*, or how the disparate pieces of the larger puzzle fit together: how the murders of the boys connected to Fox Lodge, or the temple it had been, or the monsters she'd seen there, or what any of *those* things had to do with Lawrence Jordan and the bizarre social experiment he'd tried to run at Haven House. Although she couldn't shake the feeling, having been there, that a place like The Gates would give him the perfect opportunity to run that experiment again - and maybe iron out the kinks of that first try.

But all of it meant *something*; it had to. And she was, very possibly, the only person armed with enough information to find out *what*.

It was a lonely position to find herself in: lonely and daunting. And the research she'd been doing had hardly helped to quell her nerves. Whether as a shrine to a chaos goddess (who'd sounded, to Lou, pretty fucking scary on her own terms alone), as a stretch of woodland ruled by giant birds and gold-eyed girls and sabre-toothed tigers, as an asylum set up to torture Victorian women, or as whatever portal to hell it had been when Lou had gone there herself the week before… the place that now called itself The Gates was a malevolence, and its every incarnation seemingly a catalyst for a new and unique kind of horror.

One she'd have to go head to head with on her own, if she was going to get to the bottom of anything.

Except…

There'd been that woman, hadn't there, at The Gates? The tired looking one in the dressing gown and slippers; the one who'd seen what Lou had seen, in the branches of that tree.

She'd lived there, on the estate; the doorstep she'd been standing on had been *her* doorstep, Lou was sure.

Which meant she knew Jordan - that he was, in effect, her landlord. Meant that - if Jordan really *was* messing with the people at The Gates the way he had with the students in Brighton - she'd probably want to know about it.

And if *she'd* seen what *Lou* had seen, seen it with her own eyes, and she had a vested interest in uncovering what the hell Jordan was up to…

Then she might be amenable to hearing the rest of the story, too - or, at least, the parts Lou had to tell.

To *helping*, even.

It had been a tempting thought: the prospect of an ally, of not having to go it alone. Too tempting for Lou to ignore.

Twenty minutes later, she'd been back in the car, on her way out of the university and back to Leicester, to The Gates.

She'd spotted the woman not long after she'd entered the estate; had recognised the woman's stance, the blonde sweep of her hair, now free of its ponytail, as she strode towards a gate Lou hadn't noticed on her last visit, one that could have sat comfortably at the entrance of a church, and marched up to the front door of yet another blocky new-build, this one very slightly bigger than the others around it.

Lou had followed her at a distance, kicking out pre-emptively to clear the path ahead of her of the crows and magpies that covered the ground and circled the air above it like a plague of locusts. There were flocks of them, too many - and how had *anyone* who lived here ever thought that that was normal, anyway? How had *Lou*, that first time?

The woman had knocked at the door of the house, waited, and eventually, when no response came, turned and walked back to the gateway where Lou had by then positioned herself.

"*Weird stuff,*" the woman had repeated, after Lou had introduced herself and given a splintered, allusive explanation for her return to the estate. "Can you be more specific?"

She'd sounded different than Lou had expected, after seeing her on her doorstep: more capable, in better command of herself, somehow. She'd *looked* different, too: still exhausted, the bags under her eyes still dark and pouchy, but strong and confident. A woman disinclined, Lou had thought, to take any shit from anyone. Including Lou.

"Listen," Lou had said - awkwardly, haltingly, "I'm not trying to be difficult, and I appreciate you even taking the time to stand here and listen to me, because I know I haven't given you much reason to yet, but can we go somewhere that isn't here? I just... the stuff I was hoping we could talk about - it might be better to talk about it, like, somewhere else. Somewhere a bit further away. Which I realise probably makes no sense to you all, but..."

The woman had stared at Lou for a second or two, as if she were trying to complete in her head the question Lou was asking - the real question, the words below the words.

Then, to Lou's great surprise, she'd agreed.

And here they were now, in a half-empty burger bar in the middle of the closest service station Lou could get them to in the Citroën, an orange juice in Lou's hand and the strongest coffee on the menu in the woman's.

Her name was Bea, Lou had learned over the course of their brief car journey out of The Gates and onto the motorway: Bea Alexander. And she was a curator - a former anthropologist, now coordinating some of the exhibits over at the museum in town.

"It was a *temple*?" she said, when Lou passed along what Lisa Dunbar had told her - her voice rising so suddenly that Lou had to look over her shoulder to make sure they hadn't been overheard. "I know it used to be a hospital - my next-door neighbour worked there when it was, apparently. But a *temple*..."

There was something about the way she'd said *hospital*, Lou thought - a catch in her throat, a hesitation before the first syllable - that made Lou wonder what *else* she knew about Fox Lodge, beyond what it was and what it had ostensibly done for the women in its care.

Had Bea *been* there, somehow? Had she *seen* it - or even a fragment of it - the way that Lou had, the day the shadow-things had sought her out and whispered to her in the mist?

And if she had - what exactly was it that she'd seen?

"Yeah," Lou told her. "A Roman one. I think there were ruins there, back in the day, but the Order that built the hospital got rid of them when they laid the foundations."

"I can't believe I didn't know this. For Christ's sake, I just put on an exhibit about local folklore. You'd think someone would have *mentioned* there was another bloody temple right under our noses."

"I don't think many people know about it, to be fair. I'm not sure even the people who built it wanted anyone to know it was there. The whole Nox-worshipping thing sounds like it might have been a bit of a taboo, even for the Romans..."

The coffee cup slipped out of Bea's fingers onto its saucer, spilling thick droplets of neat triple espresso onto the tabletop.

"Nox?" she said sharply, her eyes focusing on Lou's with a slightly alarming intensity. "The chaos goddess?"

"That's the one, yeah. You know who she is?"

"Yes. I mean, no. Not exactly. I know Nyx better - her Greek alter-ego, you might call her. I did Classics at university - the name came up. *Both* names. But Nox... she's not in the Roman pantheon, as such. I suppose you'd say she was *pre*-pantheon, if you had to describe her. She's primordial. Chthonic - one of the underworld goddesses, the kind you find associated with... well, some fairly dark practices. Underground chambers and ritual sacrifice, that sort of thing."

Some of her self-assurance was slipping, Lou saw; that icy composure she'd brought with her to the conversation melting at the edges as what Lou had told her began to sink in.

She was rattled; on the way to alarmed. But she wasn't frightened - not yet, anyway. She looked, if Lou had to characterise her expression, like a rookie paranormal investigator face-to-face with her first ghost; like a woman who'd been expecting to find something shocking, who'd known in advance *how* shocking that something was likely to be, but who was taken aback nonetheless by just how shocking it really *was*, in the flesh.

And then the look she wore changed. The shock was still there, Lou thought - still a bass line playing in the background. But there was something else there too, or so it seemed to Lou; a new melody, a second instinct.

She knows something, Lou thought. She's only just *realised* that she knows it - but she knows it.

Another piece of whatever puzzle *she's* been working with just fell into place.

"What is it?" Lou asked.

Bea hesitated.

"There's a poem," she said. "Or a fragment of one, I should say. Roman, Ancient Roman. I'm sure I came across it when I was a student. I don't remember who wrote it, if it was even attributed. Not one of the bigger names, I know that. But it talks about Nox, about who she is. *What* she is. You know she's supposed to have been born of chaos? Or Nyx was, anyway, but they're basically the same person. The same *thing*. It's in Hesiod, that bit. The Theogony."

"Sure," Lou said noncommittally, resolving to google both *Hesiod* and *Theogony* just as soon as she could reasonably withdraw her phone from her pocket without drawing attention to herself or her ignorance.

"Well, this other poem… it goes further. Most of the classical references to Nox that I've read are concerned with how she came about, the circumstances of her creation. But with *this* one, the focus is more on how she supposedly lives - how she sustains herself."

"Which is how?"

Bea shook her head - not as a refusal to answer, or at least Lou didn't think so, but ruefully, as if she were chastising herself for her own stupidity. For not having seen earlier what was right in front of her.

"Rage," she said. "The idea is that she's from chaos, from this sort of pre-Creation cosmic void, but rage is what nourishes her. What she feeds on."

She stared down at her cup, at her coffee-stained fingers and the small, pale indentation above the left ring finger that had been made - if Lou had to guess - by a wedding band only recently removed, and let out a slow, sad breath.

"Not just *feeds* on rage, in fact," she continued, her head still shaking, "but precipitates it. *Incites* it. Coaxes it out of the people she touches."

Or brings it to the surface when it's there already, Lou thought suddenly - remembering the way *she'd* felt under the tree at The Gates, with the apparition of the dead girl shrieking through her dislocated jaw and the shape-shifting shadows closing in around her. All the bitterness and fury, all the - yes - *rage* that had coursed through her in that moment; the crystallising sense of injustice, absolute and blinding. Of having been wronged.

"Think of it as a kind of agriculture," Bea clarified, apparently reading Lou's state of temporary distraction as confusion, uncertainty. "She needs to eat, and rage is what feeds her. So she *sows* rage, or the beginnings of it, the way you'd sow seeds if you were trying to cultivate corn or vegetables. She plants it in you - in her victims, rather - and waits for it to grow, until it's a big enough crop to harvest."

And if the soil's fertile to begin with, Lou added to herself, *then so much the better, right?*

"So," she said, something else occurring to her, something she needed to follow through to its logical conclusion, "let's say for argument's sake that she's real - Nox, that is. It'd be better for her to plant her rage-seeds or whatever in someone who's *already* a bit aggrieved, wouldn't it? Someone who's already pretty pissed off about something."

"I would have thought so, yes," Bea replied quietly, not meeting Lou's eye.

"And somewhere like an asylum, a proper old-school asylum packed full of patients having terrible things done to them in the name of science... that'd be a prize bit of farmland to sow your rage-crops in, right? Every woman there angry and frustrated and in pain, and nobody willing to help them... they'd be prime pickings. A feast, eventually."

Bea looked up from her coffee.

"What are you thinking?" she asked.

"I don't know, exactly. It's not a very well-formed idea. But let's say, hypothetically... let's say she's real, Mother Chaos. And that she's knocking around where you live because the Romans invited her in when they built their temple to her, or because there's a hole in the world there big enough to let her through - a tear in the fabric of the universe, or a hellmouth, or whatever. Doesn't matter what it is or what you call it: the point is, she's *there*."

"Then let's say, again for the sake of argument, that one day this place she's decided to call home, this place that was nothing but woodland and ruins for God knows how many centuries... it attracts the interest of an order of monks, monks who think they're doing the Lord's work by buying up the land and turning it into a hospital. Which would be all well and good, except that the people who end up running the hospital the monks build are absolute bastards even by the standards of the nineteenth-century psychiatric establishment, and *they* decide that the best way to treat the women they're given - women who are probably only there because they've got post-natal depression or are pregnant out of wedlock or something - is to torture the shit out of them. Lock them up, put them in straitjackets, pull out their teeth and hair so they don't bite the orderlies or hang themselves with their own ponytails..."

Bea shuddered, and Lou, wondering if she'd gone too far with her summary of Fox Lodge and its treatments, readjusted course.

"And Mother Chaos... she's got to be really hungry by now, after all that time without her acolytes. So she starts to feed off the anger of the women, the patients - and then she thinks to herself, why stop there? Why not sow a bit of discord in *them*, tap into some of what *they* must be feeling already, so she can *really* eat?"

"I don't know if you know this - there's no reason you would - but there was a murder at the hospital, just before it closed down. A patient went for one of the doctors, gouged his eyes out. And there's no way of knowing for sure, not now... but I'd put money on Nox having something to do with it. On her maybe giving the patient just enough of a push to act on what she'd probably been wanting to do since they committed her."

Lou stopped, her mouth dry, and reached for her orange juice.

"You said this had something to do with me," Bea asked her. "Me and the other people at The Gates. What did you mean by that? Because we're living on top of... what did you call it, a hole in the world?"

The juice was warm and unpleasantly pulpy. Lou took a final swig and placed it back down on the table.

"Again," she said, "I don't really know. Everything I'm saying, it's all sort of... embryonic. I need to sit down and think through it all before I work out what I *really* think might be going on. I've got an idea this Nox stuff has got something to do with the murders - the guy the police found where you live, and the other bodies, the ones in town. But I don't know how everything ties together yet, if it does. And I can't prove it, but I think Lawrence Jordan might be involved in some of it too, somewhere."

Bea's eyes widened.

"Jordan?" she said, incredulous.

"Sorry - look, I know he's the one in charge of the whole commune thing you've got going on, and I know he's probably, like, a friend, but..."

"He's no friend of mine," Bea interrupted her. "And I'm not at The Gates by choice. So whatever you're thinking about the man: please, just say it. You're not going to offend me."

"Like I said," Lou insisted, choosing her words carefully, "I really haven't worked it out yet. All I know is that he's creepy, properly creepy. The last co-living place he started... it turned out he was spying on the people living there. Not just looking through peepholes, but keeping tabs on them with cameras, surveillance cameras. He'd set them up in their rooms, in the kitchen, everywhere - the whole time they were living there, he'd been watching them. Which is bad in itself, obviously. But when I spoke to one of the old tenants about it... she seemed to think he was doing it as part of some sort of social experiment. Like... he was observing them. Seeing how they behaved under, you know... different conditions. I'm not saying he's doing that to *you*," she added quickly, watching the colour drain from Bea's already-white face. "Where you live... it's very different than the place he was running before. Way different."

Bea stood up, abruptly, from the table.

"I need you to take me back to The Gates," she said, not loudly but firmly, and with the same confidence and certitude she'd had earlier. "Right now."

They barely spoke in the car, Bea so evidently preoccupied with whatever task she felt she needed to accomplish that Lou was reluctant to interrupt her thinking.

She didn't park the Citroën on the lay-by outside, the way she had before, but drove straight into the estate - secure in the knowledge that, with Bea in the passenger seat, she was unlikely to be stopped and questioned. By the police, or by Lawrence Jordan.

There was a woman in the road beside Bea's house. And she was screaming.

She looked, at first glance, like somebody's grandmother, all auburn knitwear and gingery Margaret Thatcher hair, a brown canvas shopping bag hanging from her wrist. But no grandmother Lou had ever met had greeted her approach with such manifest terror. Nor had any of their hands and clothes been stained with quite so much blood.

She stopped the car a dozen feet from where the woman was standing, but kept the ignition running; wound down the windows but didn't open the doors.

"Elaine?" Bea said, addressing the woman through the passenger window - but not, Lou noticed, making any move to open the door herself.

The grandmotherly woman's head cocked up in response, and she began to stagger towards them, lurching like a zombie, the bag swinging back and forth with every step she took. Only as she came closer did Lou see that the bag wasn't brown at all, but stained with blood, like her hands and jumper. Stained, and leaking carmine fluid from whatever it contained onto the tarmac below.

"Ivan!" she howled - to Bea or to herself, Lou wasn't sure. "Please — you must help Ivan!"

"Ivan?" Bea asked, seeming every bit as confused as Lou by this turn of events. "Elaine, what *about* Ivan? What's happened to him?"

The woman lost her footing, not quite tripping but stumbling. One handle of the shopping bag broke free of her arm, and the bag dropped to the ground, exposing its contents.

There was a head inside: an old man's head, dark red and gummy with its own pooled blood.

CHAPTER 17

t wasn't kind. And it certainly wasn't normal - or, rather, wasn't at all the response she'd been conditioned to expect of herself, when confronted with the evidence of violent death.

But Bea's first thought, on seeing Elaine Davenport bend down in the road to retrieve the bag that held her husband's head, was: really? This *again*?

"You know her?" Lou asked, shakily, pointing at Elaine in the road.

"She lives next door to me," Bea replied.

She opened the door, unbuckled her seatbelt and, with none of the hesitation she might have felt before - at least, before she stepped into the Arolkers' living room to find Aarti cuddling her husband's decapitated head with parental tenderness - walked out onto the road towards Elaine, and towards whatever was left of Ivan.

Elaine was on her knees now, not rocking and weeping as Aarti had been but shaking, holding so tightly to the bag that Bea couldn't imagine how even the police would separate her from it - its handles leaving white stigmata trails along her palms as they bit into the lined, creased flesh.

"Who would do this?" she whispered, as Bea came closer. "Who would do this to my Ivan?"

So... it wasn't *you* who did it? Bea thought - finding herself, with that same slightly inhuman detachment, confused rather than relieved by the implication that it wasn't *Elaine* who'd separated Ivan's head from his body, wasn't *her* who'd killed him, but someone else. Someone currently off-screen.

"What happened?" she asked, bending down beside her, not so much as flinching now as her gaze met Ivan's blank, blood-smeared and all-too-open eyes.

"They left him like this," Elaine said softly, not looking up. "In bags, outside the door. Three bags. His legs, and his body, and his... his..."

She twisted her *own* body, with great gentility, away from Bea's, and vomited onto the pavement - a gargled spray of acrid, sour-smelling bile that made Bea faintly queasy but smelled only marginally less pleasant than the slaughterhouse stench beginning to rise from the bag.

A car door opened and closed behind them, and then Lou was there, her hand coming to rest tentatively on Bea's upper arm.

"Should I, like, call someone?" she asked, sounding entirely uncertain.

"The police," Bea told her, craning her neck around. "Call the police."

Lou reached for her phone, and then paused, not dialling.

"Something wrong?" Bea asked, conscious of the absurdity of the question in their current circumstances.

The girl extended a finger outwards, over Bea's shoulder, and Bea swivelled her head back around, until she was facing Elaine and the bloodied bag.

Luke and Amit, the Harris-Hindochas, were running towards them at full pelt, wearing twin looks of horror and concern.

Only then did Bea notice the rest of the blood: a smudged, red-wine track of it, arcing from the Davenport's porch to the middle of road in which Elaine was kneeling.

"Is someone hurt?" said Amit breathlessly, coming to rest at Elaine's back. "We just saw the blood, and... wait, is that...?"

He gestured to the bag, to what was very evidently the human head inside it, and shoved a fist against his mouth, pressing his lips closed.

He's going to vomit too, Bea thought.

He didn't, in the end - but it was, she considered, a close call. Luke's stomach was less sturdy by comparison - his tree-trunk torso bending at the waist as he retched, and the protein shake and scrambled egg he must have consumed literally minutes before spilling out of him and coming to rest in a gelatinous heap not far from the more liquid puddle Elaine had left on the ground.

"What the hell happened?" Amit asked, through the protective layer of his still-curled fingers.

Another door opened, somewhere to Bea's left. She spun in the direction of the sound, just in time to see Joan McTierney burst forth from the front door of Kajal Sawiak's semi, one liver-spotted knuckle wrapped around the pewter head of a walking stick. She was followed a moment or two thereafter by Karolina Sawiak, and finally by Kajal herself, the latter looking every bit as exhausted and downtrodden as she had on the handful of other occasions Bea had seen her.

Joan sped up as she approached the small group gathered in the middle of the road, leaning on the cane for support - then slowed down again as she saw, just as Amit and Luke had a moment before, exactly what Elaine Davenport was gripping so firmly in her bloodstained shopping bag.

Joan, to Bea's surprise, didn't shrink from the sight of it; didn't shudder or recoil. Just squinted, closed her eyes, opened them and then squinted again, as if to confirm to herself that it really *was* Ivan's head she was looking at, and not a mirage.

That's because she's seen worse, Bea told herself, the thought coming to her unexpectedly - and with it the memory of what Joan had told her about the hospital that sat almost exactly where she was standing now, the hospital that was really more of a torture chamber for the girls who'd been confined there.

About the less-than-Hippocratic interventions of the doctors and nurses Joan had witnessed, when she worked there.

It never felt right to me, how they treated them, she'd said.

It didn't sit well with me. Didn't then, doesn't now.

How *much* worse, Bea could only imagine - though she thought she might have caught a trace of it, some small facsimile, the night the walls of her living room had fallen away and she'd felt the crows at her feet and the insects on her skin. The night she was sure she'd been poisoned; that she'd been hallucinating.

She knew better now. Or thought she did.

"How did he get like that?" Joan asked her, indicating Ivan's head with her stick. "Was it *her* that did it?"

She nodded towards Elaine, the *her* in question - Elaine who was still kneeling, but crying now too, very quietly, into the crook of her arm. Pressing her forehead to her wrist, so that the wet blood there transferred to her face and painted red, panda-like circles under her eyes.

"No," Bea said, under her breath. "I don't think so."

"*Who*, then?"

"I don't know. I think she found him like this."

"What's going on?" said a new voice - this one sounding not concerned but curious, dispassionate. The voice of a man, Bea thought, content to watch a space shuttle explode in real time from the safety of his living room. "What am I seeing here?"

Jordan, she told herself. *Of* course *Jordan would want to be here for something like this. He's probably logging all of our reactions so he can review them later.*

"What do you *think* you're seeing?" she replied, rounding on him. "The man's dead. Or did none of your cameras pick up on that?"

He physically jumped away from her, almost crashing into Luke Harris in his attempt to put some distance between his body and hers - alarmed perhaps by the unexpectedness of the accusation, but more likely, she suspected, by her tone, her delivery. She'd felt calm until Jordan had made himself known to the group; as calm, anyway, as anyone could be expected to feel in her current circumstances. Now, though, she sounded murderous, even to herself.

"*Cameras?*" Joan McTierney said. "What cameras?"

"Should I still ring them?" Lou asked, warily. "The police?"

Jordan's irises expanded at this, Bea noticed; flickered left to right and back again, as if searching for a viable escape route.

He thinks she means *call the police about him*, she realised, revulsion building in her. There's a man's head in a shopping bag on the floor in front of him, that same man's wife is rending her garments next to him, and *he's* worried we're going to report him for spying on us with his bloody cameras. Worried, probably, about what the police will say when they put *that* together with *this*, and with Raj Arolker's murder, and with what happened to that boy over there in the cement mixer.

What conclusions they'll draw, when it all comes to light.

It was pathetic, she thought; utterly pathetic.

And *he* was pathetic, too, wasn't he, edging away from it all like a trapped rat trying to save its own skin? An absolute waste of oxygen.

Someone that pathetic - they barely deserved to live.

She froze; examined the thought that had just passed through her, then replayed it, realising as she did that it wasn't *her* thought, wasn't *her* judgement she was hearing.

And that she was angry. More than angry: furious, the rage in her building up to a boiling crescendo behind her temples.

"Hey," Lou said, touching her again, very gently, on the arm. "Are you okay?"

It was the smallest contact, the most minor of human connections, but it was enough to break the circuit - to draw her back to herself and away from whatever outside force had been threatening to take her over.

"Fine," she said briskly. "And... no. Don't *you* phone the police. You two," she added, addressing Amit and Luke, "do you have your phones? Can you call 999?"

"I'll do it," Luke answered immediately, pulling his handset from the wraparound phone holder strapped to his biceps.

"And can you take care of her until they get here?" she asked Amit, nodding towards Elaine.

"Not a problem," Amit said, kneeling down beside the older woman and wrapping an arm around her waist to help her to her feet, heedless of the blood that seeped from her clothes to his as she stood. He took her hand and, with that same lack of concern for himself and his own obvious discomfiture, prised her fingers from the shopping bag, lowering it - and with it, Ivan's head - to the ground.

Jordan, Bea saw out of the corner of her eye, was continuing to sidle away - his steps lengthening, propelling the rest of him further and further away from the group in a scuttling, crab-like motion that only exacerbated her revulsion.

Her rage.

Use it, then, she told herself. *Use it - just don't let it use* you.

"*You*," she said, shouting to Jordan in a bellow that would have done Ivan Davenport himself proud. "Stop. I'd like a word, if you don't mind."

It wasn't a question; left no room for refusal or negotiation. Jordan hesitated, torn between the very pressing need to extricate himself from the scene and the steely command of a woman who seemed, inconveniently, to have learned at least one of his secrets.

"What?" he replied - trying to match her imperiousness with an authority of his own. And failing.

She strode across to where he'd stopped on the pavement, out of earshot of the others. Lou chased after her, seemingly determined to hear for herself what Jordan had to say.

"You've been filming us," Bea told him. "Why?"

"I don't have to justify myself to you," he said - but it was weak, a whine rather than the assertive dismissal she thought he must have been aiming for.

"Actually, I think you do. You planted cameras all over my house, and the Arolkers' house too. It wouldn't surprise me in the slightest if you'd been filming all of us since we moved here."

"You agreed to it," he said. "All of you. You, when you signed your lease, and the owners when they committed to their leasehold agreements. Consenting to being filmed - it was one of the conditions of your being allowed to move in here in the first place. Or didn't you read the paperwork?"

He'd obviously intended this to be his *aha*! moment; for Bea to realise her error, and retreat. But she'd spent enough time lately dealing with lawyers and the ludicrous legislative loopholes they navigated to be comfortable arguing back.

"Honestly," she said, the sensation of measured calm descending on her again as she spoke, "I don't remember *what* was in the paperwork - there was so bloody much of it, the details passed me by. But I *do* remember some of the stories I've read in the papers lately about pervert landlords filming their tenants. And I can tell you now that things didn't go well for them, when the tenants found out what they were doing. Perhaps you're telling the truth about the cameras being written into the lease, I don't know. But if they were, then they were *buried* in it, *deliberately* buried. And while that may be enough to save you from a prosecution, I doubt it will do much for you in the court of public opinion. No-one likes a Peeping Tom, Mr Jordan. No-one."

"And that's without them hearing about the *other* things you've been up to. Was it you who killed the boy I saw over there on the building site, I wonder? Or did you bring someone else on board to help you do it? I'm new to this, so you'll have to help me understand: is Nox happy for you to make your sacrifices by proxy, or does she like it better when you do it yourself?"

His face froze, then hardened. *Before*, she thought as she watched the change come over him, he'd looked like nothing so much as an actor playing the part of a villain in a movie, even as he'd laughed and joked with them around the table. Now, as his lip furrowed to a snarl and his shoulders stiffened like the spine of a rabid dog preparing to attack, it seemed more than affectation, more than a performance.

"What do *you* know about Nox?" he said, sneering.

More than you *think* I ought to, she thought.

But before she could answer him aloud, the shadows fell, becoming a grey cold mist that writhed and twisted and threatened to swallow them whole - the hot, long-armed things inside it reaching and grasping and pulling them in.

CHAPTER 18

Later, when it was over, Lou forced herself to delve deeper into Lawrence Jordan's background - to figure out for herself the *how* and the *why* of the plans he'd put in motion.

She read, and dug, and read some more; drafted in a trainee solicitor friend to help her decipher some of the more complicated land ownership and property development documents she managed to acquire from the planning departments of the three separate local authorities they belonged to.

And then, finally, she arranged to speak to the few surviving people willing to talk to her about Jordan and what they knew of him - every one of them on condition of the strictest anonymity.

What she discovered was this:

Jordan had never been a scholar. He'd started work in the aggregates trade as a teenager without so much as an O Level to his name and, finding success there, had never had much cause to look back. But he'd always been fascinated by ancient history and mythology, Greek and Roman myths especially, and much of the pride he'd professed in his hometown had derived from the cultural and logistical importance of Leicester to the Romans who'd settled in Britain.

He'd also had a long-standing interest in the Fox Lodge site, long before it was ever The Gates. One of the people Lou had spoken to, a distant and estranged member of the extended Jordan family, had mentioned a great-aunt who'd spent time at the hospital as a patient in the '70s, a great-aunt to whom Lawrence Jordan was particularly close and whom he'd visited often during her confinement. Which might, the estranged relative had suggested, have accounted for Lawrence's dogged determination to acquire Fox Lodge and the land around it from the council, when the hospital folded.

And he *had been* determined; there was no doubt about it. Fox Lodge had closed its doors in 1989, and Jordan had eventually purchased the land it had occupied in the Autumn of 2018. But in the almost thirty years between those two events, he'd made no fewer than fifteen offers to the relevant authorities - his final offer accepted only after he'd added more than a million pounds to the bid that preceded it.

There'd been conditions attached to the sale, a number of them, all geared towards ameliorating the negative effects of any new housing or commercial developments on the surrounding communities. But none of those conditions, Lou learned, concerned the necessary ring-fencing of property for rental or lower-income tenants.

Bea had told her, afterwards, that Jordan had been *forced* by the council to build rental homes, as well as saleable ones, on the site of The Gates; that these rental properties were part of the *quid pro quo* that had helped to grease the wheels of the purchase.

Only it wasn't true.

What Lou deduced, therefore - though she'd been right, when she'd told Bea that it could only ever be supposition - was this:

Jordan, on one of his early-life visits to Fox Lodge, had seen something - heard something, felt something - he couldn't explain; something that had left him unsettled enough to want to investigate the history of the area. And he had come to realise, in the course of that investigation - though Lou couldn't have said *how*, exactly - that a temple to Nox had once occupied that very same spot in the universe as the hospital.

Perhaps he'd known about Nox before then; had stumbled on the name in one of the books on mythology Lou had been assured he'd once devoured. Or perhaps he'd found out about her later, once his interest in the ruins of the temple had been piqued.

Either way: he'd come to know of her. And had come to believe, through whatever means, that the land once dedicated to the *worship* of her possessed great power, some small echo of the power possessed by the goddess herself.

Had come to believe, moreover, that taking control of the land meant taking control of that power - if only he could find a way to channel it, to bring it forth.

Haven House, Lou concluded, had been a dry run for what Jordan had been planning all along for The Gates. He'd known, somehow, about the reaping-and-sowing of rage that Bea had suggested was Nox's *modus operandi*; had surmised that creating discord - bringing about a little of the choler and chaos that the goddess fed on, at the very place she was most likely to feed - was his best shot at summoning her, at drawing out her power.

And what better way to create that chaos than by assembling the most disparate group of people he could find - people handpicked, through a rigorous selection criteria of his own device, for their volatility and their bubbling frustrations, their pettiness and their irascibility - and throwing them together in a setting he could engineer at will?

It was perfect. Or so he must have thought.

CHAPTER 19

The mist was thin but soupy: a murky film overlaying every place it touched, every inch of ground its tendrils reached.

It was transparent, or so it seemed to Bea. But what showed through it wasn't the estate, or the pavement, or Elaine Davenport and her husband's head in its dripping canvas bag. It was a manor house: a crumbling Victorian pile, or a sliver of one, lying just behind the mist like coloured glass in a kaleidoscope, like a fragment of a photo seen through the lens of a broken View-Master.

It was the hospital, she realised. She was seeing Fox Lodge - Fox Lodge as it had been.

And behind it, on what felt - though she had no sense of how she'd got to the analogy - like another frequency, another sedimentary layer of time and place compressed to almost-imperceptibility by the weight of the present, was the temple: low-roofed and half-hidden by the surrounding forest, a wide stone staircase winding down from the Doric columns at its entrance.

Winding down, and underground.

In the mist, the hot, tentacled things swirled and undulated, whispering obscene incoherencies from their chitinous beaks, blindly grasping at her and Lou and Jordan with rubbery, suction-cupped limbs. She had no reference point for what they were, what they might be: neither octopus nor eel, though a little perhaps like Tennyson's Kraken, roaring and rising from their sea of fog.

Rising from chaos, she thought. *Whatever they are, they come from chaos. Just like she does - Nox.*

Jordan flailed, wild with panic, his arms chopping and whirring at the freezing vapour and boiling limbs closing in around him.

"Stop moving!" Lou screamed at him, ducking out of the path of a tentacle as it swung towards her. "Do you want to *hit* them?"

Jordan stilled, stricken, and Bea felt another surge of the anger spill up from her chest and throat, filling her face with blood so hot her skin could barely contain it.

He wanted this. He asked for it. So why stop him? Let him have it.
Let them take him.

A scream cut through the mist, one that belonged to neither Lou nor Jordan but to someone older and frailer.

Joan McTierney.

As abruptly as it had descended on them, the fog cleared, the shadows and the creatures they concealed fading away to nothing and the memory of the temple and the hospital dissolving with them, leaving nothing behind but road and houses and pavement that felt reassuring solid under Bea's feet.

She looked over at the old woman, standing on the edge of where the mist had been, and took a single, involuntary step backwards.

The most obvious change in Joan was in her features. Her mouth and lips were contorted to an animal snarl, the teeth behind them longer and sharper than any human teeth ought to have been, and tiny yellow rivulets of something Bea could have sworn was venom dripping from the points of the incisors. The old woman's skin was smoother and her body leaner and more agile than either had been only minutes earlier.

And her eyes... her eyes were gold. Solid gold, from lid to lid: iris, pupil and sclera.

"What did you do?" she demanded of Jordan - the new harmonics in her voice suggesting not one speaker but a dozen, a hundred.

And the rage of Furies behind them.

She stalked towards him, brandishing her walking stick like a cutlass, gold eyes burning and body serpentine.

"What did you do?" she repeated. "Did you spy on us, with your cameras? Watch us eat, watch us sleep? Watch us undress?"

("She heard us," Lou told Bea, fear turning her whisper to a croak. "She knows what he's been doing").

Joan raised the cane above her head and brought it down in front of her, inches from Jordan's nose, with a sound like tearing silk.

"These girls here," she continued, mockingly - the voice now scarcely recognisable as the same one Bea had heard speak up at the Co-Life Dinners, had listened to as it related the bare-bones story of the hospital and its poor, mistreated patients, "*they* think you murdered those boys."

Because it's *not* the same voice, Bea thought. It isn't Joan talking - it's something talking *through* her. Someone.

And you know *who*, don't you?

Jordan was silent; dumbstruck.

"*They* think you did it," not-Joan said. "But we know different, don't we? We know *exactly* what you're capable of. And what you're not."

She took a further step towards him, narrowing the gap between them.

"You, Lawrence Jordan," she said, and Bea imagined she could see traces of Nox in Joan now, young and ancient all at once, pulling the mask she'd made of the old woman's face into a derisive grin. "You thought you were worthy? That I'd ever make a gift of my power to a sack of bones and meat too ignorant to learn the meaning of sacrifice?"

Another step, and she was almost on him, scarcely a foot of air separating the two of them.

"Luckily," she said, the grin widening, "I'm here to teach you."

She thrust her thin arm - Joan's arm - forward, and the walking stick with it.

It happened so quickly, Bea was aware of what came next only as a heap of broken images: stills from a roll of photographs, pasted together at significant points in time.

The end of the cane - dull and flat, entirely benign - made contact with Jordan's stomach. Joan - the creature, the goddess who was *wearing* Joan - flicked the wrist holding the pewter head of it upwards, as gently as if she were flipping an omelette in a frying pan.

And then the cane was in, and blood was pouring from the torn muscle of Jordan's chest, the wood of the stick running through him: from his ribcage, where it had entered, to the exit wound it had left in his back at the moment it impaled him.

PART III

CHAPTER 20

Lou had suggested a restaurant, but Josie was immovable: if Lou wanted a second date, she'd insisted, then that second date would need to unfold at the same venue it had the first time. Same time, same place.

To put right what once went wrong, Josie had texted - following immediately thereafter with a broadly beaming emoji that had, to Lou's surprise, put a spring in her step for the remainder of that morning.

Oh, boy, Lou had replied with a smiling face of her own - hoping Josie wouldn't twig that she'd needed to google *put right what once went wrong* before she'd replied, but hoping equally that repeating lines from '90s sci-fi shows she'd neither watched nor heard of previously wouldn't evolve into a running joke between them that Lou would be expected not just to understand but to perpetuate.

The pleasure she felt at the prospect of the date was a welcome change from the anxiety that had been eating away at her guts since Lawrence Jordan's murder. And, though she had no intention of saying as much to Josie, it felt like just the break she needed from the visions of disembodied heads and harridan grandmothers with blood on their hands and gold discs for eyes that had haunted her dreams in the fortnight since.

She hadn't known Bea anything like long enough to be sure how familiar *she* was with death. Nor, for that matter, how intimately the *other* woman knew it: the prematurely-haggard Asian woman with the bad bleach job and the little girl clinging onto her thigh like a baby wombat, the one who'd been standing behind the old lady when she went for Jordan with her walking stick. *Kajal*, she thought Bea had called her.

But for Lou, who'd never seen so much as an open coffin at a funeral, it was a shock to the system: a living Chamber of Horrors entirely unlike the images she'd seen online and at a remove, but now acid-etched into her memory and, she worried, impossible to shake.

She hadn't, thank God, been arrested when the police had arrived at The Gates. Too many witnesses - the two gay guys as well as Bea and the woman with the kid - had seen the old lady go for Jordan with her stick, though she suspected that neither the guys and nor the howling Margaret Thatcher woman they were tending to had seen what had happened to the old lady just before she'd attacked, or what had been crawling in the shadows that had only cleared when the old lady stepped inside them.

But it was a close call. Not one or two squad cars but a full half-dozen had come screeching into the estate after the muscle guy had made his phone call, and an armoured van besides - working, Lou presumed, on the assumption that a *third* mutilated body turning up in the same spot warranted the attention of as many uniforms as the local force could stretch to.

The presence of a *fourth* body along with the third - a body dead and skewered, if not quite so horribly maimed as the ones that preceded it - had sent the police into a tailspin, a frenzy of interrogation and activity culminating in the arrest of the old lady, in the careful extraction by white-suited, blue-overshoe'd forensics people of the head in the bag and what was left of Jordan, and in the spiriting away (though not, Lou was happy to note, in handcuffs) of Bea, the beheaded man's widow and the half of the gay couple who'd been, by then, almost as bloody as the widow.

Bea, fortunately, had been released not long afterwards - the police convinced if not delighted by her insistence that her proximity to all four victims at the moment of their deaths, or very soon thereafter, really *had* been nothing more than an unfortunate coincidence.

What became of the others - the blood-soaked guy, the crying widow, even the washed-out woman with the kid - Lou had no idea. And what the police must have made of it all, what chains of events they'd hypothesised that could feasibly have included two unrelated domestic beheadings as well as the scalping of a casual labourer and the unprovoked impaling of a prominent local businessman by his octogenarian neighbour... *that*, she couldn't begin to imagine.

And nor, unlike before, had she wanted to know; wanted to *look*. She'd deliberately avoided the news and her inbox since Jordan's murder, and had checked her phone only to reply to texts and calls from Bea, Josie and her mother: from Bea, for what updates on the situation she could bear; from Josie, as a distraction from the dark trajectory of her own unravelling thoughts; and from her mother because Lou was reasonably sure that, if she didn't answer *her* then *both* her parents would come knocking at her bedroom door, demanding to know what was wrong and why she hadn't been downstairs for days.

She hadn't even been tempted to revisit the forums; to find out what the self-proclaimed "insiders" there did or didn't have to say about the case. The case*s*.

She'd focused instead on the date: on her own unexpected anticipation at the prospect of seeing Josie again; the possibility of conversation encompassing something more than blood and brutality, ghosts and avenging goddesses of chaos; even the small satisfactions she expected to take in choosing an outfit more alluring and elaborate than jeans and trainers and a button-down shirt. And while she couldn't ignore altogether the ill-formed disquiet she'd felt since her last, brief exchanges with Bea - *an entirely normal and natural sensation given the circumstances*, as she'd assured herself - she was certainly prepared to suppress her unease until later, when she felt better equipped to tackle it head-on.

Now, sitting down opposite Josie in the same alcove they'd briefly occupied during their first, doomed meeting, she was glad she had.

It was good to see her, she thought, unbuttoning her jacket and reaching for the bottle of Japanese beer Josie had already ordered for her: the very brand, Lou remembered, that she'd offhandedly mentioned she liked during one of their recent late-night messaging sessions. Better than good - it was something like respite, a reprieve from the paralysing dread Lou hadn't realised was engulfing her, the existential quicksand that kept threatening to pull her down into a darker place than she'd ever wanted to explore.

And she was so pretty, Josie - how had Lou not noticed that, the first time they'd met? Pretty, and kind, and - in digital form, at least - smart and entertaining, so much so that Lou had occasionally forgotten while they were talking what it was that she was trying to get away from by talking to her.

You thought she was dull, she told herself. *Safe, but dull. Sweet, but provincial. A step down from the girls in London.*

And now I'm over wanting *interesting*, is that it? she asked herself in response, sickened by the echo of her arrogance, her earlier pretensions. Is *safe* a better bet now, after what I've seen?

I don't know how safe she is, and neither do you, she replied to herself. *But I'm not sure* provincial *is exactly the safety net we used to think it was, either.*

"No other pressing engagements this time, then?" Josie said, snapping Lou out of herself and back to the present: the beer on the table and the girl in front of her.

"None," Lou said, smiling at her in a way she hoped suggested that she was, indeed, intending to stay.

"Glad to hear it."

She raised her glass - something clear and sparkling, a slice of lime floating on its bed of crushed ice - and tapped Lou's bottle.

"I've been looking forward to this all week," she added, with the same glint of amusement that had animated her face the last time they'd met. "And I didn't fancy having to chase you down the road just to get you to sit and have a drink with me."

It was going well, Lou thought, an hour and two beers later. Really well.

They'd changed their seating configuration, as they'd talked: were no longer opposite each other across the table now but side by side, Josie's leg resting against Lou's, and the toes of one of her feet pressing - by no means uncomfortably - into the bone of Lou's ankle.

"It's been a weird week," Josie concluded, wrapping up an unexpectedly labyrinthine story about one of the overzealous parents from the kids' puppet workshop she volunteered with, one who'd hidden and subsequently sabotaged a brace of emu marionettes when her son had lost out on the lead puppeteer role in the workshop's upcoming production. "And did I tell you what happened to my friend's brother?"

"Don't think so," Lou said, wondering - through the pleasant haze of the beer - whether it was too early on in the date to kiss her.

"It was awful, actually. I mean, I say *friend*, but to be honest I haven't seen her since we graduated, and we only really talk in group chats. Anyway - her brother was killed. By his *wife*, if you can believe it."

Lou froze, her leg seizing next to Josie's.

She means Raj Arolker, she thought. Bea's other neighbour - the first one of the Gates lot to die, to be decapitated. And by his wife, just like Ivan Davenport.

No, she corrected herself. *Stop. You're being ridiculous. It's not what you think. It can't be - nothing's that much of a coincidence. The woman she's talking about - she'll have poisoned the husband, or slashed the brakes on his car, or, I don't know... hired a hitman to shoot him on his way to work.*

It's not what you think.

"You alright?" Josie asked, reaching for Lou in a way that would even a few seconds earlier have answered several of the questions Lou had been weighing up as they'd talked. "Sorry - I didn't mean to get morbid on you. Probably not the best date chat ever, is it? 'Hey, let me tell you about this dude I've never met who just got murdered...'"

"What was his name?" Lou asked, abruptly.

"What?"

"Your friend's brother. What was his name?"

Josie drew back from her, puzzled.

"Raj," she said. "Raj Arolker. You've read about it, right? It was all over the news last week - he was the pharmacist, the one whose wife cut off his head when she found out he'd been cheating on her. It was horrible, really horrible. Kiran, my friend... she's all over the place about it, or it looks that way from what she's been posting..."

Josie was talking, still, but Lou was no longer listening - was thinking, instead, of what she'd just heard. Of the part of the disclosure Josie probably thought was the least shocking, the most innocuous.

Pharmacist. Raj Arolker was a *pharmacist.*

Had *been* a pharmacist.

Another health professional. A little bit like a doctor, a little bit like a nurse - enough like both, in the eyes of someone with a grudge and a score to settle, to qualify for retribution.

Lou's recent avoidance of anything that might fall even broadly under the auspices of *news* or *current affairs* meant she *hadn't* read about what had happened to Arolker, *hadn't* seen the story anywhere; that she knew only what Bea had told her, via text, about the murder.

Bea hadn't thought to mention to Lou what the guy have done for a living - why would she have? She didn't know everything that Lou did, about who the other murdered boys had been, and what they'd had in common.

Only... if Josie was right, then Raj Arolker was a pharmacist *himself*, not the son of one. Which didn't fit, did it, with the pattern Lou thought she'd picked up on before: the punishment of children for the sins of their parents.

Unless...

"Kiran, your friend," she asked Josie, with even more urgency than before. "What do her parents do for a living?"

Josie frowned.

"They're chemists," she said, slowly. "Both of them. Kiran too. It's sort of a family business. Listen, Lou, are you alright? You look sort of..."

A family business.

He *was* a son, then, like the others - and it *was* the same punishment.

And maybe it had *seemed* like his wife had been the one to kill him - hell, maybe Bea and the police were right, and his wife had even been the one to pick up the knife to cut him. But the wife wasn't *responsible*, any more than the knife itself had been. If what Lou believed was true, then the wife was just the weapon, just the vessel. Someone else had pulled the trigger - someone who'd found a way to get inside her head.

Some*thing*.

"I'm okay," she said, only dimly aware of the words as she was speaking them. "Just... drank too much too quickly, that's all."

Josie squeezed her arm - gently, supportively.

"Let me get you something to eat," she said. "There's crisps and that behind the bar - the salt might help?"

Lou nodded.

This isn't new information, she told herself, her mind still on Raj Arolker. *It's a weird coincidence, it is, but there's nothing here you didn't know already.*

But as Josie walked away from the alcove to the bar, casting concerned looks back at Lou over her shoulder, another thought occurred to her.

Ivan Davenport didn't fit. He was a victim - but he wasn't the *right kind* of victim.

She'd done a very brief search for background on the Davenports before retreating into her self-imposed exile from the world of information - and she knew, if only from the cheerful first-person biographies she'd read on their company's website, that Ivan's parents were nothing at all to with medicine. They'd been merchants, like he and Elaine had been before their retirement, and like their children were, now: importers, specialising in pineapples and bananas from South America and the Caribbean.

Not doctors, or nurses, or dentists; not opticians, or nutritionists, or psychiatrists.

Fruit importers.

Which - if the connection Lou had made between the murders held up - made Ivan an outlier.

Made him, and his death... wrong.

CHAPTER 21

n the budget hotel room that had been her temporary home since leaving
The Gates, Bea slept.

She was dreaming, and she *knew* she was dreaming. It was an unfamiliar
sensation, the lucidity, but not unpleasant: a sort of virtual reality sensation
of simultaneous immersion and disconnection, physicality and simulation.
A willing severing of herself *from* herself. Wherever she was, she thought, she
was both *there* and *not-there*; both bound and free.

And she was *strong*. Not just fit or healthy, but brimming with power: the
body that wasn't quite *her* body surging with it, overcome with it, the way it
had been that night in the cemetery when the hands that weren't quite *her*
hands had closed around the bones of the blond boy and had reached in to
pluck the teeth from his gums.

The kitchen she stood in now was large and clean and, though she was
sure she'd never visited it in her waking life, she knew instinctively how to
navigate it, and where any object she might need there would be found:
which drawer held the cutlery, which cupboard the plates, which box on
which sideboard the candles, torch and packing tape. The faces smiling at
her from the photos stuck to the refrigerator were the faces of strangers, but

were somehow also familiar: the eyes and mouths of the man and woman, the faded-at-the-edges boy and girl there eliciting from her mixed feelings of pride and protectiveness, an urge to nurture and an equal satisfaction at having set them free to live their best lives out in the world.

And the naked man with his chest carved open on the plastic-sheeted floor below her - she knew him, too.

Ivan: that was him. Ivan Davenport.

The chest cavity was open, the skin cut and the ribs pulled apart, and between her hands she held the fleshy, fatty meat of his heart. A small corner of it was missing - not torn or sliced but bitten, chewed.

She could smell the heart in the blood still smeared around her nostrils; could taste the raw, rubbery residue of it on her tongue.

He was dead now, though she knew - with the same certainty that she'd known the children who so demonstrably weren't *her* children *were*, somehow - that he hadn't *been* dead for long; that it had taken him not seconds or minutes but hours to die, to bleed out on the plastic as she straddled him with the knives and the hacksaw that, with the silver rush of her new strength flowing through her, she really hadn't needed at all.

It had excited her more than any of the others, this desecration of his body, this blood eagle she'd made of him; it had seemed to her, as she'd prised open his intercostal muscles with her now preternaturally capable thumbs, the purest and most perfect yet of her accomplishments. The pinnacle of her new, unlikely career.

And the power... dear God, it was exquisite. Intoxicating.

She no longer experienced it as anger, as an unquenchable fire burning her up from the inside, out. Rather, it had cooled and mellowed; the molten metal of it hardening around her to an exoskeleton, so tough and impregnable she felt practically invincible.

From the higher shelves of the kitchen, the crows watched her - an army of them, a sea of black wings among the hanging racks of sage and rosemary and oregano, more numerous than she could count. Her protectors; their feathers drifting over her like dust.

The heart jumped, beating an erratic final rhythm against her palms as the last of its electricity discharged, and she raised her hands. Brought it to her lips; opened her mouth and bit down.

A flash of gold light exploded somewhere behind her eyes; she closed them, trying to shield them from the brightness, and felt a press of shadow and feathers against her face and the bare skin of her arms.

When she opened her eyes again, the scene had changed.

This room she didn't know; didn't recognise. It was a bedroom, chintzy and pastel: the purple duvet spread across a king-sized mattress, worn clothes balled into a heap on top of the laundry basket and a stack of old paperbacks on the pink carpet beside the bed.

Romance novels, of all things.

It was a woman's room, she thought - a younger woman's room, perhaps.

But whose?

The door to the bedroom opened, just enough to let the dark-haired, green-eyed man on the other side of it slip in, and then she knew.

It was *her* room: the little whore's. Hers and Jeremy's room, now.

And here Jeremy *himself* was: looking leaner than she remembered, thinner and more angular, his hair artfully shaved and parted in a way that knocked five years off his face. He'd changed his glasses, she saw; exchanged his usual wire rims for a heavy-framed rectangular pair that gave him the appearance of a graphic designer or an advertising executive. His clothes were different, too: the jeans tighter, the shirt more androgynous. He wore boat shoes, but no socks, and seemed to be growing the beginnings of a beard.

That's *her*, she realised; *her* style, *her* influence. The little whore's moulding him; shaping him.

He stepped further into the bedroom, his eyes glued to the phone in his right hand. Only when he finally looked up did he see Bea. See her, and balk.

He opened his mouth to speak - to ask her, she judged from his expression, *what in God's name she thought she was doing there* - but he was just that bit too late: her fingers were already around his throat, thrumming with their new tensile strength, and she was squeezing, pressing into his windpipe.

He gasped for air, his face turning first red and then purple as he tried to prise her away from him with his own, pathetically weak hands. She raised her arm, as easily as if she were lifting a glass to toast him, and his feet left the ground - first one inch, then another, until he was a foot above her head, looking down at her in terrified bewilderment as she choked the breath from him.

It felt good to hurt him, she thought, as his body went limp and heavy and his bowels let go. Wonderful, in fact.

Right, and just.

She loosened her grip on his neck, and he dropped to the carpet like a sack of rotten vegetables, rag-doll legs folding under him as he landed.

Dead, she told herself, with no small degree of satisfaction. *Entirely dead.*

She smiled, and then the strange gold light was back, blinding her.

When her vision returned, the scene around her had changed a second time.

She was in a forest, now - or, if perhaps not quite a forest as she'd ever seen one, then a forest as a forest *ought* to be, lush and teeming with unseen life, primeval trees so high and thick and dense that the canopy they made above her very nearly blocked out the sky.

There were birds in the trees, she saw, birds of the same hybrid species she'd encountered opposite her house at The Gates: each one of them larger than a man, and some - their strange owl-eagle faces half-concealed by leaves and branches - larger still, the length of bulls, of elk or moose.

They were watching her, just as the crows had watched her in the kitchen.

The trees parted - not from some external application of force, but of their own volition, as if bending to receive the Eucharist - and a woman no taller than Bea herself appeared in the gap they'd made for her: golden-eyed and naked, her black hair tangling Medusa-like around her head and breasts in a pulsing, writhing crown, and her hand tangled in the speckled fur around the ears of the enormous fanged cat by her side. A Smilodon, perhaps. Or something older still.

"I know you," Bea told the woman. "You're her. Nox."

I am night, the woman replied - the words melding into coherence inside Bea's head as easily and quickly as they might have, had the woman said them aloud. *I am discord.*

"What do you want?" Bea asked.

I want only what you want, the woman answered her.

"And what is it that I want?"

Strength. You see what can be done with such strength. What has been done. What might be done yet.

"Jeremy?"

It can be as you have seen, if you will it to be so.

"And the other one, the man on the floor?"

A memory. A taste of what you might become.

"*Whose* memory?"

The woman shrugged, loosening her grip on the big cat's fur. It mewled at the loss of the touch, arching its back upwards and towards her hand.

The power is yours, she said. *You need only ask for it.*

"And what do I have to do to get it?" Bea said.

Because she *wanted* something, this woman. Wanted something from Bea. Wherever Bea was in this moment, *whoever* she was - she was certain of that.

The woman waved a hand, and the air around them thickened, turning to fog and shadow. And in the shadows, as black and white and flickering as a silent film projected onto a viewing screen, she saw the bodies: boys, all of them, and no older than the one in the cemetery. Some torn and bloody, others blue and bloodless and contorted, and every one of them dead.

"Who are they?" Bea asked.

Sacrifice, the woman said.

"To you?"

The woman shrugged again, and now the cat snarled in frustration, baring yet more of its tusk-like teeth.

And to others. Though my sacrifice is their atonement. As it should be.

What the hell does *that* mean? Bea thought, new confusion breaking through the dream-logic she'd thus far accepted without question.

"Do I get a choice?" she asked.

Always, said the woman. *Whatever is given must be given freely. The gift is made no other way.*

"And when do I have to decide?"

The woman smiled, and the world turned gold, and then black.

In the stiff white sheets of her budget hotel bed, Bea stirred - half aware of waking into the room, half lost in the leaves she could still feel underfoot and the moss-green canopy she could still almost see overhead.

Her, she thought - and it came to her, all of it and all at once, a sudden rush of understanding.

What, and *who*, and *why*.

Oh, she told herself. And *of course*. And *how did I miss it? How could I not have* seen *it before?*

She smiled.

Smiled, and reached for her phone.

CHAPTER 22

The Gates was creepy as hell in the dark.

It wasn't just the death the place had seen, Lou told herself, although God knew that was a factor. It wasn't just the pitch-black of the deserted, unlit countryside all around the estate, or the lingering ghosts of the girls who'd died at Fox Lodge in circumstances more horrible than she'd let herself imagine. It wasn't even the bird-thing in the tree, or the suckered squid-things in the fog, or knowing that the ground underneath her - the ground The Gates was built on - was at best a haunted ruined temple, and at worst some sort of access-point to a Greco-Roman hell.

No; it was the crows.

She'd thought there were a lot of them around before, when she'd visited in daylight. But what she'd seen then was nothing, *nothing* compared to what she was seeing now, as she rolled the Citroën past the entrance and down the road to what had been, until recently, Bea's house.

There were hundreds of them: blanketing every surface large enough to squat on, every stretch of slate and brick and grass and wood from the rooftops down to the driveways with their inky, darting bodies and their ruffling wings.

"Like something out of a horror film," Bea had said, and Lou couldn't have put it better. Whatever magnetic, irresistible attraction the area held for the birds, whatever their relationship to Nox and the temple - they seemed to Lou nothing less than monstrous. More monstrous, somehow, than the *actual* monsters that could, theoretically, leap out at them at any moment from the shadows.

"You sure it wouldn't make more sense to do this during the day?" she asked, not for the first time that evening.

"There'd be journalists everywhere," Bea told her. "They've been camped out at the entrance more or less permanently since Jordan died. They only leave to sleep. And occasionally shower, I assume."

"What about the police?"

She knew the answer to this: Bea had filled her in already, more than once. But if she'd ever needed a bit of extra reassurance, it was now.

"They're probably about, somewhere. You forget, though - I still live here, until the management company evicts me or my lease expires. And they can hardly stop me entering my own home, can they?"

"And *them*?" Lou said, pointing over the steering wheel to the mass of crows. "What are we going to do about them? I don't know about you, but I don't fancy opening the door while they're about."

"You don't need to worry about them," Bea replied, so confidently Lou almost believed her. "They'll stay out of our way."

And to Lou's surprise, they did: seeming to disband as she pulled the Citroën to a stop on the pavement next to Bea's house, and clearing a six-foot-wide path around the perimeter of the car that enabled them both to not only open their doors but step outside without landing on so much as a shed feather.

I bet we'd look like a crop circle if you saw us from overhead, she thought. A crop circle in a field of feathers.

And then:

They knew to move for us. Like someone had *told* them to - someone who knew we'd be coming.

Only two of the properties had lights on, which tallied with what she'd known already, and what Bea had told her earlier that day, when they'd met up in the lobby of Bea's slightly run-down hotel to share the conclusions they'd both, independently, reached; conclusions about how some of the recent events that had brought them together had unfolded.

Amit and Luke, the couple she'd met in the street the day of Jordan's murder, had been staying with friends ever since; they'd returned to The Gates only to pick up clothes and the various laptops and cables Bea assumed Luke needed for work. They wouldn't be back, Bea had speculated; would put their house on the market just as soon as the police and press scrutiny made it feasible for them to do so.

The old lady who'd stabbed Jordan with the cane, Joan McTierney, was being held - at least as far as Bea knew - in a secure inpatient unit at a nearby psychiatric hospital. She'd been charged with his murder, though no date had yet been set for a court hearing - but it was, in Bea's opinion, only a matter of time before the charge was reduced to manslaughter, given the woman's obviously diminished capacity.

The Arolker house, of course, sat vacant: the shell of a person who had been Raj Arolker's wife released on bail into the custody of her parents, and Raj himself now cremated, his ashes scattered on the River Soar.

The tired, broken-looking woman with the young daughter and the terrible hair had stayed, Bea had told her; quite possibly because she had nowhere else to go. *Her* house, the small semi-detached two doors down from Bea's, was lit up like a Christmas tree behind its thin net curtains: every bulb in every room of the place beaming out at the road beyond so brightly that even the crows seemed determined to keep a wide berth.

Maybe that's the point, Lou thought. Maybe it's the only thing that stops them pecking in the windows.

The *other* woman had stayed, too: the older one, the one who'd found the dismembered parts of her husband wrapped in shopping bags on her doorstep. *Why* she'd stayed after that, Lou didn't know: *she'd* seemed as if she could spare the money for a decent hotel room, even if the woman with the kid hadn't. No cherished memories were worth sticking around for after a trauma like that, surely?

It was *that* woman, in fact, that they were there to see; *that woman* whom Bea seemed to think was the key to it all, the one who could give them the answers they'd been looking for.

Though Lou wished - with a fervency growing hotter and faster with every step they took towards the doorstep that was still marked, very faintly, with traces of the butchered man's blood - that Bea had been willing to tell her *why*.

"You'll see," she'd said instead, when Lou had asked. And with, now Lou thought about it, the same enigmatic confidence, the same mystifying certainty she'd worn when she'd assured Lou, despite all the evidence to contrary, that the crows would leave them well alone.

It was a nice house, blood-traces and Medieval spiked flower-beds notwithstanding, and inasmuch as it was possible to say for sure in the nearly-dark. Nicer, anyway, than where Lou had grown up, and lovelier by far than any of the flats and shared student houses she'd inhabited during and after university. There were plant-pots below the windows; the beginnings of an ivy trellis; a polished brass door knocker in the shape of a clamshell.

And someone moving inside, in a room Lou guessed - from the silhouettes she could just about make out through the closed Venetian blinds - was probably the kitchen.

"Here we go," Bea said, with a strange joviality that did nothing to put Lou's mind at ease. And knocked.

The woman who answered the door was pale, and perhaps a little thinner than she had been that day in the street, but she hadn't exactly been sitting shiva, or so Lou thought. In the absence of a scream in her throat and without a layer of gore smeared across her face and body, she was what Lou's mum might have called *well put together*: her clothes expensive, her makeup thick enough to mask her wrinkles but not so thick as to appear clown-like or cartoonish, and her hands as neatly manicured as the garden shrubbery that framed her. She'd had her hair done since her husband's death, too: the roots looking just that bit more auburn than they had been, the bouffant very slightly more voluminous.

Everyone grieves differently, her better nature reminded her. *It's not your place to judge how she ought to be feeling.*

Still, though, the more cynical part of her responded. *She's looking pretty good, for someone who was carrying her husband's severed head around in a bag two weeks ago.*

"Bea," the woman said, with a smile so patently insincere that it would have caused Lou's mum to revise her appraisal from *well put together* to *a bit up herself*. "How nice to see you. I didn't realise you were back - I thought you'd gone, like those boys next door."

"It's good to see you too, Elaine," Bea replied - sounding, to Lou's surprise, as if she actually meant it, as if she actually cared. "How are things?"

The woman lowered her eyes; pressed a palm to her chest as if to still her own heartbeat.

"Oh, you know," she said, mock-cheerfully. "Struggling on. It's been... difficult, obviously. But our son's been marvellous, I don't know where I'd be without him. And the police tell me they're doing everything they can to, you know..."

She paused, the sentence apparently too distressing to bring to a conclusion.

She's putting it on, the devil on Lou's shoulder told her. *Playing at bereavement, at being the grieving widow.*

It's not real.

"I'm glad you've been getting support," Bea said. "It's so important, at a time like this."

She hesitated, giving every appearance of awkwardness - but it was an awkwardness completely at odds with her earlier self-assurance, with the cool-headedness she'd had about her before she'd knocked at the door.

She's acting, too, the shoulder-devil told Lou. *This whole thing is a production - some sort of weird-ass pantomime.*

Just what have you got yourself into, here?

"Do you think we might be able to come in for a moment?" Bea added.

The older woman stilled, momentarily thrown by the question, and then rallied, pulling the door fully open to invite them inside.

"Of course," she said. "Where are my manners? You must."

They stepped over the threshold, Lou more cautiously than Bea, and followed the woman as she led them into the kitchen.

It was an entirely ordinary kitchen, to Lou's mind: black and white tiles, wooden racks and cupboards everywhere, overlaid with the sort of faux-rustic aesthetic towards which people of a certain age tended to gravitate.

For Bea, though, it was evidently something more: proof of something, though of *what* Lou had no idea.

Bea didn't take a seat, not even after the older woman - Elaine - pulled one of the chairs from out of the dining table and gestured for her to sit down. Instead, she began to pace the room, nodding to herself as she took in the white goods and the spice racks, the family photographs and utensil hooks - looking, at least to Lou, as if she were cataloguing them, ticking them off against a mental checklist to which neither Lou nor Elaine were privy.

Finally, the pacing ceased, and she came to a halt - not by the table, but in the empty centre of the room.

"Is this where you killed him?" she asked conversationally, pointing down to a spot on the tiles that seemed to Lou indistinguishable from any other on the floor.

"I'm sorry?" Elaine said, taken aback.

"Ivan," Bea clarified, still so eerily calm she might have been asking about what Elaine had had for lunch. "When you killed him, was it here? Or did you do it somewhere else then move him here to cut him open, so he wouldn't stain the carpet?"

Elaine hadn't been sitting, either. But now she drew herself up to her fullest height, back straight and chin jutting in outraged indignation.

"I don't know *what* you're implying," she said slowly, each word loaded with something Lou would have read as menace in a different context, "but I very much think I'd like you to leave my house. Now."

Overhead, the ceiling lights twitched and blinked, casting strange half-shadows on the walls with every on-off flicker; from somewhere outside, Lou thought she heard a howl, then, closer by, a hiss like an aggravated peacock. Something dull but heavy thudded against the glass of the window, sending a momentary shockwave through the room.

Neither of the older women moved a muscle; had seemed scarcely to notice the disruption.

"You can stop pretending," Bea said, sounding more threatening herself now, less relaxed and more aggressive; not a lion stretched lazily out on the savannah but a tiger, coiling and tensing before attack. "I know what you did, Elaine. I saw it."

She curled back her lips in a smirk that was closer to a sneer, and there was gold between her teeth: sunflower light, a solar eclipse of it, bright enough to flood the room and force Lou to shield her eyes with the ridge of her hand to keep it from blinding her.

"*You?*" Elaine said, after what felt like an eternity had passed, and Lou saw, as her vision came back to her, that they'd begun to move around the kitchen, both women at once, circling one another like fighters, like jaguars competing for the same fallen prey: waiting for a moment of weakness, for the guard of the other to fall.

"Me," Bea answered, flexing her fingers - the nails there seeming to lengthen and grow even as Lou watched; her canines lengthening to vampiric points, and the whites of her eyes turning the same pale-gold shade that had seemed to radiate from her mouth.

And Elaine, too, was changing, Lou saw: was filling out and elongating, the veins and muscles in her wrists and neck and temples popping and swelling until she was as broad and vascular as a bodybuilder under her slacks and copper lamé sweater.

"*How*?" she said, with what struck Lou as unusual effort - as if speech itself was becoming more difficult for her as whatever the change *was* took hold.

"Same... as... you," said Bea, through sharp, gritted teeth, the act of forming the words bringing sweat-beads of exertion to her forehead. "She... made me... an offer... I couldn't refuse."

Bea smiled again, horribly, the skin and bone of her mouth shifting and slipping, and Lou was reminded of the ghost-girl she'd seen under the tree outside, the elastic click of her lower jaw as it unhinged.

"And she told you... about me?" Elaine asked, still circling.

"No. Worked it out... myself. One thing I don't... understand, though. Why... the boys?"

They stopped pacing, both of them at once, and stared at one another across the tiles from their two fixed points on either side of the kitchen - no white left in either set of eyes now, and the air around them shimmering very faintly with a heat that Lou could see but couldn't feel.

Neither spoke aloud. But Lou was left with the impression regardless - from the shifts in their expressions, the turn-taking tilts and angles of their heads - that they were communicating, somehow; exchanging signals on a frequency that she, with her ordinary eyes and fragile human body, was aware of but wasn't quite able to tune into.

Then, as suddenly as it had paused, the circling began again.

And Bea lunged forward - teeth bared, and claws extended.

CHAPTER 23

She didn't understand how it was possible; how Elaine could be *showing* her.

But, somehow, she was. And somehow, Bea *knew*. Knew what had happened, and why.

The moments - what Elaine must have considered the pivotal moments in time - came to her in flashes: clear and sequential and logically-consistent, but tinged with unreality, as far removed from her own memories and her own exposure to the world as the dreams she'd had in her hotel room bed the night before.

Of course they are, she told herself. *They're not* your *memories.*

They're hers.

Elaine's.

The first sequence - the first memory, if it *was* a memory - Bea experienced as something more visceral than cerebral: as a punch to the gut, followed swiftly thereafter by a kick to the head with the steel tip of a boot.

She was standing in a bedroom: the Davenports' bedroom, she knew instinctively, in the house they'd owned before they'd moved to The Gates. There was a photograph in her hand: a physical print, so unlikely in these days of mobile phones and digital cameras. It showed a boy in a wheelchair beside a woman very like him, a woman perhaps a decade Elaine's junior but more careworn, streaks of grey in her hair and lines she hadn't bothered to cover up around her eyes and mouth. And beside *her* in the photograph was Ivan: beaming with pride, his arm snaked proprietorially around her waist.

Ivan, who in his younger days had looked - Bea saw, as she brought the picture closer, zoomed in more intently on the details - so very like the boy in the wheelchair; the boy who looked, in turn, so very like the woman.

The boy who was, so very undeniably, the woman's son, and Ivan's.

The son they'd made together.

Flash.

Time had passed, an eternity that might have been only a handful of months, and the children - *Elaine's* children - had arrived for Christmas dinner with their own, smaller children and an armful of presents in tow.

"Where's Dad?" Elaine's son asked, puzzled by his father's absence as his mother carved the turkey.

He's with them, Elaine replied, though only to herself. *His other family. The one he thinks we don't know about.*

"He's at the warehouse," she answered, regurgitating the lie Ivan had told her with the untroubled breeziness she'd been perfecting since the day she found the picture, the day her heart had leapt of its own volition from her chest and turned to ashes on the bedroom rug. "Some hold-up or other with the Belo Horizonte shipment, I believe. He won't be long."

"He never stops, does he?" her son said, topping up their glasses. "I don't know what he'll do with himself, when the two of you retire."

Flash.

Their first night in their new home at The Gates, and Elaine, her sleeping pills not quite enough to dampen down the churning in her stomach at the sight of Ivan snoring next to her, had gone downstairs to get herself a glass of something that might take the edge off.

There was someone in the kitchen.

She could hear them, from the hallway: the stamping of feet, the rustling of fabric that sounded like feathers.

A sensible woman would have run. Called for help; torn Ivan from sleep and dialled the police, dialled Lawrence Jordan. Opened an upstairs window and called out for burly Luke Harris in his house next door.

But she didn't, though she couldn't have said why.

Instead, her hands empty of anything resembling a defensive weapon, she walked into the kitchen.

And found the girl she'd come to think of as The Lady waiting for her, naked and haloed in an ethereal gold; a flock of birds too big to be crows circling her head and a monstrous cat the size of a Bengal tiger curled obediently at her feet.

"Who are you?" she asked.

(And the part of Bea that was *still* Bea, even as she lost herself in Elaine's memory-reel, thought: *I know this. I know how this goes*).

I am night, The Lady said. *I am discord.*

"What do you want?"

I want only what you want.

"And what do I want?"

Strength.

"What does that mean?"

I will show you.

Flash.

A lurch, a moment of dislocation, and Bea was seeing not from Elaine's perspective but through another pair of eyes altogether, a third pair; was seeing *Elaine* look out at the world as someone other than herself.

In the golden half-second between the Davenports' kitchen dissipating and the scene that followed taking shape, the realisation came to Bea that she'd been on to something, after all; that the suspicions she'd woken up to in her hotel room had been the right ones.

The Lady *had* shown Elaine, after all, the same way she'd shown Bea. Had shown her how it felt to have that power flowing through you.

And she'd done it the best way she knew how: by letting Elaine slip into the skin and past the eyes of the last person who'd had that same power flow through them.

The eyes belonged, Bea inferred - from the institutional-green sterility of the room, from the feel of the almost-dentist's chair under her forearms and from the man in the white doctor's coat looming like a stone-cut monolith above her - to a patient. A patient, she guessed, at the hospital that had been Fox Lodge.

A girl, she thought; and a young girl, if the tautness of her skin and the smooth lines of her hands were any indication.

Young, and angry.

As the doctor leaned in towards her, she - or, rather, the girl she temporarily was - started, the anger she felt subsumed momentarily by a jolt of fear at what he might want and what he might do to her.

He took a small torch from his breast pocket; shone it directly into the eyes that were not quite *her* eyes. The light stung her; drew clear saltwater from her tear ducts.

Bastard, she thought, the hard inflection of the internal voice she heard unequivocally not her own. *Think you can do whatever you want, don't you?*
You'd best think again.

She felt her fists curl, involuntarily; her nostrils flare as they sucked in a last, deep lug of the room's recycled air.

Then, as the power filled her, drenching every cell of her body in turn like nectar through honeycomb, she reached for him - breaking the restraints that bound her wrists to the chair with a single flex of her tendons and pulling his face down towards hers until they were eye-to-eye.

There was a scalpel in the kidney basin on the cupboard-top closest to her: a small thing, blunt and very slightly blood-stained at the tip, discarded and left to rust since its last use.

She seized it with one hand, so quickly that she must have seemed to him - with his chin still held fast between her other hand - nothing more than a blur of motion and intent. Seized it, and drove it deep into the fibrous flesh of his eyeball as easily as spearing an olive with a cocktail stick. And then, with a second flex of her fingers, pulled the eyeball from its socket.

Flash.

Elaine was back in the kitchen, The Lady now watching her intently.

Well? The Lady asked.

"It's not just strength you're talking about, is it?" Elaine said. "It's violence. Reprisal for... something."

Strength must be exercised, The Lady said. *It exists in use, not only in potentia.*

"And how would you have me use it, exactly?"

Flash.

This scene Bea recognised, even as she saw it through Elaine's eyes. The plastic sheeting on the floor, the crows ringed expectantly around the room on every shelf and rim and surface like an audience in an amphitheatre, and Ivan bleeding out below her, his ribcage prised apart and viscera exposed. It was exactly as she'd seen it in her dream.

The Lady's dream.

Ivan wasn't dead, not quite yet. He looked up at her, pleading - to stop the pain, or to end it altogether.

And she was surprised to find, as she smiled beatifically back at him, that she was enjoying his suffering as much if not more than she was enjoying the power that now flooded her, the strength to which The Lady had alluded: strength so great that she could tear the house around her down to its foundations without breaking a sweat. Could wrench Ivan's cheating head from the wreck of his body with only the smallest turn of her wrist.

That she was more than enjoying it: was devouring it. Savouring every twitch of his limbs, every soundless plea from his shredded lips.

It was just what she needed, she realised. What she'd been wanting, if only she'd known it, since seeing the photo of the husband she'd thought was hers and hers alone standing proudly beside the other family he'd built for himself while she'd been tending, cluelessly, to theirs.

And if there were conditions attached to satiating this *need* she knew now that she had; if the strength The Lady was offering came, as she suspected it would, at a price... well, she'd be happy to pay. To pay ten times over, if she had to.

Whatever the price, it would be worth it.

Flash.

The kitchen again, and Ivan's body on the floor not a memory now, but a possibility. A promise.

"Yes," she told The Lady, licking her own - unblemished, unbroken - lips. "God, yes."

You would accept what I would give you, The Lady said.

Elaine nodded her assent.

"What do you want for it?" she added - sounding, Bea thought dimly, a little like she was haggling over the cost of a second-hand car or a consignment of papaya. "What will it cost me?"

Flash.

An empty warehouse, lit only by the faint gold glow rising in a halo from her - from *Elaine's* - bare hands and shoulders.

A boy, his chest crushed under the weight of her body as she squatted over and on him: not the boy from the cemetery but a different one, the same age but darker and more solid, and not slim but muscular. A sportsman; an athlete.

Not stoic, though. Crying - crying as she cut into him, over and over, with the keratinous blades of her fingernails. Crying as she ripped a thousand tiny cuts into his stomach, his neck, the Adonis belt of his hips.

"There, there," she told him, as gently as she'd spoken to her own children when they'd grazed their knees or bumped their foreheads on the mantlepiece. "Won't be long now."

And cut him again.

Flash.

In the space between the *now* and the *next*, Bea returned - briefly - to the theory Lou had presented to her: that Nox, who fed on chaos and fury, not only consumed but *fostered* the energies that sustained her. That she nurtured the crops of rage she'd eventually harvest.

There are ghosts here, Bea thought - not the ghosts of the temple or whatever else the Romans built on the site, but the ghosts of Fox Lodge, of the tortured girls who'd been kept there, once upon a time.

And perhaps... perhaps it isn't just the living Nox can feed on. Perhaps the dead rage, too, when they have cause to.

And perhaps their rage can be as nourishing as ours, if it's properly cultivated.

If it's kept fed, too.

And killing those boys, those boys that Lou had said were the sons of doctors, nurses, therapists: that would be a hell of a way to feed it.

Did Nox make them an offer, those angry, haunted girls-that-were, the way she did to me and Elaine?

An eye for an eye. Blood for blood. And an ouroboros chain of wrath, consumed and consuming.

Insatiable.

And Lawrence Jordan... oh, he must have tried to get The Lady's attention. Building The Gates as a temple to her; engineering the sort of environment he thought would give her what she wanted, using all of us and the problems we brought in with us to cook up his offerings of grief and gall and simmering resentment.

But what interest would a goddess have in a man like that - in giving him even a taste of the power he wanted from her? There was no rage in him; no festering grievance to be fed and watered, cultivated and harvested.

Not like there'd been in the Fox Lodge girls, or in the spirits they'd become. Nor like there was now, in Elaine.

Flash.

Another bedroom: a teenage boy's room, all Star Wars and LEGO and football memorabilia. Another boy, asleep in the bed: the brown-haired boy from the photo. Ivan's son.

And Elaine standing over him, a pillow in her hand.

She didn't mean to show me this, Bea thought - absolutely certain of the truth of the statement. The other scenes had been intentional screenings: had been montages, replayed for Bea's benefit. Explanations; justifications.

But not this one. This one, it struck her, had been sent to her entirely unwittingly; had slipped, somehow, through the net of Elaine's consciousness and outwards, into Bea.

Because there was no justification in it, she told herself, as Elaine - smiling, vibrating with the power she'd been given - lowered the pillow onto the sleeping boy's face. Nothing that could explain, convincingly, why not only Ivan but his child - and, Bea supposed, his mistress - would need to be punished like this.

Why Elaine had felt compelled to press the pillow down against the boy's mouth and nose as he gasped and flailed and cried out for his mother.

To press it down, and hold it there until he'd ceased to move, to breathe.

Flash.

CHAPTER 24

She didn't move like a person anymore, Lou thought, as Bea launched herself at the older woman she'd been circling. Nor did she move, exactly, like any one animal Lou could name, though there was a trace of something feline in the precision and agility of the leap, something simian - gorilla-like, even - in the force with which the two women's bodies collided when they met.

But no animal Lou had ever seen was *that* quick, *that* strong, *that* dextrous.

Elaine, to Lou's surprise, appeared genuinely shocked by the attack, in spite of the threats and the circling which had seemed, to Lou at least, a clear precursor to physical altercation - as if Bea had betrayed something in their unspoken exchange by turning on her. But she recovered quickly, lashing out at Bea with the ball of her foot as they rolled to the floor and landing a kick to the stomach powerful enough to send Bea flying in an arc across the kitchen, Bea stopping only when her back struck the wall above the stove, cracking the plaster and showering the tiles with a clatter of egg whisks and stainless steel spatulas.

"What... the hell... are you doing?" Elaine panted, pulling herself upright. "You've seen... why."

Bea sprung up from the supine position into which she'd fallen with an unlikely break-dancer's flip, releasing a cloud of plasterboard particles into the space around her.

"Seeing... isn't *agreeing*," she answered, eyes glowing.

"But you've... done the same," Elaine said - the fangs of her teeth, Lou noticed, now so long and curved that they jutted down and over her jaw like tusks. "You've let her... have you. You've taken... the deal. Why... are you... fighting me?"

Bea drew back an arm to shoulder height and, releasing it, drove her fist into Elaine's nose with so much momentum behind it that it would, Lou was sure, have knocked another woman's head clean off her body.

Elaine, however, only winced as it landed, a thin rivulet of blood trickling from one nostril to her philtrum.

"We're not... the same," Bea told her, rubbing at her knuckle. "You killed... those kids. And you... *liked* it, didn't you? I felt... what *you* felt... when you cut them. Suffocated... them. It wasn't just... about Ivan... for you. You... enjoyed it."

What's she saying? Lou wondered, entirely bewildered by the bizarre exchange of blows and information. That *Elaine* killed Simon Henshaw and the others? This posh old woman who could be someone's gran - who *was* someone's gran, by the look of those photos stuck to the fridge?

And that Nox *made* her do it, somehow? Offered her... what? Power?

The sort of power Lawrence Jordan was after, but didn't manage to get before he died?

"Of *course*... I bloody did!" Elaine roared back at Bea. "Just like... *you* will... when it's... your turn... to do it."

"No," Bea said, more quietly. "No... I won't."

They began to circle one another again, their straining muscles tensing and releasing like jungle cats' and flashes of that same strange, pale-gold light rippling across the surface of their skins as they whirled, around and around in a spiralling boxer's skip.

"You... will," Elaine told her, sounding to Lou almost gleeful. "You'll... *have* to. The Lady... must have... her sacrifice."

Bea tensed harder, every part of her seeming to Lou to go rigid, to tauten and stretch.

"I... know," she agreed, lengthened fangs grinding down against the more even white teeth on her bottom jaw.

She stepped backwards - crouching as she moved, transferring her weight into her legs and winding herself like a spring.

"Which is... why," she added, "I... offered her... *you.*"

She struck, the haymaker punch she launched at Elaine's solar plexus landing with such unimaginably explosive impact that it propelled the older woman not only through the plasterboard of the kitchen wall but through the masonry itself, blasting a hole in the brickwork and pitching Elaine's body through it and onto the pavement outside with the force of a cannonball.

Bea followed after her immediately, dive-rolling through the hole with the grace of an Olympic swimmer - leaving Lou to navigate her way, very cautiously, through the chunks of dried clay and mortar and the gathering fog of brick-dust.

The process took her longer than she might have hoped, and by the time she'd made it out onto the street, the fight had reconvened.

Outside, beyond the constraining walls of the Davenport house, Bea seemed to have the advantage - her blows raining down harder than Elaine's, her reflexes faster, her defensive blocks that bit more effective.

Does she have more power? Lou wondered. Did Nox give her more than she gave Elaine?

Or does she just *want* it more, the win, so that all of this can be over?

It would hit home later, Lou thought: the strangeness of what she was seeing, the two women pounding each other into the dirt like comic-book superheroes and murder upon murder of crows dancing and gyrating around them.

And when it did, she'd find a way to live with it - to reconcile it with everything else she'd seen already, on this patch of land that might as well have been a wormhole into the furnace of creation.

But for now... for *now*, she needed to understand whether Bea had meant what Lou *thought* she'd meant, when she'd talked about sacrifice. And whether, if she *had* meant that, there was any way of the fight ending without one or both of the women being offered up on a plate to the Chaos Goddess herself.

Elaine, splayed out on her back in the middle of the road, kicked out again at Bea.

And around them, around Lou, the darkness turned to shadow - to writhing, crawling mist.

They're here, she thought, as the tentacled-things in the dark rose and fell, grasping and slapping at the glowing, growling figures of the women.

Which means *she's* here, somewhere. Watching.

And not *just* her, Lou realised - not *just* Nox.

There were other things in the shadow-mists, too: girls, or the ruined remnants of what had *been* girls, gazing out at Bea and Elaine from their shifting pockets of smog.

Some were blind, she saw: their eyes no doubt burned or gouged out altogether by the doctors and nurses and orderlies who'd called what they'd practised at Fox Lodge *medicine*. Some were toothless, their gums as empty and bloody as Simon Henshaw's had been; many were bald, and others scabbed and scarred, burned and insect-bitten, their skin an incontrovertible indictment of their long-ago suffering.

Liquid anger rose in Lou, a sudden surging outrage at every injustice ever meted out to her, at every minor slight that had ever been directed her way. But she recognised it now. Saw it for what it was: not something she *felt*, some genuine resentment, but rather something imposed on her, artificially. Something seeping into her from the outside, as toxic as an airborne chemical.

Between the effort it took to quell it and the cumulative distraction of the fight, the ghost-girls and the things in the mist, she was barely aware of the sound of the front door of the other house behind her slamming open; didn't register the presence of the tired woman with the bottle-blonde hair until they were almost side-by-side, staring together into the moving shadows.

And if there was something different about the woman, a coppery aureole around her sallow-brown skin and a confidence in her face and posture that hadn't been there before, then Lou... well, Lou was too caught up in the fight and the maelstrom around it to notice.

In the shadows, Bea struck out again, catching Elaine just under her chin. But the effect was neither as dramatic nor as damaging as Lou had expected it would be. Rather than knocking Elaine back or felling her altogether, the strike seemed instead to please her - to energise her.

Elaine grinned, her mouth in the darkness nothing now but gold and tusk and venom.

Then, with the razor-tips of a hand that was all and only claw, she struck back at Bea, ramming her down into the ground and slashing open the skin between her chest and throat.

Bea's blood was gold too now, Lou noticed; an amber liquor the colour of butterscotch and whiskey.

And was so much of it; so, so much of it.

"It's the mist," the woman beside Lou said, in a hoarse, slow voice that seemed unused to speaking above a whisper. "I don't exactly know how it works, but it's doing something to Elaine - charging her up. Like a battery."

Because she's feeding off it, Lou thought. Feeding off whatever's *in* it, whatever it's made of, the same way Nox feeds off us.

The chaos. The darkness.

"And Bea?" she asked, as if the woman would know, would have answers Lou couldn't begin to guess at.

The woman frowned.

"The opposite, I think," she said. "It's draining her. Look."

Lou looked, and saw the woman was right. Bea wasn't getting up; wasn't springing back to her feet, the way she had in the house. The way she had outside, before the shadows penned her in.

It's not just about power, something told her - another voice in her head, one she hadn't heard before. *They've got power, both of them - the same power, from the same source.*

It's about something else as well. Intent, maybe?

Bea said Elaine liked *it, right? Liked the power, the suffering.*

So maybe chaos feeds off chaos - powers it, somehow.

Makes it stronger.

There was a different thought there, on the edges of Lou's consciousness - but it was interrupted by another round of movement in the shadows, another torrent of blows from Elaine's hands and feet and elbows that pummelled Bea in the chest, the head, the stomach.

"You need to get her out of there," the blonde woman told Lou. "She won't last much longer, if they keep on like that."

"*I* need to?" Lou replied, a fraction of her outrage now genuine, now legitimately *hers*. "You're not going to help me?"

"There's something else I need to do," the woman said.

Lou gaped at her in disbelief.

You don't have time for that, the voice told her. *Get pissy with her later, if you have to. But she's right, and you know it. Bea's dead if you can't find a way to get her out of that fog.*

And what about *me*? she thought, angry even at herself. Aren't *I* dead, if that madwoman in there catches hold of me?

If the voice had been real, been something more corporeal, it would - Lou was almost certain - have shaken its head and sighed at her.

Then don't let her, it said.

Another kick to the stomach, and Bea groaned, so loudly that not even the fog could muffle it.

And Lou, against every better instinct she had, ran towards her.

She took the fog at a sprint, bracing herself as she broke its surface. The shadows inside were cold, as cold as she remembered them being the first time they'd enveloped her, and the burning-hot things inside it... there were more of them than there had been, maybe twice as many, packed into the fog like sardines.

And they were bolder now - reaching for her, *grabbing* for her, no longer content just to whisper in her ears.

She pushed at them - pushed *through* them, the touch of them scalding her skin - and they fell away, only for more to take their place.

It's like something out of Lewis Carroll, she thought grimly, as she hacked at them with her elbows, with the bones of her forearms. *And thick and fast they came at last, and more and more and more...*

Aeons later, and what was probably less than ten feet from where she'd begun, she reached Bea - took hold of her wrist and yanked her, as hard as she could, in the direction she'd come from. Out of the mist.

Too slow.

Elaine saw her; threw her the same condescending smirk she'd offered Bea, before she'd ripped her open.

Lou tugged harder at Bea's arm - at the leaden, inert body it belonged to, weighing as heavily on Lou as a Sisyphean boulder - and picked up her pace, using her one free hand to clear as much of a path as was possible through the ever-thickening crop of tentacles.

But Elaine was faster.

They reached the edge of the mist, and with a final surge of effort that caused something in Lou's triceps to tear like crêpe paper, she hurled Bea's body over the threshold, towards the clear patch of darkness in which she and the blonde woman had been standing only a minute before.

And felt Elaine's clawed hand tighten around her shoulder; felt the nails puncture the layers of jacket, shirt and bra there before they pierced the meat of the arm below.

I won't bleed gold, she thought, as the hand spun her around, towards the mist and the things it held.

But at least it'll be quick.

She closed her eyes, waiting for the hammer to fall - and felt something *else* pull at her from behind. An arm, hauling her backwards and out of the shadows.

She let herself be pulled; broke the cold, damp crust of the mist a second time and collapsed onto the tarmac, blood seeping out of her into the cotton of the shirt and the denim of the jacket.

And then Bea was there, reaching over and past her for Elaine, snatching at the stretched collar of the older woman's sweater and pulling her from the mist, just as she'd pulled Lou.

Elaine struck out at her; scratched at Bea's face with her nails, kicked at Bea's shins with the points of her toes.

But there was *less* of Elaine, somehow, outside of the shadows - her connection to whatever energy source had been powering her severed, lost from the moment she'd tumbled back out into the warm summer air.

And Bea, restored to her earlier power - the edges of her chest wounds closing and knitting together, beginning to heal even as Lou watched - had no reason at all to be merciful.

She seized Elaine by the hair, dragging her head downwards, and drove a knee into her face. A crunch and a snap of bone that Lou thought would probably haunt her until the day she died, and Elaine soared backwards, as fast and far as Bea had in the kitchen - crumpling down only inches from the bed of spikes that bookended the path to Bea's front door.

Bea took off after her, so quickly and with such ferocity that it very nearly knocked Lou off her feet as she raced past.

She stopped by Elaine's fallen body; picked her up from the ground in an overhead press, as fluidly as a bodybuilder lifting a barbell, and dropped her, with the force of a freight train, down onto the spikes.

No part of Lou wanted to see what happened next. But she found, equally, that she couldn't look away: that the compulsion to know was too great, too overwhelming.

Elaine's body, she saw, had been not just stabbed by the spikes, but speared: their metal tips skewering her arms and legs, her head and torso in a hundred different places, rising up through the skin and fat and muscle in a mess of yellowish blood and organ meat and brain matter.

Vomit rose in Lou's throat. She swallowed it down, but it stuck in her throat, choking her, as the body began to dissolve, turning first to a thick, red-gold soup around a liquefying scaffolding of bones, and then to nothing but the ragged, soaked remains of the clothes Elaine had worn.

Bea stood over the spikes, over what had been Elaine's body, watching: her breath coming hard and her shoulders shaking.

She was... contracting. *Shrinking*, in fact, was the only word Lou could think of that came close to describing the change in her. The gold in her eyes was there, still - but it was receding, or it seemed to be, and the hazel of her irises was returning as the gold dwindled away. Her teeth were *just* teeth again now, as small and straight and off-white as they'd been before; her nails were *just* nails, or beginning to be, retracting back into her fingers with a faintly metallic whir.

It's leaving her, Lou thought. Whatever was in her, whatever power Nox gave her... it's on its way out.

Very nearly gone completely.

Bea turned in Lou's direction - not speaking, barely able to move, and looking to Lou like she might pass out at any second - and tilted her head, quizzically.

What now? Lou supposed she was asking. *What happens next?*

Lou didn't have an answer for her.

She took a step closer to Bea, intending to reach out to her - to reassure her, maybe, inasmuch as Lou had any reassurance to offer.

And then the blonde woman was there again - standing between them and blocking Lou's way.

Kajal, Lou remembered now. Her name was Kajal.

"You need to leave," she told them, told both of them - and was it Lou's imagination, or was there something in her voice that hadn't been there before, something harmonised and amplified and multitudinous? "She's coming. And you shouldn't be here when she comes."

God, Lou thought. Her eyes...

They were gold - the same gold Bea's and Elaine's had been. But there was something else in them, too: a depth and a movement and an age that gave Lou the distinct impression of looking not *at* them but *through* them to somewhere else entirely, a *somewhere* to which she had no desire whatsoever to travel.

Chaos. It's chaos in there.

"She?" Bea said, so raggedly Lou worried the fight might have permanently damaged her larynx. "The Lady?"

She means Nox, Lou told herself. *I don't know where this* Lady *stuff is coming from, but she means Nox.*

Nox is on her way.

And golden-eyes is right - I don't know about anyone else, but I really don't want to be here when Mother Chaos makes her entrance.

"What about *you*?" Bea replied, her own eyes - now completely hazel again - fixed on Kajal, on the change in her.

"Don't worry about me," Kajal said. "Karolina and I... we'll be fine. She's promised us we will be, and I believe her."

"She came to you?"

"To both of us. Me and Karolina."

This revelation, it seemed to Lou, made Bea more uneasy even than she was already.

"Karolina's a child," Bea said. "You can't... she shouldn't have to do it - what The Lady asks. She's too young. She won't understand what she's agreed to."

"She understands," Kajal said. "Your Lady - what she's asked for from us isn't what she wanted from you. From you *or* Elaine. It's... something else."

"I don't understand," said Bea.

You and me both, Lou thought. Though something tells me you understand a hell of a lot more than I do about all this right now.

Kajal's eyes widened very slightly, and Lou's earlier sense than she was somehow seeing *through* them intensified.

She looked away.

"It doesn't matter now," Kajal said - gently but firmly, and with such quiet authority that Lou couldn't imagine arguing the point. "All that matters is that you're gone before she gets here. So, please, go. And quickly."

Lou studied Bea; saw her struggle with herself, with the questions she was desperate to ask.

"Be safe," she told Kajal eventually. "Both of you, you and Karolina - be safe."

And Lou, taking the cue she hoped she hadn't misread, looped one arm as gently as she could through Bea's and began to steer her, slowly and steadily, back to the car.

EPILOGUE

The flat was small, cramped and scruffy: the ceilings too low, the fittings worn and dusty, the sofa too short and hard to be sat on comfortably for any longer than a few minutes at a time. Two of the halogen bulbs in the kitchen had blown, and were proving virtually impossible to replace; the bedroom door-handle was loose and had a tendency to fall to the ground whenever it was turned with any kind of vigour; both the toilet and the shower-head were leaky, and apt therefore to flood the bathroom with a symphony of drips and splatters at unpredictable intervals throughout the day and night.

Bea absolutely loved it.

It wasn't cheap - nowhere, certainly, as cheap as its myriad inefficiencies suggested it should be - but she could afford it, just. For all his solicitor's bluster, Jeremy himself had proven in the end surprisingly accommodating in the claims he'd made to their mutual assets, willingly ceding her half of the value of their marital home when it went to market and improving her previously dire financial situation considerably in the process. She'd appreciated the gesture - even if it *had* been prompted, as she suspected it had, by his need to expedite the Decree Absolute before the girl she was trying very hard not to think of as *his little whore* went into labour, and Jeremy's life became a never-ending whirligig of soiled nappies and sleep deprivation.

That the flat was neither appreciably haunted nor home to any primordial chaos entities was also, she considered, very much to its advantage.

Not that The Gates was either, anymore.

The night of Elaine Davenport's death, and of Kajal Sawiak's transmutation into whatever it was she'd become, a suspect or suspects unknown had (according to the news reports Bea had read and the murky dark-web forums Lou had apparently mined for information) broken into the developed portion of the site and planted on it a number of unusually powerful plastic explosive devices, scattering them around the perimeters of the eight properties already constructed on the land.

The explosion precipitated by the detonation of these devices was reportedly felt not only in the next village along, but in the village on from *that* one - with men and women in towns as far from The Gates as Market Bosworth claiming to have felt the tremors as the buildings collapsed in on themselves like angry dominoes. When a dozen or more representatives of the local constabulary arrived at the scene some ten minutes later - primed by the earlier murders they'd encountered there to expect something requiring a heavy and immediate emergency response - there was little left of the site but flame and smoking brickwork and, in the centre of the rubble, an enormous rectangular trench in the ground that was more crater than hole. The trench looked, as one anonymous junior officer had sworn blind to his friends on the internet, as if it had been paved at the bottom with cracked tiles, blue and white and faded. Old ones, he'd said: the kind you only ever saw in museums.

The provenance, and indeed the specific makeup of the devices used remained thus far unknown, not just to police but to the forensics, ballistics and counter-terrorism units the local constabulary had drafted in to assist with the investigation - all of whom, upon examination of the ruins of the site, had professed themselves baffled by the total absence of any of the chemical and material traces of the C-4, Semtex and more specialist military explosives with which they commonly dealt.

Nor had the bodies of Elaine, Kajal or Karolina Sawiak been discovered during the many, fine-tooth comb searches of the area that followed - although all three, having failed to respond to police appeals or show themselves elsewhere, were presumed dead, their remains lost to the explosion.

Investigations into the murders of John Seward, Philip Knight, Simon Henshaw, Hadrian Dawson and Ivan Davenport continued - but, though all of them but Dawson's were understood to be the handiwork of the same killer, little progress appeared to have been made by any of the officers involved, and not a single arrest had been announced.

Joan McTierney, as far as Bea knew, remained in the care of doctors at the secure Keystone Unit of the Lady Jane Hospital in Loughborough, and was - Bea had been told, when she'd called to ask after her - in no condition to receive visitors. Aarti Arolker, conversely, was out on bail and due to stand trial any day now for the manslaughter of her husband; supported by a legal team sufficiently skilled, or so Bea had gathered, to negotiate for Aarti a prison sentence of no more than ten years that would, with good behaviour, see her out in five.

Lawrence Jordan had been buried in a small cemetery in the Aylestone area of the city, close to where he'd been born and raised. Both Bea and Lou had attended the funeral, in part to satisfy their mutual curiosity about who he'd been, before he became the man he was in his final months and years, but had left the service with no more answers than they'd entered with - only a lingering sadness at how few other people there'd been in the pews at the church, and how few mourners Jordan seemed to have left behind.

In the kitchen of her new home, useless halogen bulb in hand, Bea thumbed thoughtfully through the small pile of mail she'd found in her letterbox that morning.

It was mostly junk: circulars for Chinese restaurants and pizza delivery places, a phone bill she'd already paid, a council tax demand addressed to the previous occupants of the flat.

Junk, and a postcard.

The quartet of scenes the card showed was pretty but nondescript: a beach, a lighthouse, a country road and a round-walled Medieval castle, all - according to the banner that ran across the centre of the montage - attractions located on the Isle of Anglesey, North Wales.

The text on the back of the card was sparse and elliptical, printed in the neat, careful script of someone unused to writing by hand but at pains to communicate that they *could*, should they need to.

Don't worry about us, it read.

K and I are fine and carrying the torch.

We're keeping Her happy, and that's the important thing. As long as She's happy, it'll all be alright.

We hope you're staying safe yourself.

And please - don't look for us.

KS

Bea took a long, slow breath to steady herself, flicked on the kettle and allowed herself to fall into one of the stiff-backed dining chairs she'd inherited along with the rest of the flat's furniture.

We're keeping Her happy - what did *that* mean? Assuming the card was from Kajal and Karolina - and it had to be, there was nothing else to be inferred from its cryptical handful of sentences - and assuming the Her it referred to was Nox... *how*, exactly, were they *keeping Her happy*?

What were they doing, to placate her?

And what, specifically, were they offering up to her, that would keep her satisfied?

She considered calling Lou - less to seek out the girl's opinion on the message than to offload her own anxieties to the one person who might possibly understand them. Then she remembered: Lou wouldn't be able to answer. She was tied up all afternoon, she and the other young girl she'd been seeing but was hesitant to call her girlfriend, recording the first few episodes of the podcast they'd devised together: a book, film and TV-review series that had, Bea had been relieved to note the first time Lou had mentioned it, nothing at all to do with true crime, local history, unsolved murders or the Greco-Roman pantheon.

It hadn't sounded, from Lou's description, like something Bea would seek out under her own steam. But creating it seemed to be making Lou happy, or at least to be diverting her attention from the memories that would, no doubt, be playing on her mind more acutely than they were in the absence of distraction. And that, surely, was the important thing.

She wondered what Lou would say, when Bea *did* eventually tell her about the postcard; whether she, like Bea, would consider it cause for alarm, or whether she'd be happy enough to take Kajal at her word and leave the whole business alone.

Probably the latter, Bea thought. She didn't know the girl that well, but she'd learned enough from the conversations they'd had since that last night at The Gates to believe that Lou was more than ready, for the sake of her own sanity, to try to forget that any of it had ever happened.

And perhaps Bea could learn a lesson from that herself.

She wasn't happy - not altogether, not yet. The wounds were too raw, still: from what had happened to her at The Gates, from what she'd *done* there, and from Jeremy, too. The loss of him, and the melancholy ache that had crept in to fill the empty places in her that the rage and bitterness had left behind, when she'd eventually let them go.

But she was calmer. Calmer, if not entirely at peace - content enough to sleep, to rest from time to time in the silence of her own skin.

And perhaps - perhaps for now, that was enough.

ABOUT THE AUTHOR

TC Parker is a writer and researcher based in the fox-ravaged wilds of Leicestershire, where she lives with her partner and their two extremely energetic children.

The author (as Natalie Edwards) of the *El Gardener* series of feminist heist books and (as TC Parker) of the horror novel *Saltblood,* she's been a copywriter, a lecturer and, very briefly, an academic; now she runs a semiotics and cultural insight agency by day and dreams up horror and crime fiction at night, when the kids are asleep.

Visit her online at www.tcparkerwrites.com